Elf Circles

By
R. D. Hemenway
&
Joan Sherwood

PublishAmerica
Baltimore

First printing

ISBN: 1-60441-862-1
PUBLISHED BY PUBLISHAMERICA, LLLP
www.publishamerica.com
Baltimore

Printed in the United States of America

Dedication

I would like to dedicate *Elf Circles* to those that inspired me to write such a great book. It was in the middle of a winter storm with heavy snow and strong winds and we were driving home. I knew my wife Paula my daughter Bridget and my son Michael were afraid of the storm, so I decided to talk to them just to pass the time. I asked them if you were to write a book what you would write about. They replied Elves and Dwarf's. It was at that moment that *Elf Circles* came to life. I thought about what both my children and my wife had said to me, and after several months of pondering the thought I started to write the story. So to the three most important people in my life I am honored to dedicate *Elf Circles* to each of you. I love you guys so much and to have your children inspire you as much as you do is such pure joy.

Thank you.

Your husband and father

R. D. Hemenway

Acknowledgment

I would like to acknowledge my great friend Joan Sherwood. Her ability to edit and embellish *Elf Circles* has made story telling such an adventure. She and I have a perfect writing connection that has allowed us to produce a story that all can enjoy. Thank you Joan, you will always have a special place in my heart.

R. D. Hemenway

Foreword

It is a world nestled between tree roots and rainbows, waterfalls and deserts. A place of soft breezes and warm sunshine...of bursts of storm and raging peril; of forever friends and mortal enemies; of sweet, tempting aromas drifting from steamy cookfires—and empty knapsacks with stomachs begging for crumbs.

It is a special place where I long to be, where flights of fancy set me adrift in a sea of wonder, hope and imagining. I am free—I am on wings of the Phoenix—plunging to the depths of destruction—then soaring triumphantly to be re-born to the wonders of life and love.

It is the Land of Zin; it is my Village of Okon.

Travel with me.

Prologue

It was a different time, not of now, nor of then, but when the lands belonged to *another* time. Zin was a powerful kingdom ruled by a wizard named Zupan, *King* Zupan, and guarded by Light Elves who protected the land using their Elf Circles. With their supernatural powers, this handful of Elf Spirits kept the peace and fostered goodness within the Kingdom.

Zin was home to both elves and dwarves, two races of little people who were outcasts from other lands of that other time. King Zupan, a Druid who came from afar, was cast out from his own country because…well, gentle reader…let us keep that for another time, and another place!

We come now to the beginning of our tale, when the Kingdom of Zin has been hidden from view and from the evil of Syffus, the Dark Elf. Zupan has mysteriously disappeared and now Syffus seeks to find, and destroy, both the Kingdom and the protector, the Light Elf. If he succeeds, the darkest evil will rule the land, holding all the innocents in its grasp.

There is but one hope for escaping this unspeakable fate. The old Light Elf, Kailon, must awaken and guide the Elf spirits in their search for the new Light Elf. Kailon has been suspended in time for these four hundred years. He awaits the birth of Quill Okon, destined to be the new warrior of the people, the new Light Elf. Now the time is at hand, for Quill has come of age. Kailon must summon Quill and convince him of his destiny for the power of Zin to return.

During the sleeping centuries, Syffus has terrorized the land; continuously searching for the one he knows will come. He is unaware of who the new protector will be, or of the time for his coming, but he must not let down his guard: he must destroy all that is good if he is to survive!

Introduction

Tales of a People

Long before the Kingdom of Zin was hidden under the valley of Okon, there were numerous villages within the many valleys, each with its own leader and some form of discipline or laws, but all ruled by the good and peaceful King of Zin, a powerful wizard. The elves and dwarves trusted him with their lives, and honored his every word.

As this great Kingdom grew, it became difficult for Zupan to rule alone so he selected a powerful council to oversee the land. This group consisted of carefully-selected elves, with each member being given special magical powers. However, only one of these members at a time could walk the land with such power! The first to become a guardian, or Light Elf, was Tercal, son of the King's personal bodyguard. Light Elf Tercal would be responsible for ensuring that goodness prevailed throughout the land. His potential for power almost equaled Zupan's, but would of necessity be earned in steps, and over a period of time. Zupan was well aware that as long as he had the ability to *create* a powerful Light Elf, he must also be able to maintain *control* over him!

To this end, King Zupan constructed a special place within the Kingdom where each new Light Elf would train and study in order to receive their first level of power. It was a chamber made of oak, the tree which tradition said gave all elves strength and magical power. This chamber was hidden from curious eyes and only revealed to those who had been selected by Zupan to enter.

At the same time, Zupan also created an ultimate, impregnable armor for each Light Elf—armor that would pass from one to the next and be held forever in the grasp of time—invisible to all. This armor surpassed any that could be worn for it consisted of the spirits of past Light Elves—those who had gone on in mortal death. But, because Tercal was the *first* Light Elf, he would be without the power of the spirits, or the protection of the magical armor. Realizing this, Zupan took a root from the great oak tree that stood at the entrance to the chamber and fashioned a cane from it; this would serve as Tercal's armor. Tercal carried this gnarled cane, his protection from all evil, until the day he died. But death to a Light Elf was not an end, but rather a new beginning! Tercal became the armor and power for all those who would follow him. His spirit became a mystical, invisible aura around the next Light Elf, and continued in succession for each one to come. In this way, evil could not harm the keeper of peace.

As required, when each new Light Elf throughout the years entered the hidden chamber, known as the Elves' Power Room, to claim his position, he received his first power at the entrance—the power of his Elf Circle. As a reminder of his achievement, each was presented with a special rope that would forever signify his particular power levels. His Circle would tie a knot in the rope for each level achieved, but no more than ten knots, the highest level. And for this, it could take many years of struggle. As wisdom comes with time, so too did the knots of the Elf Circle.

King Zupan Disappears

Not long after Zupan created the Light Elves, an incredible thing occurred—Zupan vanished! It was rumored throughout the Kingdom that the great King had died, but no one really knew what had happened. Not even Tercal, who was the only one left with King Zupan's magical power! With their founder gone, leadership now had to come from the Light Elf, a difficult task for Tercal. He soon made it known that his immediate quest would be to search the land in hopes of finding Zupan. Tercal had forgotten why the Elf Circle had been created so ignored his responsibility of ensuring that the balance of goodness and caring remained constant throughout Zin. As time passed, Tercal, and the Light Elves who followed him, were unaware of their real purpose. These were the times that brought about change.

It is said that where there is good, evil also dwells. And so it came to pass that a venomous black viper attacked and bit one of the Light Elves. This elf, Syffus, turned to the dark side of the spiritual world, cloaked in the evil ways of the Master of Darkness. He became known as the Dark Elf, one with destructive powers beyond anyone's control. The Elf Circle was forced to summon another Light Elf for protection for the people. And so Kailon was chosen. Once again, the purpose of the Light Elf had changed. Now it must defeat the evil of Darkness.

Hiding the Kingdom

Though Kailon was young, he recognized the extreme difficulty of fighting the older, wiser and more cunning Syffus. It would mean certain death for him and destruction of the Elf Circle, a chance he could not take at this time. He also feared for the Kingdom of Zin—that Syffus would destroy it in order to rid the land of all Light Elves. Kailon's only choice was to hide Zin until such a time that a greater power would arise and be able to lash out against the Dark Elf, once again conquering evil.

Kailon chose the small valley of Okon in which to hide the Kingdom. And, if it were underground, no outsiders could ever possibly enter. He also sealed off the valley as an extra measure of protection, calling upon powerful winds to stand guard over all of Okon. These winds from the mountaintops surrounding the valley prevented both man and beast from entering or leaving.

And yet, still fearful that all of this were not enough, in another valley Kailon created a place called the Elf Treasure, where all future Light Elves could retreat in safety from the powerful Syffus—a place where only goodness could enter! Here a Light Elf could be suspended in time until once more called upon to defend the honor of his station and Elf Circle.

The Light Elf Sleeps

Kailon knew full well that eventually he would have to do battle with the Dark Elf. He sensed Syffus hunting him like an animal and it was not long before he was discovered. A vicious battle between the two tenth-level Elves, between Good and Evil, was fought, with Syffus managing to destroy Kailon's Elf Circle, sending each of the chosen Spirits into the darkness of the evil side! Kailon's only hope was to seek refuge in the Elves' Treasure, where he remained for four hundred years, suspended in time, frozen in a deep sleep. But now it is time for Kailon to waken—to return to Okon Valley—to find and train the *new* Light Elf. This chosen one will replace Kailon, for Kailon's time to join the Spirit World has also come.

The Populous

The Elves

Quill Okon	The new Light Elf of Okon Valley
Kailon	The old Light Elf
Syffus	The Dark Elf
Lore Okon	Quill's father and leader of Okon Valley
Kara Okon	Wife of Lore, Mother of Quill
Luna	Friend, girlfriend and wife of Quill
Tercal	First Light Elf of Zin
The Golden Elf	The most powerful of Light Elves

The Dwarves

Burt Hobil	Quill Okon's best friend
Okar	Okon village priest
Tobble Hobil	Burt's father and the village carpenter
Solla Hobil	Burt's mother
Tran	Dwarfen warrior
Hyslop	Mohan with evil players
Woba	Mohan spiritual leader
Tiad	Mohan King and leader

The Druids

Kobar	Protector of the Light Elf
Molik	Kobar's brother

Dark Warriors	The evil soldiers of the Dark Elf
Zatto	The Red Wizard
Zupan	King of Zin

Others

Tworek	Tworek is a cricket that Kobar carries
Hawk	The Hawk is Quill's eye from high above

Chapter One

"Burt, move toward the left side of the pit so I can see," Quill whispered.

"I don't think I can. If I move, it'll bite me," the Dwarf whispered. Then he grumbled to himself, "I'll wet my pants if he doesn't do something soon."

"What was that Burt? I didn't hear you," Quill said.

"Nothing. Just do something will you?" Burt hissed in a hoarse whisper.

"Well, if you'd turn yourself to the left a little, I might be able to get a shot at the thing," the elf snapped impatiently. "The only way I can see is through the hole you made when you fell into the pit!"

Suddenly, out of the darkness another deadly viper slipped down into the bottom of the pit. Not making a sound, the poisonous intruder slipped toward Burt. The short, plump dwarf began to squint as beads of sweat formed on his large forehead. Terrified and trying not to move, Burt raised and lowered his thick brows in an attempt to prevent the perspiration from rolling into his over-sized dark brown eyes. His big ears quivered as several strands of long, scraggly brown hair fell across his face and came to rest on top of his bulbous nose. Continuing its descent, the sweat found the outer edges of his eyes, sliding over his pudgy cheeks, as it approached each corner of his heavy lips. He would then patiently scoop up the moisture with the tip of his thick tongue, knowing that any kind of movement, even droplets falling from his dirty chin, could provoke the menacing viper to strike.

Quill, shocked by the events taking place, could feel the anguish building in the base of his stomach as he looked into the pit. The young elf knew the pit was originally meant to trap wild boars or small deer. Now, however, it contained two deadly vipers and his best friend. Quill had no idea how to stop what he thought was surely going to happen. He pushed his blonde hair to the side, his piercing blue eyes riveted in fear as he watched the danger envelop his friend. Quill's thoughts ran rampant. Why hadn't he been the one to fall into the pit rather than Burt? As an elf he might have had a better chance against the snakes. Elves are taller than dwarves and have much more strength because of their muscular structure. Elves intelligence allows them to learn and solve problems much faster than dwarves too. Quill knew he would have the edge if he were in the pit instead of Burt!

They had grown up together in this valley; yet this was the first time either had seen a viper. Quill recalled stories that the elders of the village told of these snakes, but the stories had always been regarded as tall tales. Something told around the campfires to pass the time and enthrall eager listeners. Quill remembered hearing that if you ever encountered a viper you were bound to meet your death. It was believed that vipers guarded the evil Dark Elf who continuously looks for the lost kingdom of Zin, a tribe of Elves and Dwarves such as Burt and Quill. The Dark Elf looks for them because they are the keepers of the power tomb, a magic place that holds the power of the Light Elves. The little people of Zin were hidden from the rest of the world. No one ever knew why, but it is said that Zin holds the power to destroy the Dark Elf. All of these stories, heard for so many years, were now flooding his memory. Quill couldn't believe it. And with memories came fear and concern for his family and friends.

Quill looked at Burt, a friend for life, someone who would die for him. Burt, a dwarf, is the son of the village carpenter. He is not the best-looking friend someone could have; but he has a big heart. Quill had long-since learned that looks were highly overrated! Burt's big ears, and nose to match, made him a target when they were young. He stood about four feet high with a face showing the wear and tear of being a dwarf. His soft brown eyes still held the sparkle of youth. Yet, the wrinkles around them were proof that life was not easy. Burt was not a very likeable dwarf; he grumbled a lot and was sometimes very slow. He also possessed a bottomless pit for a stomach—and was almost as round as he was tall!

"Burt! Don't move! There's another one crawling right next to you. I think I can get a shot," Quill warned.

Hardly daring to breathe, Quill held his bow as steady as he could. The sweat was by now running down the middle of his forehead and flowing the full length of his nose. He took careful aim knowing that if he missed he would kill his best friend. As soon as he released the arrow, Quill heard it find its target. Although the viper's head was pinned against the bottom of the pit, it looked as if the snake was still alive. He knew he hadn't missed. The arrow was buried half way into the ground below with the viper's head skewered in the middle of it all.

"Burt, when I say move, I want you to take a full step back so I can get a shot," Quill said, reaching into his quiver to remove another arrow.

"Wait! Wait! Are you sure you can hit the darn thing?" Burt asked, still trembling in raw fear and filled with panic.

"If I don't, you had better grow some wings, or that snake is going to eat you." Quill paused and then shouted…

"Move!"

For the split second it took Burt to move, he could see the viper start to strike. At that very instant the arrow hit its mark again. The viper fell to the bottom of the pit, twisting in circles around the shaft of Quill's arrow. Its efforts to release itself were pointless and the would-be attacker quickly died.

"Oh no!" Quill gasped.

Looking down he saw Burt lying on top of the first snake but as yet unaware that a third was making its way from the hole in the side of the pit. >From what Quill could see, this new intruder was three times the size of the other two. Quill saw it coming but there was no way he could get a good shot. His weapon now thrown to the side, Quill hung over the pit, both arms outstretched, straining for Burt's hand in a frantic effort to pull him out.

"Burt, hurry!" The tone of Quill's voice told Burt that this thing wasn't over yet. He never turned around, but scrambling to his feet, lunged toward safety. Quill's hand squeezed hard as he began pulling him up and out of the pit. Burt sensed a presence behind him and knew something was terribly wrong.

"I've got you, Burt! I've got you" Quill panted as he struggled in a last frantic effort to land his friend beside him at the edge of the pit.

The slithering, treacherous evil began its ascent from the dark bottom, silently closing the distance to its prey. Quill and Burt were oblivious to the incessant pursuit.

"I'm okay," Burt said, slowly getting to his feet. Then turning, Burt stared into the dark hole and quickly became aware of Quill's face, a face frozen in pure fear. Burt felt his knees lock and his body start to tremble as he stared into the eyes of the viper. Not more than two feet from his face, the reddish-brown twisting snake continued its slow rise out of the depths until it towered about five feet above Burt. Burt could not move or speak, seemingly transfixed by the serpent's gaze. Quill began to back up, but stopped after realizing Burt was in trouble.

"Burt, back up!" Quill screamed.

Quill had to do something—and do it fast—or Burt would die. Skillfully, he reached into his quiver for another arrow. Positioning it in the bow, he took careful aim. His arm shook ever so slightly from the tension on the bow as he drew the arrow slowly back as far as it would go. The viper swayed back and forth getting ready to strike, its mesmerizing hold on Burt unbroken. Quill followed its movement, knowing the only thing between life and death for Burt was this one shot. Just as he was ready to release the arrow, he was shocked to see something eerie about this adversary—it seemed to have four eyes! And then the arrow flew as he aimed for its head. Time seemed to crawl with the arrow making its way toward its target in slow motion. At that same instant those eyes turned and looked at Quill. For a split second he too became frozen from the power emanating from this personification of evil. Quill then realized what control the viper had over Burt. No wonder Burt couldn't move from the first second their eyes had made contact. But then, in that moment out of time, that scarce fraction of an instant, Quill's arrow hit its mark and the terror reeled backward into the black abyss.

"Burt, are you okay?" Quill yelled.

Burt could hear Quill but still could not move or talk. Quill slowly moved over to Burt and placing his hand on Burt's shoulder, gave him a firm shake.

"Burt, Burt—snap out of it! Are you all right?"

Burt turned slowly and looked at Quill. Tears streamed down his cheeks as Burt searched Quill's eyes. "I wet my pants Quill. I couldn't help it, but I wet my pants. What happened, Quill?"

"I'll tell you later. Let's just get out of here," Quill said softly as he gently put his arm around Burt's shoulder. Without a word, they both turned and looked into the pit. Quill realized that not only was the largest of the vipers gone, but the other two as well. The only evidence remaining were his three arrows.

"Look Quill! Even the hole that the vipers came from is gone." Burt continued, "You don't think we were dreaming all of this do you?"

"Well Burt, I don't believe dreams leave things behind," Quill answered.

"What are you talking about? What things?"

"Look down there." Quill matter-of-factly pointed to the center of the pit.

Burt looked to where Quill was pointing and saw a small pool of blood. In the center of the blood he saw two small black stones.

"Where did those stones come from, Quill?"

Then Quill remembered the viper with four eyes. They weren't eyes after all but these stones!

"Jump down there and get those stones," Quill ordered.

"Are you crazy? I was almost killed in that pit three times today. Then as if I didn't already have enough problems, I wet my pants," he said looking down into the gaping hole. "I'm not ever going down in there again, not for you or for anyone else. If you want those stones then I suggest you jump in and get them yourself," Burt snorted as he stared at Quill in disbelief.

"Do you know what's going to happen now? My new leather pants are wet and they're going to shrink," Burt mumbled as he spun on his heels and stalked away.

Quill started laughing as he moved to the edge of the pit. "Come over here and help me get down there. I wouldn't worry too much about those new pants. If they shrink, it could help your looks because you're too fat anyway." He chuckled to himself as he reached for Burt's hand. "Come on, lower me down, will you?" he asked with a flicker of a smile still on his face.

"Okay. Get ready," Burt said.

Quill held on to Burt as tightly as he could while he was slowly lowered into the pit. Once down, he looked to the spot where the viper hole had been, not believing it was gone. He looked again just to make sure then bent down, picked up his three arrows and placed them back into his quiver. He then remembered why he was down there in the first place. The stones. He turned back and quickly located them. After a quick glance up to make sure that Burt was still waiting at the rim, he knelt next to the stones to get a better look at what the viper had been wearing on its head. Sure enough, they were some kind of a stone, but like nothing Quill had ever seen before. They were the same size as a person's eye but solid, jet black.

"Quill, grab those things and get out of there. Those vipers might come back," Burt whispered urgently.

Just as Quill reached for the stones, a brilliant bolt of light flashed from his fingers the instant he touched them. It was as if the big viper were still there. He could not let go of the stones. They had almost become a part of him!

"Burt, Burt, I can't see! What's going on? Get down here and help me!" Quill was screaming as blinding light still arced from the stones he held in his hand. It was as though the stones themselves were being disturbed and their anger was being unleashed. Quill scrambled to the wall of the pit, waving his arms in the air, waiting and hoping that Burt would be able to reach him and pull him out.

"Burt, get me out of here!" yelled Quill.

Burt was already lying on the ground at the edge of the pit. He stretched his small, short arm down as far as he could and tried to grab Quill's hand, as he screamed loudly for Quill to grab on.

"Burt, do something! I can't see anything," pleaded Quill.

Burt made every effort to avoid looking directly at the stones—still shooting out blazing streams of light. If they made Quill go blind, they would surely make him blind as well. He remembered the food pouch that was tied to his belt, reached down, untied it and dumped the food on the ground.

"Give me your hand—the one with the stones in it," Burt commanded.

Quill stretched his arm into the air toward the direction of Burt's voice and as he did, felt the reassuring grasp cover his hand. In the same motion he felt himself being pulled from the pit.

"Come on Quill, get up on your feet," Burt said as he helped Quill stand. "My food bag is over your hand so I won't be looking at the stones. Let go of them so I can remove the bag."

Burt reached out and grabbed the small leather pouch, shaking Quill's arm a little to encourage him to release the stones. Finally, the iron grip of his hand relaxed and the stones fell free. Burt slid the bag from Quill's hand and quickly secured the leather thongs so that no light would escape. Dropping the bag to the ground, he placed his arm around Quill in order to lead him away from the edge of the pit.

"Come on Quill. I'm going to help you walk. We need to get away from here." Burt gently led his friend to safety. "I still can't see," Quill whined.

"Here Quill, sit down and let me take a look."

Quill sat on the ground and instantly felt Burt's hands touching his face. For the first time in his life Quill felt lost and alone. His hands were touching the ground and he could feel the weeds and dirt under him, but it was very unnerving not being able to see them.

"Burt, what do you see? Are my eyes burned out? Are they?" Quill asked, almost afraid to get an answer.

"Nothing. I can't see anything. It doesn't look like there's a thing wrong with them at all. We have to get out of this place before something else happens. I'm going to lead you. I want you to stand up and give me your bow and quiver. I'm also going to need your food pouch so I can put my food in it too." Burt was taking charge of this situation now.

Quill stood and removed his bow and quiver, dropping them to the ground. He tried but could not untie the pouch. "Burt, give me a hand with this knot will you? I hope you won't have to use my bow for anything. Remember the last time I let you shoot it? You shot the water bag hanging on the side of your father's hut." A smile broke across his face.

"You always have a way of making me feel better, even when things are going badly for us. How do you do it Quill?" Burt was genuinely amazed.

"Life is too short to let everything bother you. 'You can't let the hard times get you down,' " answered Quill, quoting an oft-repeated phrase of his father's, at the same time trying to believe it himself!

Burt then walked back to the edge of the pit and gathered the food he had dumped on the ground. Placing it in Quill's bag, he fastened it to his belt. Going back to where Quill was sitting, he picked up the bow and quiver, placing them over his head and around his shoulders.

"Quill, stand up and give me your hand. Now follow me so I can get us out of here." He grabbed Quill and started walking down the trail.

Quill's only thoughts were on the loss of his sight. Burt was thinking that it would take them much longer to reach their village if Quill couldn't see. They had come four days just to get to this place. Now they were looking at six or seven to get home. Burt slowed just enough to take one last look at the gaping pit. As he turned around he saw the other food bag containing the two stones that were the cause of all this trouble. His first thought was to leave them where they lay but Burt knew that if Quill realized they were still there he'd go and get them himself.

"Quill, stop. I forgot the bag with the stones. Stay here while I get it."

As Quill waited, he listened intently to the sounds around him; Burt's lazy feet scuffing the ground with each hesitant step he took; the wind rustling the leaves in the trees as if shaking out the day's dust; frogs croaking in the distance but seeming so close. Then, another sound—different, yet familiar—the call of a large bird, yes, a hawk, flying low overhead! Briefly, Quill forgot his sight was gone and he instinctively raised his head to look at the powerful bird. Only then did reality strike once more—he was blind!

Burt retrieved the bag and as he did so, he glanced into the pit, a chill running down his spine. That eerie feeling signaled that this was only the beginning. There was surely more to come. Quickly turning around, he returned to Quill, tied the bag to Quill's belt, took his arm and walked away from the forbidding hole in the ground.

"There. At least we got something out of this trip," Burt mumbled to himself.

"Come on Quill, let's try to pick up the pace. This place gives me the creeps and I don't want to be anywhere near it when it gets dark. And that won't be too long either. In just about two or three hours the sun will be setting. How do you feel anyway? Do your eyes hurt?" Burt had hardly taken a breath and was practically pulling Quill along.

"Burt, all you ever do is complain. You mumble and say things you don't mean. I do thank you for saving my life, and for being my best friend though. But to answer your question, I feel fine. As a matter of fact, I feel better now than I have in years. Isn't that strange? It seems to me that I should be worried or full of fear. But I'm not. And maybe my eyes should be hurting or something. But they're not. I don't feel anything but good, really good, and full of strength. Thanks again little buddy. Thanks for making my day complete."

Burt stopped and turned to look at Quill, a quizzical expression on his face as he wondered if maybe Quill had bumped his head or something. He sure was talking about some strange stuff! He just grunted an answer and then looked away. He was also wondering if he was going in the right direction. But then again, all that mattered to him at that moment was that they were heading *away* from trouble.

Chapter Two

They had been walking for three hours now and it was getting dark. They had to stop soon and make camp.

"Quill, we've got to find a safe place for the night. It'll be dark soon and I'm really getting hungry. I feel like I haven't eaten a thing in days." Burt rubbed his ample stomach and looked around trying to spot something familiar.

"O.K. Burt, you can get some firewood and start a fire, we'll eat and then rest," Quill agreed.

It wasn't long before Burt realized he had gotten them lost but he didn't want to say anything to Quill—he had enough problems with his eyes and all. Anyway, things would look different in the morning. Burt helped Quill sit down then set off to find a place of shelter for the night. Not far away he found a small clearing with plenty of wood all around it. He noticed a huge pine tree with limbs all the way to the ground. It would make a perfect shelter. Just crawl under the limbs and they would be safe. Burt walked over to the tree and moved some of the branches back to take a look underneath. It looked like it had been made just for them—just big enough for the two of them to curl up to sleep and, it was dry. After this inspection, Burt made his way back to where Quill was patiently waiting.

"I've found a wonderful place. Stand up and I'll guide you there."

When they arrived at the clearing, Burt sat Quill next to the big tree. He told him that if he wanted to lie down all he had to do was crawl backwards and he'd be safely under the tree. Burt then set the bow and quiver next to the opening, knowing that Quill would feel better if it were near him even though he couldn't use it right now.

"I'll make a fire and get something together so we can eat. Just relax and it'll be done soon," Burt said reassuringly.

As Quill sat there, he began to feel very strange. He was seeing things in his mind—things he couldn't understand. He was able to see the clearing in front of him, Burt walking around collecting wood for the fire, and, turning his head to the left, he saw his bow and quiver next to him. Without even turning around he knew what the shelter behind him looked like. He didn't want to say anything to Burt about this; Burt would think he was going crazy or something. Then Quill was aware of another image in his mind. It was a of great room full of gold and treasure, very bright and colorful, with statues of gigantic people. They wore brightly-colored robes with jewels hanging from around their necks. There were crowns of highly-polished gold and jewels beyond belief. The picture soon faded but Quill knew he had never seen anything to rival the splendor of that room. Scared and uncertain about all of this, he reached for his bow and quiver, taking them into his arms. The familiar feel was comforting and soon he was able to lay down in the opening and drift into sleep.

"Quill, what do you want to eat?" Burt asked as he was stacking wood in a small pile.

He turned around as he spoke and then realized Quill was asleep. Burt feared for his long-time friend, knowing that if he did not regain his eyesight soon he would never be the same. Burt always followed Quill. Now it was the other way around and he was not comfortable with it at all. Unlike Quill, with his well-built body and blond hair, Burt didn't even look like a leader. Quill is an elf, much different from Burt. He's smarter and a little bit taller and his pointed ears and good looks always made Burt a little jealous. Burt knew that Quill was a born leader. Quill always had the right answer and knew exactly the right thing to do, and when it had to be done. Quill's deep blue eyes mirrored his very soul and strength of spirit. Burt was sure he didn't have the same qualities. He saw himself as a short, fat, ugly kind of guy. His hair was always a mess; he never shaved and very seldom bathed. But there were two things that Burt knew he did well; eating was one, always being there for Quill was the other! "How strange," Burt thought, "Why did Quill want me as a friend?" It just didn't make a bit of sense. He knew that the two of them had nothing in common, not a thing, except that they liked each other and got along really well.

Burt knelt down and arranged some of the small sticks he had found nearby into a neat pile. He took some of the dried grass he had also found and placed it under the sticks. After reaching into his pocket to pull out a piece of flint stone, he slid his knife from its leather case and began striking the knife against the stone to make a spark. Coaxing the fire to life, Burt put several more pieces of wood on the growing flames. He knew it would get cold as the night grew longer. As it was, darkness was already upon them and the flickering light from the fire was now their only lantern. Burt crouched near the fire warming himself, chasing away the dampness that came with the night. He thought of home, a small village in the middle of a group of mountains that were known as the Great Mountains of the Wind for the simple reason that no one had ever made it out over the tops of those mountains. The wind was so strong that it would not allow you over the top and out of the valley. The elders always said that no one could leave by order of the King of Zin who would not allow it. The people had somehow angered the king so much that all in the valley were kept as prisoners. But that fact didn't bother Burt right now. He had other things on his mind.

A smile came to Burt's face as he thought of his mother and father. How good it would be to get home and be with them. Burt's father was a strong man—the village carpenter. He had built most of their village himself. His mother was as gentle as a brook flowing on a hot summer's day. Burt thought she was the best cook in the village—and he could prove it by his size! Just thinking of her cooking made him hungry!

He walked over to Quill and gave him a firm shake. "Quill, wake up. How do you feel?" Burt asked. To be truthful, he was thinking more of his stomach than about Quill's well-being at that moment!

Quill opened his eyes and sat up. He still had his bow and quiver clenched in his arms. "I feel fine," he answered sleepily.

"Let's eat something before we settle for the night." Burt suggested as he untied the food bag emptying its contents on the ground next to Quill. They were running low on food, but there was still enough for the two of them to enjoy a good meal before they went to sleep. Burt reached down and took one of the small bundles wrapped in cloth and untied its leather strings. Taking out a piece of dried meat that his mother had prepared, he handed it to Quill.

"Eat this," Burt said as Quill reached out for the meat.

Burt then took a piece for himself and sat next to Quill.

"Have you still got the water pouch?" asked Quill.

"Yes," replied Burt as he pulled the moist, leather canteen over his head and handed it to Quill. "This is all the water we have until I can find more so let's try to take it easy with it," Burt cautioned.

Quill pulled the wooden peg from the top and took a small drink. He handed it back to Burt who also drank and then replaced the peg carefully.

They continued eating until they were satisfied and then Burt picked up the leftovers and put them back in the bag. He took inventory as he did so and felt confident that there was enough food for one more day. If they didn't get home soon, they would have to hunt for food. Burt was very concerned about the food stores because going hungry was not one of his favorite things in life! With Quill unable to see, it would be Burt's responsibility to provide. It seemed a bit odd to him because when it came time to hunt, it had always been Quill's job. Quill was by far the best hunter in the village—and they never went without food. Now it was Burt's job and he was lost as to how to go about it.

Facing Quill, he said, "We have enough food for one more day but then I'll have to find something for us to eat."

"Well, I guess my sight had better come back soon or you and I are going to go hungry aren't we?" Quill's grin let Burt know that his friend really was feeling better and was good naturedly teasing him.

Burt reached over and put his hand on Quill's shoulder, and gave him a light shake and said, "I'm trying as hard as I can to get us through this. If you continue to pick on me, I'm going to leave you right where you're sitting, but, for now, I think you had better crawl under the tree and get some sleep. It's going to be a long day tomorrow."

Quill turned around, slipped under the tree shelter and was soon fast asleep. Burt decided he would sit up for a while so he could keep an eye on the fire. Again his mind drifted to thoughts of home and how nice it was going to be to get back. He started thinking about the rest of the village and all of the people in it. He could see Quill's small home, which was across from his own, and then started thinking about how he and Quill had been friends for as long as he could remember. Their fathers were best friends. Quill's father was the village leader and a great hunter. Quill's mother was as strong and smart as Quill's father and also the best looking woman in the village. She was the power behind Quill's family, and everyone knew it. The village had several families. There were as many young people as there were elders. Half of the young ones were the same age as Burt and Quill, around twenty-two. Burt had no other friends than Quill. It had been the same his whole life. Everyone would pick on him because he was fat. The only person who didn't was Quill. Burt decided a long time ago that he was not going to be friends with anyone who made fun of him. As Burt sat there going over each member of the village in his mind, he started thinking of what each one did that made them special to the life of the village. Some cooked. Some helped his father build things such as tables and chairs. Others made clothes and collected food. Some farmed the land. As Burt was reflecting on each one he realized that he made no significant contribution to the village. He thought about this for a moment longer and then it came to him. He was Quill's best friend and right hand. Quill would be the next leader and Burt was to be his assistant. That was good enough for him!

Looking up, Burt noticed that the fire was going out. He got up and walked over to the stack of wood that he had collected and began to put more wood on the fading embers. It was then that Burt first heard a noise. He couldn't tell what it was, but something was moving around in front of him in the woods. Burt became very much afraid and grabbed a big stick lying on top of the woodpile. Slowly he took a few steps toward the edge of the trees, his right foot becoming tangled in some fallen limbs and he tripped and fell. In a flash there was a tremendously loud noise over the top of him and something landed on his chest. Terrified, he began gasping for air and screaming. It was a gigantic wolf and Burt was staring straight into its eyes as it started to chew and bite at his chest and arms! The pain was excruciating! Each time the wolf snapped its jaws it tore another piece of Burt's flesh away from his body.

By now Quill was wide awake and reaching for his bow. Something was wrong and Burt was in trouble. He could hear the cries for help and although he couldn't see, his mind's eye saw the wolf on top of Burt. Quill sprang from his hiding place taking an arrow from his quiver as he moved. Quickly he raised it to his bow and took aim. He couldn't help but think about the visions in his head. Were they real or imagined? Quill knew that if they were not, then he could kill Burt if he missed this shot. He was facing the direction from where the sounds of Burt's pain were coming. Quill drew back on the straining bow, again wondering if he were doing the right thing or if he were going crazy. The arrow flew—the two-hundred-pound wolf fell dead on top of Burt.

"Burt! Are you all right?" Quill yelled.

Quill could hear only the wind and the trees moving. He walked over to where Burt lay on the ground and knelt.

"Burt, say something. Please, Burt. You have to be all right!" Tears filled Quill's eyes.

Still the only sound was the rustling of the leaves on the trees and the whistle of the wind. Quill, by now, was trying to push the wolf off Burt. He couldn't see it with his eyes, but could in his mind. He managed to get the wolf off and started to feel for Burt's face. Finding the familiar, round face he lightly slapped him to see if he could rouse him at all.

"Burt! Burt, wake up! Wake up! You have to be all right." The tears that had instantly filled his eyes now streamed down his face.

A long, slow moan gave indication that Burt was coming around. Feeling Burt's face Quill realized that Burt had been badly bitten. He started to search the rest of Burt's body with his hands and it seemed that everywhere he touched there was blood and chunks of flesh missing. Quill's heart pounded like a blacksmith's hammer. His hands began to shake out of control as fear set in. His best friend was dying and there was nothing he could do to save him. Quill knew that the wolf had ripped away much of Burt's body and that he was bleeding to death.

"Quill, are you there?" asked Burt weakly.

Quill cradled Burt's head in his arm, placing his hand to Burt's mouth. "Sh-h-h, yes, little buddy. I'm here."

"Am I going to die? I am aren't I? I know it. I have no feeling in my arms and legs and all I want to do right now is sleep," Burt whispered.

"Burt, you know that you're my best friend and I wouldn't let anything hurt you," Quill responded as he held back the tears that threatened once again.

"Quill, do me a favor. I know that all of the trouble we have gotten into has something to do with those stones. I knew that when I had to go back to the pit and get them. If I am to die, I would at least like to hold my half of them. May I hold one?"

Quill couldn't hold it back any longer. He let out a loud wail and began sobbing like a baby. His best friend was dying and he couldn't even see him one last time. Quill reached down and untied the bag from his belt. The bag contained the two stones. He undid the leather thongs holding the bag tightly closed and then reached in and grabbed one of the stones. He placed it in Burt's hand and made no effort this time to keep from crying.

"Burt, you know that I'm going to miss you. You're my only true friend. You're like a brother to me," Quill said as he laid his head on Burt's chest.

There was no more sound from Burt. As the night wore on, Quill stayed there with him. He lay with his head on Burt's chest so he could hear him breathe, not realizing that he would soon fall asleep.

As the morning sun made its way over the tree line, Quill felt a light breeze softly stroking his cheek. At first Quill thought he was at home, but fear soon gripped him once more when he realized that he was still laying across Burt's chest. When Quill opened his eyes the brightness of the sun shocked him. He couldn't believe it! He could see! He turned quickly to look at Burt. As his eyes fixed on Burt's body, Quill's heart began to pound. He thought it would explode! He saw nothing wrong with Burt other than his ripped clothes. Stretching out his hand, he gave Burt a firm shake.

"Burt, Burt, wake up! Come on lazy bones, it's time to get up," Quill said excitedly.

Quill was practically leaping in the air for joy when he saw Burt's arm come up and scratch his nose. Quill couldn't believe his eyes; Burt was alive and what was even more surprising was that there wasn't a mark anywhere on his body. Quill was so happy that he was jumping up and down, his arms waving in the air and a smile on his face so big it stretched clear up to the corners of his eyes!

"I don't believe it! My little buddy is alive," Quill yelped in amazement.

Quill looked over at the wolf and saw anything *but* a normal wolf. It appeared golden, and the biggest wolf that he had ever seen. Yes, definitely a bright gold in color. His shot had hit with deadly accuracy, one of the best he had ever made, right through the heart. He approached the dead animal and pulled out his arrow. After cleaning it, he replaced it in his quiver knowing full well he could not waste any arrows. His father had taught him how to make the best arrows in the village and Quill's trademark was the arrowhead itself. He made them from a clear stone that only he knew where to find. Quill then walked back over to Burt and with his foot, gave him a firm kick. Burt's eyes popped open and he started mumbling.

"Quill, do you always have to wake me up when I'm dreaming?" Burt sat up and scratched his head. Suddenly he sprang to his feet like a nervous rabbit in a lion's den!

"I'm not dead! What happened Quill? I know the wolf killed me. How come I'm still here? Just look at me, not a mark on me!" Burt examined every inch of his small body looking for any signs of the attack. and then he looked down and opened his hand. There in the center of his palm was the black stone. Without saying another word he knew this stone had saved his life.

"Quill, you can see can't you? Your head was on my chest all night wasn't it?" Burt asked quietly, seemingly awestruck by this realization.

"Yes Burt. I stayed with you through the night and the power in that stone must have cured us both." He put a friendly arm around his friend's shoulder.

"What do you say we try to find our way out of here, seeing that you managed to get us lost yesterday?" Quill asked good-naturedly as he led Burt to the big tree where their food and water still lay.

"Burt, I don't understand the power of those any more than you do but I do know one thing for sure, whoever they belong to is surely going to come looking for them!" Quill remembered that he had left his bow and quiver, as well as the bag with the other stone in it, next to the wolf.

"Burt, get the food and water will you?" It was more of a direction than a question.

Quill returned to the wolf, picked up his belongings and hung them over his shoulder then, without hesitation, he took out his knife and cut the tail off the wolf. He turned around, picked up the bag with the stone and walked back over to Burt.

"Burt, put the stone in the bag with the other one."

Quill held out the bag and opened it. As Burt placed the little black stone in the bag, Quill smiled at him. He tousled Burt's hair with one of those "you're all right" shakes that said everything was going to be better now. After tying the small leather bag to his belt, he reached into his left pocket and pulled out a small strand of leather. He tied one end around the wolf's tail and handed it to Burt.

"I think you should be the one to have this trophy. After all, you were the one who earned it, not me."

Quill scoured the camp with his eyes making sure they hadn't left anything behind, kicked more sand on the almost-out fire, and started off into the woods.

"Quill, wait for me," Burt yelled as he tried to catch up, with water pouch, food bag and wolf tail all swinging in opposite directions!

Chapter Three

Quill led the way all day, stopping only once so that Burt could catch his breath. Quill couldn't understand it but as the day passed he kept hoping to find a reference point of some kind that would give him an idea of where he was. There wasn't a thing that he recognized so far. It was almost as if he and Burt had somehow walked out of the valley; but, that couldn't be. Quill knew it was impossible to leave the valley because of those powerful winds at the tops of the mountains. The wind was there to keep *them* from leaving and to prevent anyone else from coming *into* the valley. He finally decided to face the reality of the situation; they were lost.

Quill kept pushing on, and as he did, he noticed that the trail started to resemble a place in the southern tip of the valley where his father had taken him long ago. The terrain looked almost the same, but Quill knew it couldn't be the same place. They were at the northern part of the valley now; at least they were when Burt fell into the pit with the vipers. Quill then remembered something that his father had once told him while they were hunting. If you ever get lost, take note of the sun, the stars, and the moon and, if there is water, note the direction in which it is flowing. Quill stopped and looked up to see if he could find the sun, but realized that the trees were so thick he couldn't see through them. He began to look around at the forest and noticed that the trees everywhere were much thicker than he had ever seen. He could also see that there was much more brush, brush that appeared to be ten feet high and so thick that he couldn't even see into it. He also noticed that there were vines growing everywhere, climbing over everything. As Quill stood there, he saw something else strange about this forest. There was no sound. The only noise was the slip-slap of Burt's feet shuffling along the trail as he approached him. Quill tilted his head as if trying to listen from a better angle. This time he heard another sound. It was the sound of his own heart beating, pounding and pounding as if it were about to explode. Fear had him in its grip. He was lost, lost in a place that he didn't know or understand. He took a deep breath, and then another, trying to fight back the fear that had tied knots in the base of his stomach. He couldn't allow Burt to see that he was afraid.

"Quill, it's getting dark and I'm getting hungry. Can we make camp for the night?" Burt asked as he flopped down to the ground to grab a few moments' rest.

"The trail is too narrow. If we stay here there's the danger of animals like that wolf that almost killed you." Quill tugged at the water pouch hanging around Burt's neck.

"Wait, wait. Let me get it off," Burt snapped as he removed the pouch and handed it to Quill.

Quill pulled the wooden peg from the top and took a long drink. He handed the pouch back to Burt and asked for a piece of meat that Burt had already pulled from the food bag. Burt looked first at Quill and then at the meat. He held the meat up in the air and looked at it for a few moments. Quill knew what Burt was doing. He had gone through the same routine for years. He ripped the meat down the middle, but as always, Burt somehow never could do it right. He always had one piece bigger than the other. Quill understood though. He knew Burt would get the biggest piece because that's the way he had always worked it.

"How far do you think we have to go before we can camp for the night?" Burt asked as he hung the water pouch back around his neck and tied the food bag to his belt.

"Burt, I don't know how far we have to go. As a matter of fact, I have some bad news. Somewhere between the time I lost my sight, and when I got it back, we got lost."

"How can we be lost? You know this valley like the back of your hand. You've never been lost," Burt wailed.

"I don't know what happened. I was hoping that *you* could tell me how we got lost," Quill answered as he placed his hand on Burt's knee and gave him a reassuring pat.

The look on Burt's face gave Quill the answer without Burt speaking a word. Burt had no idea where they were or how they had gotten there. He couldn't even remember in what direction they had traveled when they left the pit.

"Quill, I don't understand. We can't be lost. I know we were going in the right direction when we left that pit. You remember don't you? We didn't go that far. We only walked for about three hours," Burt remarked as he got to his feet.

"Burt, I don't want you to worry about this. You and I both know that all of the trails in this valley go around in big circles, and sooner or later we'll make it home." And he actually felt very confident with this answer.

As Quill got to his feet, he looked at Burt's face and knew that Burt was not going to handle this well at all. Burt's greatest fear was being lost and Quill knew that. He also knew that Burt was already letting the fear get to him. It was written all over his face. Quill put his arm around Burt's shoulders as they both started to walk down the trail together. Nightfall was almost upon them and it was getting harder to see any distance in front of them. By now Burt had moved ahead of Quill, about five yards or so, and could be heard mumbling to himself every now and then when he would trip over some of the loose branches lying across the trail. Quill was beginning to feel closed in. It was the trail. It was becoming narrower. So narrow in fact that he could feel brush hitting his arms as he increased his pace. Quill noticed that Burt had picked up his pace as well and it was getting harder to keep an eye on him.

"Burt, slow down! I can't see you anymore," Quill yelled.

Burt didn't respond to Quill's plea to slow down and then Quill could no longer see him. Burt was losing control and the only way to stop him was to catch up to him. Quill started running. All he could think of was that his little friend was in trouble and could become separated from him, or even hurt, because of his deep fear of being lost. Quill felt his breathing become more rapid—his heartbeat more noticeable—the faster he ran.

"Burt, stop! Stop running! Stop and wait for me!" Quill shouted.

The branches at the edge of the trail were hitting Quill in the face now. He even had to close his eyes a few times lest he might lose an eye. He could feel the pain as the brush slapped and dragged across his whole body and he felt blood running down his cheeks. If he didn't slow down, he knew the brush would cut him up even more. So he slowed to a fast walk and just started catching his breath when he heard Burt scream "Quill! Help me! Help me, I'm falling!"

Quill raced in the direction of Burt's screams, not even giving a thought now to the battering branches. He was trying to listen as he ran, but it was difficult. His bow was hitting him in the back of his head and the two stones in the food bag were banging together so loudly that he could hear nothing else. He slowed to listen. As he did, his legs came right out from under him and water rushed around him. Quill tried to get to his feet but kept slipping and sliding. He couldn't get back up. It was then he realized the water was sweeping him away in a downhill torrent. Quill began to grab at whatever he could find, a stick, a vine, anything that might stop him, but it was of no use. He couldn't stop. He was speeding ever faster as the water washed over his face and head. He rolled over on his back to avoid drowning but then knew that he was being swept away in a nonstop surge toward what appeared to be a waterfall!

Quill screamed Burt's name as he was carried over the edge. There was no way of stopping and for the briefest of instants he was sure he was plummeting toward certain death. As he plunged toward the bottom of the falls, he felt himself colliding with the face of the cliff. As his body smashed brutally against the outcrops of rock the pain overpowered him and, mercifully, he blacked out.

When he woke water was falling all around him. The full realization of what had happened had not yet hit him. He was in so much pain from the fall that all he could think of was getting to a safe, warm and dry place. Moving his left foot, and then the right to make sure they were not broken, he saw he had landed upon several years' accumulation of branches and tree limbs which had apparently met the same fate at the bottom of that waterfall. Not much more was visible because of the deluge of water flooding over him and the growing darkness of the coming night. He took a couple of deep breaths and got to his knees. Everything hurt, but it seemed that there was no real damage. He would leave it to sunlight to reveal the bruises!

As he moved, the clutter under him shifted. It rocked back and forth as if it were going to tumble over. Quill stopped moving for a moment. It was obvious that in order to get off this pile of wood he needed to take his time. It was now dark and the cascading water made everything much more difficult. The wood was slimy and slippery making it hard to hang on without falling off. He remembered that Burt had fallen first and must also be down here somewhere. Quill moved to the right, a little at a time in order to get out from under the waterfall. As he reached up and wiped water from his face, his heart skipped a beat. He had fallen onto the outer rim of a ledge—a ledge covered with years of debris washed down by the falling water. He moved a little more. This time the pile *didn't.* He was still on his knees so he decided to lie down and roll the rest of the way off, making sure that it was toward the cliff! As he rolled down the pile, he heard snapping and cracking as some of the clutter broke loose and dropped over the ledge. He hit the rock wall of the cliff and came to a jolting stop. He again raised to his knees and looked around.

"Burt, Burt! Are you down here?" Quill yelled. His echo carried for several moments.

There was not another sound except for water splashing against the pile in front of him. Grabbing a piece of wood, he threw it over the side. Again he listened. Nothing. Just an eerie silence. Either it had landed in water or the bottom was so far down that sound couldn't carry back up to him. As he sat down, he felt for some of the loose sticks and branches that seemed to cover the floor of the ledge. Reaching under himself he started throwing large clumps of these over the edge. In a short time, he had cleared an area large enough for him to move around. He didn't want to trip over anything and be in danger of falling over the edge himself!

Now that he felt somewhat safe for the time being, his thoughts turned again to Burt. No one could have survived a fall any farther than the one he had just taken. There was no sign of Burt anywhere on this ledge. Quill felt tears fill his eyes as he thought of his little companion. Burt was the best friend any man could have and Quill would be lost without him. He lay down as these thoughts filled his mind. He tried to fight off the urge to sleep which was overpowering him but it was impossible.

His energy gone, and knowing he wouldn't be able to do anything else till daybreak, he closed his eyes, giving in to the darkness, and quickly falling into a fitful sleep.

Chapter Four

As the morning sun's light made its way into Quill's face, he opened his eyes to a new day. He struggled to sit up, feeling pain in his back and legs. He realized that he must have bounced against his bow during the plunge over the waterfall. Quill removed the bow and quiver and leaned them against the rock wall of the cliff, then reached around and began to rub his back, trying to relieve some of the pain that was making it so difficult for him to move. As he was moving his hand all around his back and lower legs, he felt the small leather food pouch and remembered that it contained the small stones that he and Burt recovered from the pit. The pouch must have become twisted and was now behind him. He untied the strings holding the pouch and pulled it around to the front where he stared at it for a moment. As he squeezed it, he thought to himself that it was those stones that caused the mess he was in. He gave the pouch a few small shakes and heard the stones knock against each other. He opened the bag and retrieved one of the stones.

As he fingered the stone, he recalled how they had cured Burt and how they had returned his eyesight. But they had also been the cause of his going blind in the first place! It didn't make sense to him that two small stones could hurt someone and at the same time be the source of healing as well. Pulling the black stone from the bag, he exposed it to the sun's golden rays. This was the first time Quill really had a chance to look at what he and Burt had risked their lives for.

Gazing at that stone, he tried to decide what it was. He knew the stone had a power he didn't understand, and had never known or even heard of before. There was a feeling of fear, fear of the unknown. As his fingers gently rubbed over the stone, he noticed that it was about the same size as a human eye. It was pure black and as smooth as churned butter. Quill rubbed the stone between his fingers, and eased into a feeling of peaceful calm. It was pure delight such as he had not felt for a very long time and he couldn't understand why he felt this way now of all times. Suddenly he realized that the soreness in his back and legs was gone and he could feel his strength returning. Quill closed his hand around the stone and squeezed, enjoying every minute of this blissful experience. Just as he thought these strange feelings would never end, he began to feel dizzy and sick to his stomach. He dropped the stone into the pouch and the dizziness seemed to pass. When he put his hand back in and grabbed the stone again, the dizziness returned. As soon as he released the stone, the feeling was gone. Yes, this was indeed very weird. But for the first time Quill began to understand how to use the power of the stones. He knew that the stones would cure sickness if held separately and that if he held them together they would release a great power that could harm him. He realized that if he needed this power to cure, he could only hold *one* of them for a short time.

****

Quill sat there for a few minutes looking around. He enjoyed the pleasure of the sun as it covered his face with warmth that gave a great feeling of comfort. His eyes scoured the face of the cliff. He was looking for anything that would give him a clue as to how to get off the ledge. He could see that there was no way he could climb this vertical slab of rock. He stood up and peered over the rim of the small ledge, trying to find a way down. Again, he concluded that it was impossible to climb down. Quill looked into the waterfall that was in front of him. As he stared through the water he couldn't believe his eyes. He saw a valley—one he had never seen before! The valley appeared very rugged and dry, almost as though it were dead. He could see nothing that seemed alive; no trees, no grass, no water. Looking down at a pile of tree limbs and brush hanging at the rim of the ledge, he saw more than just brush and wood this time. He noticed that tangled throughout this huge pile of woodland clutter were the remains of several small animals. He also noticed several piles of bones all over the ledge. It then dawned on him that he was standing in the middle of a graveyard of sorts—victims who had fallen into the small stream above.

He was beginning to foresee his own ultimate fate. Being a prisoner here meant certain death. The thought chilled him to the very bone. But along with the terror, anger was building inside, a singular rage at the prospect of his entrapment in this place! He viciously kicked at the bones lying at his feet, then reaching down, grabbed one and threw it into the waterfall with all the might he could muster. He spun around and lifting his arms as high as he could, began pounding at the rock wall that held him trapped! A piercing scream tore from his throat as all the frustration of the moment overwhelmed him and poured forth in one gigantic protest to this unfair turn of events! He slammed and pounded against the rock until blood from his punished knuckles and hands trickled down the face of the cliff, seeping into the cracks of the rock. He was devastated—alone, lost and forgotten.

Exhausted by this passionate outburst, he was about to lie down and give up, accept whatever it was fate had ordained for him. But then, something hit him in the middle of the back. When he turned around to see what it was, he saw that the bone he had thrown into the waterfall had reappeared. How could that be? It was easily a three hundred foot drop to the bottom of the cliff. He reached down and took the bone into his hand. This time he would make sure it made it to the bottom! He tossed the bone back into the waterfall, but nothing happened. He looked at his hands. They were covered in blood. He watched as the pile of bones at his feet slowly turned scarlet, bathed in his blood. The droplets formed a small pool at his feet and mysteriously he could see a vision of Burt lying across some logs. Burt was alive and nearby! He felt it to the core of his being! This was indeed a true vision! Instinctively he knew as he looked up at the pile of tree limbs in front of him that he would find Burt on the other side!

Quill frantically began climbing to the top of the brush-covered pile unaware as he did so, that the tree limbs had begun to shake. He slowed down, waiting for the pile to stop moving back and forth. As he entered the waterfall from the top of the pile, he heard the distinct crack and scrape of branches giving way and falling over the edge. Peering through the water just enough to see over the top, he spied his little buddy Burt, hanging helplessly over two cris-crossed logs!

"Burt! Burt it's me, Quill, up here!" He yelled as he started waving his arm to get Burt's attention. He was so excited at this discovery he almost lost his grip, slipping a bit on the soaked pile.

Burt looked up at Quill and raised his arm in the air to show Quill that he could hear him over the rush of water pounding all around him and then pointed to his leg. Quill could see that Burt had obviously broken his leg and that it was covered with blood. He knew he couldn't go any further, lest he, the pile, and Burt would plummet to the bottom of the cliff. There had to be a way to help Burt. But how, without causing everything to cascade over the face of the ledge? Backing up a little to get out from under the waterfall, Quill looked down and thought that if he could lower the pile of wood a bit, he might be able to take some of the weight off and crawl out to Burt. He began frantically grabbing at the tree branches and brush, throwing them over the side. Quill had managed to lower the pile about five feet when he stopped dead in his tracks.

He had uncovered a skeleton; but no normal skeleton! These were the bones of a giant! A sword and shield lay next to it. And around the neck of the leather-clad giant was a necklace containing a single black stone. He pulled the gruesome discovery up against the face of the cliff—moving it out of the way but being careful not to push it over the edge. He then continued toward Burt.

Quill crawled out through the waterfall. Very carefully he inched along toward his little friend stopping repeatedly to make sure that the remaining pile of clutter didn't shift. When he was about five feet from Burt, he grabbed a long branch and reaching out yelled, "Burt! Burt, wake up. Grab the branch!"

Burt roused, and weakly stretched his hand out to the shaking lifeline. He was able to grasp only the very end of the branch but he held on with all the strength left in his sore and battered body. Quill managed to haul him over the debris and through the waterfall. Grabbing Burt under the arms, he pulled him to the face of the cliff where he leaned him up against the rocks. Quill himself then collapsed against the security of the stone face.

"Burt, are you all right?" gasped Quill, the effort of this rescue now taking its toll on his bruised body.

"My leg is killing me. Can you do anything for the pain?" Burt asked, his quavering voice telling Quill that the pain was almost more than Burt could endure.

"Here. Reach into the pouch and take one of the stones into your hand. It will take away the pain in your leg," Quill answered as he opened the bag and held it out to Burt.

Burt reached in and grabbed a stone. As he fell back against the rock wall, he closed his eyes and drifted into an unconscious state.

While Burt slept, Quill again inspected the humongous skeleton. How long had this giant been lying there? He reached over and taking the huge sword in his hands, picked it up and held it in the air. As tall as he was, the sword was almost as heavy. He leaned it up against the rock wall next to his own bow and quiver. As he picked up the shield, the dirt and slime from years of being under the water oozed through his fingers, making it almost impossible to get a good hold. He dragged it over next to where Burt lay and started cleaning it, occasionally glancing at his still-sleeping friend to make sure he was all right. As Quill rubbed years of grime and sludge from the shield, strange markings began to emerge, markings which Quill didn't understand. These marks, or symbols, looked like they told some kind of story, but Quill had no idea just what! So he laid the shield next to the sword. Next he removed the necklace from the fragile bones. When Quill held it up to the sun, he noticed that the stone in the center of the setting was the same as the two he had found earlier when the viper was destroyed! The only difference was its size. It was at least three times larger than the other two! He placed the necklace around his own neck and sat back down against the wall. He would rest and wait for Burt to waken.

****

It had been almost four hours since Burt had fallen asleep and Quill was becoming worried. He reached over and gave Burt a firm shake.

"Burt, wake up!" Quill said.

Burt slowly opened his eyes and rubbed the sleep from his face.

"Quill, why do you always have to wake me up?" Burt asked as he realized that he had one of the stones in his hand.

Burt looked down at his leg and saw that it was completely healed. He opened his hand and looked at the stone lying there.

"This doesn't look like a stone. It looks more like someone's eye," Burt remarked holding it up to the sun.

"I know, Burt, but whatever they are, they have the power to heal," Quill said.

Then Burt saw the giant's skeleton and, jumping back in fright, started screaming, "Quill, what *is* that thing?" Burt's howls of panic were almost comical but Quill knew better than to mock his friend's genuine fear!

"I don't know *who* it is but I can tell you this much, that it's the remains of a great warrior and an incredible giant," Quill answered, his own mood now reflecting this puzzling situation.

Burt scrambled to his feet, gently trying out his leg, gingerly putting more and more weight on it. He wore a smile from one end of his face to the other. Now completely ignoring the skeleton before them, he looked around the ledge and asked Quill if he had a plan for getting them down from there. He more or less assumed that Quill had already thought of everything.

But to his surprise he heard.

"Burt, I have no idea how we're going to get down from here. I've tried to come up with an idea but nothing strikes me."

"Look, there's got to be a logical way of getting out of this mess," Burt said, his voice a little edgy to think that Quill hadn't figured this out yet. As he spoke, he scoured the rock face of their trap and suddenly he saw something leaning up against the rocks. The sun's rays were glinting off what looked to be a sword. Leaning forward a bit, and cocking his head to get a better look, he saw that it was indeed a sword and, at a crazy tilt next to it, a shield.

The sword was huge—taller than Burt, and the shield was gold with ten glistening jewels mounted around the outside edge. He didn't know what kind of jewels they were, but they sure were pretty.

"Quill, were those with the giant?" Burt asked.

"They must have been his. And this necklace was around his neck," Quill said as he held it up so Burt could see. Then Quill noticed that Burt still had the food pouch tied to his belt. He was very hungry so he reached over and tugged at it. Without saying a word, Burt removed it and they both sat down and finished the rest of the food. When he was done, Burt started scrounging around the ledge, collecting small dry twigs and sticks.

Quill just sat there looking, and wondering what Burt was doing. He knew Burt could do strange things but what now?

"Dare I ask just what you are up to?" Quill asked.

"I'm going to build a fire. It's getting dark and I don't want to be cold. Maybe someone in the valley will see the fire tonight and come to our rescue," Burt answered.

"I don't believe it. After all these years you've finally come up with a good idea!" Quill teased as he joined Burt in his search. He was definitely beginning to feel more confident that they would indeed find their way out of this jam. They had faced problems together before and would eventually be able to sort through this one. Morning would shed a different light on everything.

It wasn't long before Burt had a warm and comforting fire blazing and they were both sitting by it, enjoying the welcomed heat. Quill could feel sleep creeping up on him like a soft, warm blanket as he leaned back against the rough rock wall. His head slowly drooped and he nodded off. Burt sat staring at the dancing flames for a while before he too drifted into sleep.

****

Daybreak burst upon them without warning interrupting a deep, dreamless sleep. Quill was cold—the fire long since burned out. He tried to warm himself by curling up into a ball but it didn't help. He opened his eyes and looked at the smoldering ashes. Rising curls of smoke were all that remained of last night's cozy fire. Then he noticed something very strange about the smoke. It was not drifting up as it normally would, but rather was being sucked into the cracks in the face of the cliff. He carefully got to his feet, moving closer for a better look and couldn't believe his eyes. "The smoke is going into the side of this mountain. How can that be?" he mused to himself. He reached down and felt the cracks in the solid rock, then looked around for something to use as a pick. Spotting the sword, he grabbed it and began poking the sharp, pointed blade into the cracks. To his amazement, the sword didn't meet with resistance when jabbed through but easily passed into the rock! There was hope after all! Perhaps this was a way out! Quill excitedly kicked Burt, trying to jostle him awake.

"Burt, come on, wake up! I found something!"

Wide awake now, Burt jumped to his feet sputtering "What? What is it?"

Waving his arms and the sword, Quill pointed in the direction of the wall. "Look at these cracks then watch the smoke from the fire. It's being sucked into them! There has to be something on the other side!"

Burt knelt down and with his fingers traced the cracks to the bottom of the ledge. "Give me that sword Quill. I think I can dig out some of these loose rocks from here."

Burt worked as he had never worked before. He wouldn't even stop to take a break; just kept mumbling about getting off the ledge because he wasn't going to die in a strange land. Using the sword as both pick and shovel, Burt furiously dug out the rock, chopping away with all his strength and heaved the loosened chunks over the side of the cliff.

This went on all day long, the two of them taking turns with the makeshift pick, but it was now growing dark again. Burt had managed to dig out a space big enough for him to sit in. Quill wondered whether the cracks in the rock were just that—cracks, never-ending cracks. Just as Quill was about to suggest that they stop, Burt shouted "We did it! We did it!"

Backing out of the space, he spun around saying, "It's there! There's a cave in there!" Quill moved forward to get a better look. Stepping into the space that Burt had worked so hard to open, he could see a small hole, a hole just big enough to reach your arm in and move it about freely. Quill backed out and grabbed Burt's shoulder giving him a firm shake. His way of saying "Good job little friend".

"Burt, you've saved our lives. Now I think we should rest to build our strength. Tomorrow we can finish widening the hole and get ourselves off this miserable ledge," Quill said as he settled down next to his bow and quiver.

"Quill, I'm going to build a fire and this time I'll be sure to keep it going because we'll need one to see what we're doing when we *do* get inside the cave." With that, Burt set about collecting wood.

After a few minutes Quill stood up, stepped over to the waterfall and removed his clothes.

"What *are* you doing?" Burt asked between his puffing attempts to blow the small sparks into useful flames.

"I haven't taken a bath for days now and something on this ledge has a foul smell. I just want to make sure it's not me," Quill answered as he stepped into the waterfall.

Quill knew that Burt didn't like even the thought of using water to get clean. He preferred to let the air clean him! Quill tried to do everything he could to politely suggest to Burt that it was *he* who had gone foul and smelled up the ledge. If he came right out and said it to Burt, Burt would get angry and not even think of cleaning himself. Quill started singing. It was a song learned by everyone in their village to just pass the time. Burt was still tending to the fire and started humming along. As the fire caught, Burt reached down into his pocket and grabbed his ocarina, a small potato-shaped wind horn, that he could play very well. He began to play along to Quill's singing, and as he did, the echo carried for miles. The soft melody brought comfort to one's heart. After Quill finished taking his bath under the waterfall, he stepped out and motioned to Burt that his turn had come. Burt looked at Quill quizzically at first, then adamantly shook his head telling Quill to forget it!

"Burt, you've got to get cleaned up. You always look like a mess. Besides, you don't know what type of strange things we could catch out here just from being dirty," Quill offered as he pulled his clothes back on.

"Who knows what I'll catch if I put myself in that icy water!" Burt countered in a half whine, half pleading voice. But he stood and moved over to the waterfall and reached his hand into the cold water. "No way!" shivered Burt, quickly pulling his hand from the water.

But Quill had had enough. "Burt, I'm not going to argue with you any more. Take off your clothes and get in there!" he ordered.

Burt had a way of doing what he was told whenever Quill would take that tone of voice to him and at this time he knew Quill meant business and it would do him no good to argue further. Burt struggled out of his clothes almost as if he had forgotten how to do it! Meanwhile, Quill moved over to the fire and put a few more sticks on it. The satisfied smile on his face said that he knew he had won that round with his friend. Burt stepped under the water mumbling to himself "I hate this. Only fish enjoy this kind of stuff!"

Quill almost laughed right out loud but instead contented himself with a smirk and started humming the song again, trying hard to remember all the words that the elders had taught him. They should have been easy to remember, they went easily with the tune, but they just wouldn't come to him.

"Burt, do you remember any of the words to this song?"

"I don't remember anything," Burt snapped in reply.

Quill knew Burt was upset with him, but having him clean for a change would be worth the effort and definitely more pleasant than the living with the smell!

"Quill, you are my best friend but right now I don't want to talk to you. I have just done something that I don't believe in; I took a bath. Only fish do that," Burt grumbled jumping out of the water. He quickly dressed trying to ignore Quill.

"Burt, someday you are going to want to take a wife but if you don't keep yourself clean there will be no woman who will have you," Quill said as he poked at the fire with one of the sticks lying next to him.

"Are you out of your mind? Women are nothing but trouble. They won't let you do what you want, and all they make you do is work. You know me, work is as bad as taking a bath!" Burt moved closer to the warmth of the fire. "How can you even think of such things? I will not take a woman. I look at how my mother treats my father. The poor guy. He's going to die at a young age, all because someone, namely your father, told him he should marry. No thank you! This is one dwarf who is not that stupid. I'm going to live my life doing what *I* want to do. One thing is for sure, taking care of a woman is *not* in my plans!" Burt was emphatic, punctuating his statement with both hands crossing in front of him repeatedly, signaling his absolute denial of this insane thought of Quill's.

Quill had not expected such an outburst but pursued it anyway. "Tell me Burt. What is it that you *do* want to do with your life?"

"I know I'm not much good at anything, and believe me I have thought about this before, but I *am* good at helping you. I want to be your assistant, your helper, for life. I can't see myself doing anything else. Can you understand that?"

"Burt, I'll always be proud to have you by my side." He reached for Burt's hand which was readily offered and they shook on it. There was no use prodding Burt any further. He was loyal and trustworthy—what more could Quill ask for?

A crash broke the mood and they both jumped to their feet in a flash. Something had fallen into the pile of tree limbs in front of them. They cautiously looked around and then Burt exclaimed, "Look here! It's a rabbit! Breakfast!" He joyfully picked up the unexpected bounty.

Quill had forgotten about all of the bones that were lying all over the ledge. He thought about it for a moment. If this happens every now and then, someone could live on this ledge for quite some time if they weren't hurt. He then glanced at the skeleton of the giant trying to understand what caused his death. Quill knew that the giant was more than likely a great warrior but, where did he come from—and how did he die?

"Quill, get that fire stoked up. I'm cooking us some rabbit! It's a good thing the fall killed him or he'd have been afraid and run right off this ledge trying to get away from us. You'd better hope another one drops over the cliff soon, or you're going to starve," Burt joked, his mood instantly improved now that the prospect of a good meal had presented itself. Why, he didn't even mind the work of skinning the little beast!

Now as Burt squatted next to the fire holding the stick-skewered rabbit over the coals, Quill returned to his spot next to his bow, sat down and stared up at the stars brightly twinkling in the dark night sky. He knew in his mind that whatever it was he and Burt were going through had a purpose. The vipers, the wolf, and now this ledge in a strange land; all were connected somehow. What was it that drew them to where they were—and why? He remembered the strange visions of the room full of gold. It all must mean something. Quill then dropped his hand to the leather bag containing the two stones that looked like eyes. He squeezed the bag feeling their round shape and he felt that they would play a part in his future. He was aware that because he was an elf he would someday have certain powers that others like Burt wouldn't have. His father would never tell him what they would be or how he would receive them. But oddly enough, Quill now sensed a change taking place inside of him. The elders of the village often talked of elves and the magic power they possessed. Quill would listen quietly and many times wondered why, if elves had such powers, didn't his father and he have them. But each time he would just dismiss these tales as just stories. Nothing to be believed. Most of the time they had something to do with a so-called "lost kingdom of Zin". Whatever that was.

As Quill continued staring off into the sky, he began to recall those strange stories in more detail; they had been told and re-told so many times, of how the good Elf protected the people of Zin from the bad Elf, and how the bad Elf finally won over the good Elf and destroyed the Kingdom of Zin. Everything Quill knew about elves and dwarves he learned from living with them in his village. In all those years he had never seen any of them with special powers. He thought of how nice it would be to have magical powers; powers that could help the people of his village live a better life, a life where survival would not be so hard. After all, most of the men of the village died before the age of fifty because they worked so hard to keep themselves and their families going. All those stories were just that—stories told to entertain and give a fantasy life to children and adults alike. A pleasant piece of hope in an otherwise very difficult life. Nothing more.

Burt jolted Quill from his reverie. "Quill, do you want some of this rabbit or not? I've been standing here asking you for several minutes now. I don't understand you; your mind seems to be somewhere else. What were you thinking about?" Burt stood over Quill offering him some of the rabbit meat.

"Nothing, nothing. Just daydreaming. If I told you what was on my mind you'd throw me over that ledge!"

"Tell me anyway Quill. I could use a good story and after what we've been through these past few days, I'd believe anything," Burt pleaded sitting down cross-legged next to the dreamer.

Quill explained in detail all that had gone through his mind, adding that he was also thinking about this journey and how they had been drawn to this strange land. They ate as they talked and it felt good to share his feelings and memories with this life-long friend.

"Better wrap the rest of the rabbit and save it in the food pouch. We may need it tomorrow if we can get inside the cave," Quill advised as he picked up a rather heavy stick, about two feet long, and began peeling the bark with his knife.

"What are you making?" asked Burt.

"Well, if we get into that cave, we're going to need some kind of light to see, so I'm making a torch. Hand me some of that cloth we had our food wrapped in."

Quill made the torch while Burt packed the rest of the rabbit. Burt, his stomach now well fed, was ready to bed down for the night. It wasn't long after he laid down that a soft snore told Quill that he had fallen asleep. Quill put a few more sticks on the fire and sat back down next to his bow. Without really thinking, he picked it up, feeling to make sure nothing had happened to it when he fell over the cliff. That bow was his life and he would be devastated if it were damaged. Other than Burt, the bow was the only friend Quill had. Satisfied that all was well, he leaned the bow back against the rock cliff and laid down, letting thoughts of the elders' stories take him into a deep, dream-filled sleep.

Chapter Five

Quill woke to the sound of Burt hacking away at the rock with the giant's sword. Sitting up, he saw that Burt had kept the fire going and had also packed all their gear, placing it in one pile. It was obvious Burt was ready to leave the ledge. Quill stood, went to the waterfall and splashed his face trying to erase the sleep from his eyes. He then moved over behind Burt and began throwing loose rocks from the ledge. Without saying a word, each of them worked for the next four hours. The opening was now big enough so Burt could put his head and half of his shoulder in, but more cutting needed to be done. Every now and then Burt would stop and try to look inside, but he couldn't make out anything familiar. Strange. As Burt worked he began to get a feeling about going into this cave that made his stomach tie up in knots. He knew that something wasn't right. He could smell the air coming from inside; cold, so cold that it burned his nose as he took a couple of deep breaths.

Burt stopped for a moment to listen, trying to hear anything that would give him a clue as to what lay ahead. At first, he could hear nothing. Then, the sound of water dripping; as if there was a lake inside there.

"Burt, what are you doing?" Are we going to get inside today or not?" Quill questioned as he stepped behind him to get a better look. But as he said this, he stopped and listened. A familiar sound, coming from overhead. He looked up just in time to see a huge hawk as it hung on an updraft of air, then quickly passed from sight over the top of the cliff. For a moment he had a crazy notion of how wonderful it would be if only he and Burt could fly! He laughed to himself. How ridiculous. "Get a grip on yourself, Quill old boy. Back to reality!"

"I don't like it Quill. I have a bad feeling about this. There is something inside this cave that scares me," Burt said as he pulled himself from the hole and stood up. Then he took Quill's hand, placing it on his face. Burt's face was cold as ice from being exposed to the temperature inside of the cave. Quill felt a chill go through his own body.

Quill knelt and crawled into the hole. He could feel the cold and could also sense something ominous inside this cave—and it had to do with him! He couldn't explain *how* he knew, but the feeling was intense. He backed out and stood up.

"Burt, we have to get inside. Keep working. Let's finish this. There is something in there waiting for me. I feel it pulling at me, drawing me in. I've sensed it for the past two days. There is a power that wants me to enter." He picked up the giant's sword and handed it to Burt.

The look on Quill's face at that moment told Burt that Quill understood. He got down on his knees once more and crawled back into the hole, then started again to cut the rock away from the opening. He couldn't believe that the rock was so hard and the going so incredibly slow. However, it wasn't much longer before the opening widened enough to get through. Burt didn't want to go in first; he would leave that honor to Quill! Backing out of the entrance, he stood up and signaled Quill: "It's big enough. You can go on in anytime you want." The tone of Burt's voice was not lost on Quill. He too was hesitant to plunge into the unknown but squared his shoulders, took a deep breath and grabbing his bow and quiver, knelt in front of the enlarged entry in the face of the cliff. Burt gathered up the food and water, placing the straps over his shoulders, leaving his arms free to carry the giant's shield and sword.

With one last glance at the strange valley below, Quill began to crawl into the hole. But he stopped and backed out again, which completely unnerved Burt!

"Nothing's wrong. Don't panic Burt. Just light the torch, and when I get inside hand it to me, O.K?" Although it was cold, Quill could feel sweat forming on his forehead once again, a nervous reaction. A feeling of dread, fear of the unknown, filled him as he entered the cave. Quill got to his feet yelling to Burt to pass him the torch. He couldn't see much at first, but as his eyes adjusted to the inky blackness of the cavern, he could see what looked like a lake. The light coming in through the hole reflected off the water's surface, revealing a huge body of water. Hearing Burt struggling at the entrance, Quill instinctively knew that Burt was trying to squeeze torch, sword, and shield along with his short, fat body through the hole all at the same time.

"Burt, hand me some of that stuff. If you don't, you're not going to fit!"

"Very funny, ha, ha, ha," Burt snorted as the shield clanged against the rock, the noise echoing throughout the cave.

When Quill heard the echo he realized that this was one huge cave! He knelt to help Burt get inside. Burt gladly handed over the torch and then the shield. Quill helped Burt to his feet and they both stared in amazement.

Huge stalactites hung from the ceiling, ever so slowly dripping lime-rich water as they stretched to reach the growing stalagmites beneath them. Iridescent colors danced in the torchlight eerily giving life to these enormous rock formations, even as their reflections cast upon the underground lake doubled the effect. The lake laid still, not a ripple in the water, a perfect silvery mirror of the majesty of growth above and around it. The only sound an occasional drip of water as it fell from the very tips of the stalactites into the small pools made by time in the floor below.

As both Quill and Burt's eyes became better adjusted to the dimly-lit cave, they saw outcroppings of colored crystal, the torchlight piercing through these valued stones, the shimmering colors reflecting back at them. Surely they had walked into the base of a rainbow! Colors of the entire spectrum were dancing around the cave, on the floor, the walls and the ceiling. Quill and Burt were awestruck—their breath deep and heavy from the excitement! Such spectacular beauty was overwhelming.

Then Quill noticed the smoke from the torch. It was floating across the lake and being sucked into a huge hole in the side of the cave, just above the water's edge. He knew as soon as he saw the smoke going in that direction that freedom was near at hand. But how would they ever cross this underground lake and climb the wall of the cave in order to get out? For all its beauty, the lake presented an awesome challenge. It seemed as though every time Quill took one step forward, something pushed him two steps back! And yet, he could still feel a force drawing him, pulling him closer to the unknown. Now Quill somehow knew that all of his answers lay within the walls of this cave. His fear gone, it was replaced by an urgency to seek out this power and take it for himself. For some reason, he felt it was rightfully his.

But for the present, reason won out as Quill and Burt began making preparations for yet another night lost in a strange and ever-changing world.

"Let's get some wood and lay a fire for the night Burt," Quill prodded.

Burt set the sword, water and food bag down next to Quill's things. Quill then laid the shield on the top of the pile of gear and both began the task of settling in for the night.

About an hour later, Quill stopped Burt from sending any more wood through the hole. There was enough to keep a fire going for two or three days. Burt came back in and fussed with the fire while Quill walked over to the edge of the lake and knelt down for a closer look. He reached his hand into the water and made a cup with his hand so he could drink. As he raised the water to his lips, the unexpectedly icy cold slammed against his teeth. Quill had never felt water this cold before except in the dead of winter. Why was it so frigid and where was it coming from? He stood up, retracing his steps to where Burt was adding some bigger sticks to the growing fire, coaxing it to sparkling flames of red, yellow and orange. Burt took great pride in making the fire and knew he was good at it. The cave was now well lit and the two stood silently enjoying the leaping colors bouncing all about them from the crystal outcroppings that were everywhere. With the only sound the crackling of the burning sticks, the friends savored this unique spectacle.

Suddenly, Quill noticed what appeared to be a trail running along the edge of the lake—a trail that seemed to head toward the far end of the cave. He couldn't see that far but he instinctively knew that he should walk the trail to see where it led.

"Burt, make me a torch. I'm going to take a walk along the edge of the lake. Maybe I'll find some thing or some way to get out of here," Quill explained as he picked up his bow and quiver and hung them around his neck.

"Don't you want me to go with you?" asked Burt, handing Quill a hastily made torch.

"No, I'm not going far, besides, you should take out the rabbit and fix us a bite to eat. It's late and we have a long day of exploring ahead of us tomorrow. I won't be long. While I'm gone, maybe you could make about five or six of these torches for tomorrow, O.K?"

Burt nodded a silent resignation to this assignment, trying to hide his disappointment. Being left behind wasn't his idea of a good time!

Quill made his way toward the other end of the lake walking between and around the stalagmites that also followed the trail. He couldn't quite shake the feeling that something or someone could be hiding behind one of these huge monuments to time. All of the formations were two and three times taller than he. By now he had slowed considerably, inching along so he could listen and look with caution. Now almost at the other end of the lake, he turned to take a look at Burt standing next to the fire at the far end. Turning back, he picked up his pace once more, mindful of time. Then he saw that the trail seemed to lead to a great tunnel. Walking up to the entrance, he peered inside. As he did, the rush of cold air became stronger. Now he understood why the water in the lake was so cold; the air coming through the tunnel kept the temperature in the cave very low. A few steps into the tunnel showed him that it didn't look at all like the rest of the cave. It looked almost as if someone had carved it out centuries ago. He reached out, caressing the rock with his open hand. It was much warmer than the air in the tunnel and smooth to the touch. This made Quill even more suspicious. Whatever was at the end of this tunnel was colder and more frightening than anything he had ever known.

Reversing direction, he started to make his way out of the tunnel. As he did, a strange sensation of warmth flooded over him. It was a feeling of contentment and welcome. He was having a hard time moving toward the outer cave. He knew that he was not ready to enter the tunnel yet; he needed time to think, time to get his thoughts together before he was to accept what was waiting for him at the other end. Quill could feel a presence; it wasn't far from where he stood. The force was tugging at him and his mind raced back to the elders of his village and their stories of the wolves and their power. Quill reached up and felt his left ear. It was cold from the rush of air but that wasn't the reason for touching it. All elves had pointed ears so just to reassure himself that he hadn't changed, that he was still an elf, a good tweak of the ear was definitely in order!

****

Now standing at the entrance to the tunnel, Quill thought again about those stories which he had been told as a young lad. Stories of good and bad elves, and, if this had anything to do with his being an elf, then, he wondered, what was he—a good elf or a bad one? Thoughts of his father and mother also flooded his mind and as they did, he knew he had to be a good elf. After all, that was the way his parents had raised him. Quill couldn't be evil and he knew it. He reached to his side and clutched the leather bag containing the two black eyes. He was sure they were not stones. They were the eyes that were guiding him, bringing him to this final place, a place where Quill would get his chance to become the first elf in his village to possess magical powers. It was all becoming so very clear. All Quill could think of were the stories of the powers told over and over by the elders. Were they just stuff of legend or were they actually true?

He made his way back to where Burt was waiting. "What did you find Quill?" Burt asked as Quill came to a stop right in front of him.

"Burt, this is the place, the place where I am to find the elf power, the same power the elders taught about all these years!"

"What are you talking about? I don't understand a thing you're saying Quill." Burt walked around Quill scanning his head for extra holes or something that would explain all of this nonsense.

"Burt, you don't understand it, you can't understand it—you're a dwarf! The feelings I'm getting from within this cave are different from anything you will ever feel. Think for a moment of all those stories that we were told as young kids, the ones about the good elves and the bad elves. I can even remember you and I going off into the woods and playing elves; you were always the bad one and I was the good one. Remember?"

Burt stood there for a moment holding his chin in his hand. He was trying to think of some of those stories. Then, as if someone had hit him in the head, he snapped his arm down and started dancing around the fire mumbling something about the elf circle and the bad elf.

"What *are* you doing?" Quill asked, astonished at his friend's behavior.

"I'm dancing. I'm trying to conjure up an elf circle. Remember? You and I did this all the time when we were young," Burt said as he came around the fire near Quill for about the third time.

Quill did recall the elders saying if you danced at night in a circle it brought you good luck, but only if you were an elf.

"Burt, stop dancing and tend to the fire. We've got to get some sleep. Tomorrow we have to find our way out of here." He ate some rabbit, laid down, and stared into the fire. His eyelids began to droop, sleep washing over him like a comforting blanket. He surrendered to his dreams, curling up in a warm ball.

Burt sat up for a while working on the torches for tomorrow, thinking of what Quill had said. He was traveling back in time, conjuring up memories of those incredible tales that were so much a part of their heritage. They *were* just stories, weren't they? How could Quill *believe* all that? Sitting opposite Quill, he gazed through the fire at the sleeping form. He swore to himself that no matter what, even if Quill were going crazy, he would stand by him until the end of time. Burt felt satisfied with that vow and soon curled up and drifted off into a sleep filled with dreams of giants and elves dancing together in a huge circle of fire.

Chapter Six

Quill's eyes opened upon a velvet blackness and for a second he was unsure of where he was. He had forgotten that he and Burt were deep inside a cave. At first he thought he had gone blind again, but then the previous day's events flooded his mind. The fire was cold and he could hear Burt snoring—still sound asleep. As he looked around, Quill noticed the opening that Burt had made in order for them to get in off the ledge. A new day's sunlight glistened off the multi-colored gems throughout the cave, their reflections dancing on the smooth rock walls. Quill rose, kicking at the coals left from the evening fire. He knelt and piled some of the sticks that were lying next to him onto the coals, coaxing new life into the still-hot ashes. A new fire would soon flicker and catch. He stood, walked over to Burt and impulsively gave him a swift kick in the pants, startling him awake.

"What are you doing? *What* is the matter?" a very startled Burt demanded as he sat up, rubbing the sleep from his eyes.

"We've got to get going. It's time to find out what's in this cave," Quill stated as he picked up the giant's shield. Leaning down next to the small fire that was struggling back to life, Quill held the shield up to the light in order to get a good look at it. The shield was in the shape of a circle, about two feet across and made from some kind of metal that Quill had never seen. The face of the shield was plain except for ten colored stones that were mounted around the outer edge. He turned the shield over and noticed that in the center was a leather strap mounted so that a hand could hold it comfortably. Quill also saw that the shield looked like it was made in two parts, an outer ring and an inner solid circle. The colored stones were mounted in the outer ring with the inner circle left plain, but rounded out toward the front. What kind of warrior carried such a thing? There were certainly more questions than answers in all of this and he was determined to find those answers!

Burt was now up and walking toward the underground lake. Quill angled a few more sticks on the fire and joined him at the edge of the water.

"Quill, that stuff you were talking about last night. I want you to know that I don't believe any of those stories." Burt proclaimed as he knelt down next to the lake and splashed some of the cold water on his weather-worn face.

"Burt, I understand what you're saying. And I can't blame you for feeling this way 'cause I find some of it hard to believe myself." Quill looked down into the water and continued. "But you have to understand what I'm feeling inside. I *am* an elf and I believe that there is something special about me. I can't explain it, but I know that inside I am not the same as I was before we found the black eyes." Quill moved next to Burt and knelt down.

"How can you say that those two eyes, stones, or whatever they are, have anything to do with you? I agree they have some kind of special power—they *did* cure both of us—but that has nothing to do with you." Burt got up and moved a couple of steps away, just staring out across the lake.

"First of all Burt, the two black eyes in this bag are just that. They *are* eyes that have been leading you and me to this cave, and they do have something to do with why we are here and what happens to us for the rest of our lives," Quill explained as he untied the bag from his belt, reached in and grabbed one of the eyes. Quill withdrew his hand and held the eye out so Burt could take a good look at it. But, as Quill opened his hand, both he and Burt gasped in amazement. Neither could believe what was happening. The eye had turned a brilliant light blue in color, making it appear as if it were on fire; and yet streaming from the eye was a soft blue light—a magical, mysterious light that slowly encircled Quill like a wisp of curling smoke.

"Quill, what did you do?" Burt asked, his voice a mere whisper as he backed quickly away.

"Burt, I'm telling you, these two eyes have something to do with this cave and us, whether you want to believe it or not!" Quill answered as he watched the light spiral around him. Slowly he put his hand back into the bag and let go of the object that had drawn him to this place inside of a mountain. The light disappeared.

Shaken by what had just occurred, yet more determined than ever, Quill turned, walked back to the fire and picked up the torches Burt had fashioned the night before. Tying them in a bundle, he shouldered them then stooped to retrieve the rest of his gear. His mind was made up. He had to know what was at the end of the tunnel. It was his destiny and now he was ready to discover whatever fate had in store for him.

Picking up the food bag and the sword, Burt's eyes followed every move Quill made. He took one of the torches and lit it. Not being able to carry the sword, Burt had to drag it, holding the handle with his free hand. Quill gripped the shield tightly after lighting his torch.

"Are we ready little buddy?" Quill asked as he started for the tunnel. Burt nervously nodded and followed closely behind him.

****

As they made their way in and around the enormous stalagmites standing at attention, like sentinels, along their way, Quill listened to the sword scraping along behind Burt. He couldn't help but smile to think of how useless that huge sword would be to Burt if something *did* jump out in front of him. Burt would never be able to lift the sword in time anyway! Constant thoughts of what might lie in store for them kept flashing through Quill's mind so that when they finally reached the entrance to the tunnel, he was almost surprised. Burt's labored breathing, huffing and puffing from dragging that sword, was the only sound now.

"Quill, can we leave this sword behind? Neither you nor I can use this thing anyway, and it's just too heavy. Look how long this thing is!" Burt complained as he dropped the awkward load. The clanging of the sword hitting rock echoed repeatedly throughout the cave. Startled by the intensity of the sound bouncing off the walls, Burt turned in circles, his legs shaking and his breathing and heartbeat faster than ever.

"Quill, do I have to go in there with you? I have to be perfectly honest with you; I'm so afraid that my knees are knocking together." Burt's voice was shaky as he sat down next to one of the giant stalagmites that majestically guarded the tunnel entrance.

"You can stay here, Burt, but I want you to go back for some firewood. Bring it back here and build a fire. I'll leave the sword here with you, but I'm taking the shield with me." Quill turned and started into the tunnel.

Quill walked at a steady but slow pace down the dark passageway, clutching the shield in one hand and the torch in the other. The tunnel remained straight for about two hundred yards and then curved to the right just enough so Quill could not see the entrance any longer. For the first time in his life, he felt confident about himself. He knew that whatever was at the end of this dark, cold shaft was waiting just for him—for Quill Okon.

Suddenly, the end of the tunnel came into view as the sputtering light from the torch exposed an opening within ten feet of him. And light was coming from that opening! He stopped and lowered the torch. Quill Okon took one more look behind him, got his bearings and confidently stepped through the portal.

Life as he had known it would never again be the same!

****

He found himself in a small chamber. Several small slivers of light knifed their way through the ceiling of this small room hewn from solid rock. It looked as though someone had purposely made these small holes that penetrated to the room below allowing the light to enter. It was then that he noticed a blanket of fog floating about six inches off the floor. He took a few more steps and could see the fog moving all about the chamber, drifting with such ease that Quill could almost feel its satiny caress against his legs. The room was round—perfectly circular in shape. Again Quill sensed that nature didn't form this place. As his eyes moved across the chamber, they fixed on an object that stood in the middle of the rock floor. Quill couldn't help but notice the unusual shape of this object, obviously made from stone. It too was perfectly round. There appeared to be a circular base about three feet thick and three feet high. On its top sat another stone, flat and oval. It looked like a table, but as Quill approached it for a better look it became obvious that it was definitely *not* a table. He was surprised to see that there, on the surface of the flat stone, carved into the rock, was what appeared to be a map.

Quill knelt and sat the shield on the smooth, but cold, rock floor, removed his bow and quiver, and laid them on top of the shield. Rising, he placed his hands on the edge of the flat stone. The first thing he noticed was that the majority of the carvings on the surface were covered with years and years of dust. He could see only part of the carving through the dust. It was very familiar. Of course! It was the valley he and Burt called home! He began brushing away the dust. As he did, he found that two of the beams of light from the ceiling were shining directly onto the center of the flat rock. At first the dust was difficult to remove. Quill had to take the knife that his father had given him and use it to scrape away the dust hardened by time. The more he scraped the more he was convinced that the carving was a picture of his homeland. It even detailed the mountains. There are no other mountains like those that surround that valley. His heart hammered in his chest from excitement. He couldn't believe it. What would his valley, the wonderful place where he grew up, have to do with this chamber? As Quill worked on removing the dust, the picture became clearer. Carved along the outside edge of this oval flat rock was a rope with ten knots. Standing just on the inside of the rope were *his* mountains. It had never occurred to him before that his valley was perfectly round—like this chamber and everything in it! He continued to work away at some more dust exposing the center of the picture. As he worked his way to the spots where the light struck the surface, he felt his fingers sink. Quill brushed the dust away and saw what appeared to be two small holes, each about one inch in diameter. He couldn't understand what the two holes were or why they were there. He finished scrubbing the remainder of the dust away and when finished, he took two steps back to get a good look at it. He was puzzled! What did it mean?

Then Quill remembered that Burt was waiting for him back in the outer cave. He turned around and stepping out of the chamber, called to Burt. The echo could be heard for several moments. Finally Burt responded.

"I'm coming Quill. Just wait a minute," Burt yelled.

Quill reentered the chamber and decided to walk around the small space for a closer look. He was hoping to find some more clues. As he made his way around he heard Burt scurrying down the tunnel, the sword bumping and scraping as he came. Quill stopped. Kneeling, he found something else. It looked like a door. He followed the crack in the rock as it made its way from the floor of the chamber up and around and then back down, just as a door would. But Quill could find no way of opening it. He kept running his hands all around it but there was nothing. He stood up and turned toward the opening of the chamber and saw that this door was directly opposite it. Quill heard Burt getting closer and moved back to the entrance. He waited for Burt.

"Come on, you're slower than a turtle," Quill shouted.

"Stop yelling will you, I'm right here," Burt grumbled as he walked inside.

Burt dropped the sword as soon as he entered the room. The sound echoed eerily throughout the chamber and well into the tunnel.

"Where are we Quill?" Burt asked as he dropped the bundle of torches he had also carried with him.

"I don't know Burt, but wherever it is, it has something to do with our home," Quill responded pointing the way to the picture.

"What are you talking about?" asked Burt moving over next to Quill.

"Look at this. It's some kind of a carving of the valley we live in," Quill said showing Burt the mountains.

"You're right. Those are the mountains around our valley. But I don't understand why someone would carve a picture of our valley and then leave it underground where no one could ever find it." Burt looked puzzled as he studied the chamber and the would-be map.

"Look, at least there's light in here. We won't have to carry these dumb torches around with us," Burt said as he threw his torch on the floor.

Quill looked at Burt, slowly shaking his head in disbelief. "Burt, it'll be getting dark soon and that light will be gone before we know it. Let's go back out to the cave and get wood and some water."

"We don't need water. I filled the water bag before I came." Burt handed it to Quill who gratefully took a long drink. He put it with his bow and quiver.

"Well, we still need firewood. Let's go. We should be able to make it in one trip. How about lighting one of those torches you didn't think we'd need." Sheepishly Burt agreed.

It wasn't very long before they had returned to the round chamber and had a warm fire blazing. Night had already come and the shafts were no longer sending the sun's rays down. Firelight alone lit the room and as the warmth chased away the cave's damp chill they talked for a long time. About home and about this chamber. About adventures past—and about those yet to come. As time passed, they tired and Quill decided to get some sleep. Burt said that he would stay awake a little longer so he could keep the fire going.

"Burt, I don't think we should keep a fire going. We should save the wood. We may need it another night."

Nodding as he reclined against the rocks, Burt agreed. It wasn't long before the fire died down, not even the embers adding much light. Burt found himself sitting there in the dark. As he was about to lay his head on the rock floor, he realized that it wasn't totally dark in the chamber. Where was light coming from? It hadn't been noticeable with the firelight and it wasn't bright, rather dim and soft. Burt walked over to the center of the room where the carving was and when he looked at the surface he saw that it was moonlight coming down through the shafts and casting its soft bluish light all around the carving. Burt had seen this color before, but just where didn't come to him at first. He returned to the still-glowing coals and lay down. He was comforted by the lunar display. Just as he was about to fall asleep, he remembered something—and bounded to his feet.

"Quill, Quill, wake up. I think I've found a clue!" Burt yelled as he shook Quill from his dreams.

Quill woke with a start and was on his feet in an instant. He followed Burt to the carving. When he looked down at it and saw the two holes lit by the moon, he knew what they were. He reached into the bag containing the two eyes from the viper's head, took one and held it over one of the holes in the center of the flat rock and dropped it in very gently. Quill put his hand into the bag and grabbed the remaining eye. He turned to Burt. Sweat was rolling from Burt's brow. The look of apprehension in his face told Quill that he still wasn't sure about all of this. Quill then held the other eye over the remaining hole and let go. There was dead silence in the chamber now. Neither moved a muscle for several seconds. Quill then leaned over the carving and peered into the two small holes. All he could see were the two bright objects casting their light up toward his face.

"What do you see, Quill?" Burt asked as he tried to see as well.

"Just light coming from the holes."

Burt was having a hard time reaching up over the top of the rock because of his big stomach. He had to grab the rope carved on the outside edge of the rock surface and pull himself up. As he did so, the entire rock turned. Rock grated on rock as the top moved about six inches!

"Burt, what are you doing?"

"I'm just trying to get a look. I couldn't see so I leaned on the rock a little so I could see over the edge and the thing moved!"

At that moment a huge flash of light exploded from the two small holes. It bounced off the ceiling lighting the entire chamber as if it were the middle of the day. Trembling, Burt backed up next to Quill as they simply stared at this new light. The sound of grinding rock began again. Only this time it wasn't coming from the object in the center of the chamber; it was the door that Quill had found on the other side of the room.

It was opening.

Chapter Seven

The chamber was now filled with the sound of rock grinding on rock as the huge door groaned and scraped open. Quill and Burt moved back up against the wall trying to keep clear of anything that might be harmful to them. The heavy stone slab came to a slow, crunching stop. There was so much dust floating about the chamber that neither Quill nor Burt could see anything until it settled. But then, to their amazement, another room was revealed. Quill took a few steps forward, cautiously, yet with growing curiosity, and saw that it was even smaller than the one in which they stood. And he felt a presence—someone, or something, looking at him! Quill didn't move a muscle. He froze in his tracks for several minutes trying to listen—he felt that someone was on the other side of that doorway.

Burt was still pushed up against the wall and not about to move until he was sure that nothing would jump out at him! Reaching down he pulled out his knife. For the first time, Burt could also feel that there was a strange power behind that door. Whatever it was, he was ready for it! He kept silent, just standing there as if his back were frozen to the rocks. His thumb rubbed back and forth on the blade, making sure it was honed to a keen edge. He got his answer as the knife cut his finger! He watched blood trickle along to the tip of the knife, then drip to the floor. He pressed his wounded thumb against the flat surface of the five-inch blade to stop the bleeding and remained frozen, his eyes firmly fixed on Quill who was still standing in the now-open doorway.

Quill still wouldn't move. He tried to look beyond the door, straining his eyes to catch a glimpse of whatever it was pulling at his inner self, drawing him ever closer to his destiny. Sweat ran down his face, even though the temperature inside the chamber was so cold that he could barely stand it. The sweat was the product of pure fear. Then, just as he was about to take another step forward, Quill heard a sound coming from further inside this new room. Was someone walking toward the door? Quill retreated a few steps, moving behind the door, out of sight of whatever, or whoever, was approaching. He shot a look at Burt, noting the terror on his face as the footsteps grew louder. Quill leaned forward enough so he could peek around the door hoping to see into the darkness beyond. The steps grew ever louder, the sound carrying throughout the chamber, down the tunnel and into the cave. Quill's legs were trembling and his heart pounding. Burt was one tiny sound from bolting back down the tunnel to comparative safety! But it was too late.

It had arrived.

Quill slowly looked over his shoulder and standing next to him was a figure that towered at least seven feet high. Quill's only thought was that he was about to die at the hands of this huge thing hovering over him. He had no way to defend himself. His only defense his knife. He quickly drew the weapon, holding it tightly in his hand, ready to die. The giant was carrying a sword and shield—identical to those he had discovered on the ledge.

Quill backed away and as he did so, the giant turned toward him and raised his sword, the tip pointing straight at Quill's nose! Then the giant turned his head and looked over at Burt, who instantly dropped his knife and fell to his knees, a choking sob escaping from his tightly sealed lips. The giant's gaze returned to Quill and, as if recognizing something familiar in the quaking elf, he lowered his sword. Quill stared at him, not wanting to make a move. Fearful it would be his last!

Nobody did or said anything. Quill studied this imposing giant of a man, dressed in leather from head to toe, with cautious interest. He had never encountered someone like this before. He wore boots that went to his knees, laced about half way up, and a leather shirt with no sleeves, in spite of the cold. It was obvious why there were no sleeves on the shirt—his arm was as big around as Quill's waist! He had more muscles in one arm than both he and Burt had together! Quill raised his head to get a good look at the giant's face. But a leather mask covered all but the eyes and ears. Yet the eyes were compelling and as he held those eyes with his own, he felt a calm come over him and a realization that the giant would not hurt them. There was a peace and tranquility that emanated from those deep blue eyes that spoke more than words ever could.

The giant turned and motioned to the stone object in the middle of the room. He walked over to it and gazed at the light coming from the center. He laid his sword across the top of the carving and with one hand grabbed the edge of the flat rock returning it to its original position. With that, the two stone eyes lifted from the holes where Quill had dropped them. The giant gathered them into his huge hand, turned around and walked back into the small chamber. Quill noticed that the giant left his sword lying on the carving; why? He could only wonder, what would happen next?

"Are you all right?" Quill whispered to a still-kneeling Burt.

"I think so. But what should we do?"

"Just stay put and don't do anything stupid," Quill ordered as he once again looked toward the door.

****

It seemed like hours had passed. Quill and Burt never moved an inch, waiting for whatever was next. Quill knew that it wouldn't make one bit of sense to run; there was no place to go. He stood there trying to think back to the tales of the elders, trying to remember if any of them ever said anything about giants, but he couldn't think of any. And what was *this* giant doing here? And what about the two stone eyes? More questions, but still no answers.

He couldn't wait any longer. He had to find out what the giant was up to. Quill took a deep breath, went over to the door, and entered the small anteroom.

He wasn't prepared for what he would encounter. The giant was kneeling over what appeared to be a stone altar, upon which lay the small body of an elf. The giant rose, looked at Quill, and without saying a word, stepped back motioning with his arm for Quill to come forward. Quill hesitated, but took two or three steps toward the altar—close enough to see that the body was covered to the shoulders with an emerald green robe. Quill had a sense of the power that had been leading him when he looked upon the very still form. There was also a feeling of familiarity with this elfin being that swept over Quill for the briefest of instants when his eyes first took in the pointed ears and light-colored hair. The little person lying before him was an elf, like himself. Quill looked deeply into the soft eyes and knew at once where the two stones had gone. They belonged to this elf, whoever he might be. Quill remained as he was for several minutes, contemplating every detail of the prone figure. He was definitely an elder—the wrinkles of time were etched carefully on the pale skin of his little face. If his eyes had not been open, Quill would have sworn that he was dead.

Gingerly reaching out, (he couldn't help himself, he *had* to touch this incredible being), he placed his fingers against the ashen skin of the still face. It felt very cold at first but as Quill's touch lingered, he could feel a warmth returning to the waiting body.

It was magic! Life seemed to pour into the little elf right before Quill's eyes. Gradually, he sat up and stretched his two small arms above his head in a strained attempt at dispelling the stiffness of time.

As the old one struggled to a sitting position, still on the altar, Quill noticed a wooden cane lying next to him. It appeared to be made of oak, bent at the top, with a carving of a falcon's head. Quill was baffled by the cane's twisted shape, looking more like a snake that had wrapped itself around the trunk of a small tree. As the robe fell from the waking elf's shoulders, a brown tunic made of a woven fabric totally unfamiliar to Quill became evident. Around his waist was a thick rope with knots tied at even spaces along its length. The ends of this rope dangled in front of him, swinging back and forth. Several more knots were at the ends of the rope. As Quill's eyes strained to take in all that he was seeing, his gaze rested on a small leather bag dangling from the neck of this small wonder. Quill could only imagine what magic power was inside that little bag!

"Quill Okon! I have been waiting here some four hundred years for you to wake me from my sleep," the ancient one said in a very matter-of-fact tone, as he edged to the side of the altar letting his legs hang over the side.

"Four hundred years!" thought Quill, now fully at attention and heeding every word that was spoken.

"You don't know me, but I know everything about you young man. It is written that you would be the one to waken me from my enchanted sleep—sleep forced upon me by the Dark Elf." He removed the robe completely now and laid it on the altar next to him as he continued.

"I know it will take you a while to understand what I am going to divulge to you in the days to come, but I want you to know that everything I will say to you is absolutely true. You must trust me."

Quill remained speechless. All he could do was stare into the dark eyes of this stranger and wonder what was going on. Who was he and why had Quill been chosen to wake him? All Quill needed right now were more questions with no answers! His head was reeling and he felt that this must all be some kind of dream. Things like this weren't possible, were they?

"But first, let me introduce myself." The words snapped Quill back to the present.

"I am Kailon, the Light Elf. Behind you is Kobar, my friend and personal guard." With all that had just occurred, Quill had completely forgotten about the giant! Kailon struggled to climb down from his perch on the altar, then turned and retrieved his cane and robe.

"Come, let us leave this place and find your friend Burt," he said motioning in the direction of the rock doorway.

Burt! Quill thought. He's still in the outer chamber! What will he think of all this?

Quill shook his head in disbelief. Kailon knew him, *and* Burt, and knew that he would one day come to wake him. How could that be? Quill moved out of the chamber and signaled to Burt.

"Burt, don't be frightened," Quill soothed as both Kailon and Kobar walked out from behind him.

"Burt! It is so good to meet you. I am Kailon, the Light Elf from the Kingdom of Zin. I want to thank you for assisting Quill in finding me." Kailon held out his hand to Burt.

Taking the hand offered to him, Burt held it as firmly as he could, primarily out of fear. As soon as he started squeezing his hand, Burt felt something special about Kailon's handshake. It was the handshake of brotherhood. He didn't understand why or what gave him this feeling of friendship, but it was all very real. Burt looked into Kailon's eyes knowing that before him was a kind and gentle individual.

Quill interrupted Burt's thoughts as he asked, "Tell me something Kailon. What were those stones that Burt and I found? Were they your eyes?" Kailon broke into a strange laugh and turned around in a circle three times. When he stopped, he reached into the right pocket of his tunic. "Quill, you mean to tell me that you thought *these* were my eyes?" Kailon chuckled as he held out his arm and opened his hand.

There in the middle of his small palm lay two acorns. Quill looked at them and said, "Those are *not* what Burt and I found!"

"O but they are Quill. Tell me this. Would you have picked them up from the bottom of the pit, risking your life one more time, if you saw only acorns?" Kailon reached for Quill's hand and placed the two acorns in his palm.

"No, I know that I would not," responded Quill, examining the plain acorns.

"That is *why* they did not look like acorns. You never would have taken the effort to pick them up," said Kailon.

Quill stood silently for a minute. How could these acorns possess so much power? Kailon was right. He was still having a hard time believing!

"Are these acorns some kind of magic charm?" Quill asked.

"Come, sit and I will explain it to you," Kailon said as he shuffled over to the pile of glowing coals from the earlier fire.

Kailon sat down. Quill and Burt followed, seating themselves next to the fading warmth of embers on the rock floor. Burt suddenly realized how low the fire was and jumped up to collect a few more sticks. He would stoke the fire into new life. Kobar moved to a position just behind Kailon where he remained standing, a silent guard.

"Quill, the first thing you must understand is that all you are about to hear must never cross your lips. No one but your successor must ever hear what I am about to tell you. Do you understand me?" Quill quickly nodded in acknowledgment of their agreement.

"That goes for you too, Burt. I do not want you to say anything either. If you do, it could mean the end of your life." Kailon shifted his weight a bit as he spoke. Burt sat very still, fear spreading across his face.

"Four hundred years ago I fought a terrible battle with the Dark Elf, Syffus. Syffus is one of our greatest enemies. His only charge in life is to destroy the Kingdom of Zin. He knows that if he can destroy Zin, he will also be able to destroy the Power Room from which Light Elves create their elf circles. Syffus was a Light Elf once himself, in a time long ago when peace prevailed throughout the land, and evil was hidden by the power of good. Then one day, when Syffus journeyed to visit a friend, he discovered the Black Temple. How he stumbled upon it remains a mystery. The Black Temple is the other side of the good power, namely evil, and all its diabolical power. From that day on, Syffus has been seeking to destroy all Light Elves."

Quill and Burt hardly took a breath as they listened to Kailon's words.

"Are you the only Light Elf left?" Quill asked.

"I do not believe so. Quill, you must understand that this is a big land that we live in. I know you have never left your valley so it is hard for you to imagine the size of our entire country. But I can tell you this much, Kobar is not from our land. This leads me to believe that there are more places and more elves," Kailon said as he faced behind him for a brief look at Kobar. He continued.

"Syffus has been searching for the Kingdom of Zin since the day he became a Dark Elf. It was during our last battle to keep him away from Zin that Syffus destroyed my Elf Circle, my key source of magical power. All Light Elves must build their own power level over a long period of time. The Elf Circle is what provides us with our magical powers. Both the Light Elves and the Black Elves must maintain that circle in order to survive. If your Elf Circle is destroyed you will lose the internal life you are given upon its creation, and you will die. The only way an Elf Circle can be destroyed is through the magical power of another elf. When Syffus destroyed mine, I had no successor to replace me and had no way to protect the Kingdom. So I hid the Kingdom and suspended time for Kobar and myself until the new chosen Light Elf came of age." Kailon stood and moved to the other side of the fire. Pointing directly at Quill he pronounced, "You are that chosen one."

It was an incredible amount of information for Quill to absorb all at once. He almost felt out-of-time and out-of-place himself!

"Are all elves able to perform magic?" Quill asked.

"Yes. Elves, dwarves and some Druids have limited powers, but most of the time they do not use the power because they do not even realize they possess it. If they do not use their magic for several years, they will lose the ability to call upon it," Kailon answered.

"You mean *I* have magical power?" Burt asked. The very idea of having a magic power excited him!

"Yes, Burt, you can perform some magic. I do not mean to make you feel bad, but you will never have the ability to perform the type and amount of magic that Quill will." This bit of information didn't deter Burt's enthusiasm at all. *Some* was far better than *none*!

"Kailon, you said something about Druids. I've never heard that word before," Quill said.

"A Druid is an extremely intelligent being. Some are great priests and others are advisors in other kingdoms. They are not like you or me. Their appearance is a lot like Kobar's. And they are very big in stature.

"How was I picked to be the chosen one Kailon?" Quill asked.

"You were chosen by the King of Zin long ago, appointed to become a Light Elf, as I am, even before you were born. It is written in the great Kingdom and it will be so. Your time has come to learn, to seek out the knowledge that is hidden in the Power Room of the Light Elves."

"What is this 'Power Room' you speak of, and where is the Kingdom of Zin?" queried Quill.

"The Power Room is the source of all good power. It is a place within the Kingdom of Zin where all Light Elves begin their Elf Circle. The Kingdom is hidden in a special place, safe from the Dark Elf. I will reveal it to you when the time is right," Kailon explained, giving a knowing glance to Kobar.

"Quill, the tomb that holds the Power Room is also your beginning—your first step toward building your own Elf Circle. It holds all the knowledge and wisdom of the Kingdom of Zin. Look here Quill. See this rope that I wear? It has knots tied in it, each knot representing a level of power, power that must be earned. That is why Kobar and I are here—to help and guide you as you begin to earn your knots." Kailon held up one of the loose ends of the rope, showing it to Burt and Quill.

Quill absentmindedly picked up a couple of sticks and threw them into the fire. He then stood up and paced in a circle, deep in thought.

"Ropes, Power Rooms, Black Elves, Light Elves and hidden kingdoms—I'm confused—and afraid. You tell me that I have been chosen to fight a Dark Elf so that I can protect a kingdom I know nothing about. What makes you believe I'm going to do as you say?" Quill demanded as he moved over to the center of the chamber and stared at the rock carving of his valley.

"Quill, you cannot control what is going to happen. You could fight it, but you would lose anyway. The power of elf magic has already invaded your heart. How do you think you got here? You felt the power drawing you even if you did not realize it at the time! The two acorns still in your hand are nothing more than magical tools used to awaken the power from within your spirit. Sure those snakes were real. But only *you* could have killed them. It is written that the Black Temple is guarded by vipers, and if this is true, then you and Burt came very close to the inside of the temple, a place from which you would never have returned. Hand me one of your arrows, Quill, I want to show you something that will surprise you," Kailon offered.

Quill moved to where he had earlier stashed the shield, bow and quiver. As he bent to pick up the shield, moving it out of the way, Kobar charged at him, grabbing the shield from Quill's hands. Kobar raised the shield high above his head, an ear-piercing scream bursting from the very depths of his being! Icy chills ran down Quill's back. Burt scrambled to his feet, tripping over himself to get next to Quill. They watched in horror as Kobar dropped to his knees clutching the shield in his arms. Kobar sobbed the word Molik, Molik, Molik over and over.

In a hushed tone, and with deep concern in his expression, Kailon explained, "Molik was Kobar's brother. They were very close. Only in death would he be parted from his shield. Tell me, where did you find it?"

"We found a skeleton under the tree limbs and brush on the ledge just outside this cavern," Quill answered.

"Did you find anything else?" Kailon asked as Kobar jumped to his feet and expectantly waited for his response.

"Yes, I found a sword and this necklace," Quill replied, pulling the necklace from under his leather vest. He quickly removed it.

Kobar reached over and took the necklace from Quill's outstretched hand. Tears filled Kobar's eyes and, to Quill's surprise, he spoke for the first time.

"Where is my brother's sword?" The deep, husky voice resounded throughout the system of caves and tunnels.

Quill went to retrieve the sword from where Burt had dropped it, near the entrance to the chamber, and silently returned to where Kobar stood. He looked into Kobar's eyes and could sense the deep sadness hidden behind the leather mask. Using both of his small hands, he lifted the sword as high as he could and held it out. Kobar bowed as his enormous hands seized his brother's sword. He stood for several moments staring at the sword, then moved to the other side of the chamber and laid the shield, sword and necklace on the rock floor. He sat next to them in silent vigil. Quill and Burt quietly returned to the fire, sitting down across from Kailon.

The heavy silence was broken by Kailon's words. "Quill, we must leave this place soon as we have a long journey ahead of us."

"Where are we going?" Quill questioned.

"Back to the valley where you and Burt were born. Back to your home. There I will look for a clue to help us find the Kingdom of Zin," Kailon said.

"I thought you knew where the Kingdom is," Quill stated, a bit puzzled.

"Quill, it has been four hundred years since I have seen the place where I hid the Kingdom. In four hundred years a lot of things change; the land, lakes, trails and even the mountains. I must start somewhere. I am familiar with that valley." Kailon stood even as he spoke.

"I'm for leaving this place! I could eat my father's best cow right now, the whole thing," Burt said as he jumped to his feet. Going home was the best news he had heard all day! Well, maybe that thing about his magic was better, but not by much!

"Well Burt, if you were hungry, why did you not say something? What do you want to eat?" Kailon had a kind manner about him.

"Do you have some bread covered with gravy, and maybe some potatoes?" Burt asked hopefully.

"Sorry, I cannot make food appear but I will promise you this; when we get to your mother's table, we will both eat what you wish!" Kailon smiled warmly at the little dwarf.

Quill, now on his feet as well, joined the others next to Kobar. Kailon put his hand tenderly on Kobar's shoulder and said, "Kobar, we must leave this place. Our mission has begun. I am sorry about Molik and I really do understand your pain in losing him. He was a good friend to me also, and we will miss him. Come, my friend. Walk with us."

For the next two hours the four collected their gear and cleaned the chambers so virtually no trace of them would ever be found. Kailon remarked that he must leave the chambers as he found them. This was not his place. It would be used some other time, maybe even by Quill. Then they emerged from the chamber into the tunnel, slowly making their way to the outer cavern. Quill couldn't stop thinking of what Kailon had told him. He replayed it over and over in his mind. How could he fight a Dark Elf and save a kingdom?

He was hoping to find answers and instead, found new challenges, new friends, and a new direction for his life.

These were indeed confusing times—with no end in sight!

Chapter Eight

As the unlikely foursome made their way down the tunnel leading to the cavern, Quill realized he was still holding the two acorns that Kailon had put in his hand. He stopped and opened his hand, but couldn't see them because of the dim light.

"Kailon, do you want these two acorns back?" Quill asked as he moved next to Kailon.

"No Quill, the power in those two acorns has nothing to do with me. The power in them belongs to you. If I were you, I would put them in a safe place so you will never lose them," Kailon suggested.

Quill opened the food bag tied to his belt and dropped the strange acorns in, tied it shut and reattached it to his belt.

By now Kobar was some distance ahead. He was almost in the cavern. Burt was close behind Kobar and Quill was next to Kailon, holding up a torch to light the way.

"Kailon, how are we going to get out of this place? Burt and I couldn't find anything that seemed to lead out," Quill said.

"Son, you have a lot to learn. Kobar is not only a great warrior, but he has powers that even I do not understand; if anyone is going to get us out of here, it will be him." Kailon stopped and looked at Quill.

"But I thought you said that only elves had power."

"No, what I said was that you have more power than Burt. I never told you anything about Kobar's power and the reason for that is simple; I do not know much about Kobar *or* his power," Kailon replied as he reached up and tapped Quill's shoulder with the end of his cane.

Just then Quill remembered the skeleton he and Burt had encountered on the ledge outside. The thought of it being Kobar's brother sent an icy chill running down his spine. They should at least remove the skeleton of Molik and find a proper place to lay it to rest. Maybe inside the cave would be good.

"Kailon, do you think we should bring Molik's bones inside the cavern and bury them?"

"I think it is something you should discuss with Kobar. After all, it *is* his brother—he should be the one to make any decision." Kailon continued on toward the end of the tunnel.

Quill moved ahead of Kailon so that he could talk with Kobar. As Quill neared the end of the tunnel, he could see Kobar standing behind Burt. He was trying to tie Molik's shield to Burt's back. Kobar stepped back and Quill saw the beginning of a smile creep across his face. As Quill looked at Burt, he understood why! With the shield tied to his back, and given the fact that Burt was so short and stocky, it made him look like a turtle! Quill laughed heartily at the unusual sight, as did Kailon, pulling up short next to Quill.

"What's so funny?" Burt asked, not a little indignantly.

"Burt, you look like a turtle with that shield tied to your back," Quill chuckled as he walked over and slapped the shield a couple of times.

"Well, Quill, I'm glad my situation amuses you!" snapped Burt. "You always find something to laugh about, but I don't find this one bit funny! Kobar tied it there so I wouldn't have to carry the thing. It *is* heavy you know, but then, how would *you* know? You aren't the one who's been lugging it around, are you?" Burt turned in a huff and saw that Kobar was laughing too but now quickly stifled any further laughter at Burt's expense!

"I'm sorry Burt. We really aren't laughing *at* you, just at the silliness of the whole situation I guess. There hasn't been much to laugh about these past few days! We really should thank you for giving everyone a few minutes of release from the tension of all that's been happening. You're a good sport, my friend. Come on, enjoy the moment."

Burt kind of shuffled his feet while studying them, and then gave a heavy sigh, agreeing that he certainly did look pretty ridiculous. A smile returned to his face and the incident was forgotten.

"Kobar, how do you think we should take care of your brother's body?

Do you want us to help you bury him?" Quill asked, getting back to his original train of thought.

Kobar shook his head emphatically, then disappeared in between the stalagmites that almost completely surrounded them. He proceeded in the direction of the hole that Burt had made in order to get into the cavern in the first place.

Quill and Kailon followed after him. By now the torch Quill carried had died out, so he threw it down. Walking in the darkness, feeling for the huge stone sentinels, was difficult at best. Suddenly a ray of light shone through the hole. Daylight! A welcome sight as Quill realized that he and Burt hadn't had any sleep for two days now. He felt good, though, knowing that he would soon be getting out of this cavern and going home. But then it dawned on Quill. He hadn't even thought of this before. His father and Burt's father must be out searching for them at this very moment! It had been several days now since he and Burt had left on their hunting trip. How worried their parents must be!

"Quill! Quill! You won't believe this but by the time I got to Kobar he had already buried his brother's body. I still can't figure it out though. How did he squeeze through that small hole?" Burt was in a half run, half trot as he returned to Quill and Kailon, his breath coming in short gasps.

"Easy Burt. I told you that Kobar has powers that are beyond my understanding. You should stay here with us now. Leave Kobar alone to do what he must," Kailon said.

"Burt, while we're here, why don't you go fill the water pouch?" suggested Quill.

Still panting from the run, Burt went to the edge of the underground lake and removed the pouch. As he was about to kneel down, he caught sight of his reflection in the still water. Sure enough, Quill was right! He *did* look like a turtle. Then, as he stood there smiling at himself, Burt saw something move in the water. He leaned over for a closer look. It was a fish! A big one at that, and barely moving. Burt very slowly slipped his hand into the water starting at the water's edge so as not to scare the fish, which, on closer inspection, looked like a trout. He eased his hand forward. His stomach instantly reminded him it had been quite a while since they had eaten a decent meal. This fish was not going to get away!

He had now positioned himself on one knee while using his left arm for support. Slow and easy was the name of the game if he was to nab this slippery fellow! It was further out than he first thought so he tried to move closer, adjusting his weight and moving ever so carefully. But, as only his luck would have it, as he grabbed the fish in his right hand, he fell off balance and tumbled unceremoniously into the icy water! His leather pants quickly filled as Burt realized he couldn't touch bottom! He screamed for help as he felt himself sinking fast. The shield's weight was pulling him quickly under the surface.

"Help! Help! I'm sinking!" Burt screeched as the swirling water washed over his head.

Quill and Kailon raced to the water's edge. By the time they arrived, Kobar was already holding Burt high in the air by the back of his shirt, water gushing everywhere. But! Burt still had the flopping trout in his hand! Kobar gently lowered Burt to the ground and took the fish from the clenched fist. Walking over to one of the flat-topped rocks, he laid the fish across it, drew his sword and with one quick motion, cut off the hapless trout's head. He then presented the trophy to Burt who looked up at Kobar and smiled his thanks. He had indeed found a friend.

"Kobar, I owe you my life. To show you how grateful I am, I'm going to cook us the best trout dinner you've ever eaten," Burt announced as he walked over to the pile of sticks left over from the first fire he and Quill made upon entering this cave.

"Well Quill, I believe we should enjoy our meal before we depart from this haven for elves like me," Kailon said while walking toward Burt who had already started the fire. "But before you do anything else, dry off in front of that fire before you catch your death of cold!"

Before long, Burt had dried sufficiently to begin preparing the food. Kailon, Kobar and Quill sat down around the fire and for several minutes no one said a word. They just watched as Burt tied the trout to a stick and began turning it over the crackling flames. As Quill sat, he once again allowed himself the luxury of enjoying the beauty of the many different colors dancing around the walls of the cavern.

"Isn't it amazing how many colors become evident in these rocks by the light of the fire?" Quill asked of no one in particular.

"The rocks are really gems and they all contain a certain type of special magic," responded Kailon. "Look here." Kailon removed the leather bag from around his neck and emptied the contents on the ground in front of him.

The small shiny gems were beautiful. There were various shades of yellows, reds, blues, and even one or two clear gems.

"I keep these with me to help fight off cold and hunger. They have a secret power, one that you will become familiar with someday. Here Quill, I think you should get your own magic gems so you can always have them with you." Kailon tossed Quill a small leather bag.

"Hey, what about me?" Burt whined.

"Yes Burt, you too can enjoy having and using the magic in the gems," Kailon said as he tossed another small pouch to Burt.

Quill hurried off to gather a few of the colored gems that studded the walls of the cave.

"Quill, just so you know, there are other powers in those rocks as well. I do not think this is the time or the place to explain what that power is, but you will learn of it as time passes," Kailon said.

Quill stopped and turned as soon as he heard Kailon speak. "Is there anything else about these colored rocks that I should know now?"

"Yes, there is. This cavern is a special place. It is what Light Elves call the Elves' Treasure. This is a place where you can rest your power, a place where you can come to reflect, to be refreshed and console your tired bones from the stress of fighting the black power. This cavern is called the Elves' Treasure because it is the only place left where the Dark Elf cannot enter. These colored rocks, as you like to call them, hold a magical power that prevents the Dark Elf from entering. Quill, someday you will come to appreciate this place. You will actually *need* this place. You must understand that once you leave here you must always be on guard. Once outside, you are at the mercy of all other known powers. But in here you are safe." Kailon spoke quietly, knowing it was difficult for Quill to understand all of what was happening.

Quill looked into Kailon's eyes and felt that he was being truthful. He then moved over to the colored rocks and knelt down to gather a handful. Sifting through them Quill found ten gems of mixed colors and gently placed them in the pouch Kailon had given him. Sitting back on his heels, he hung the small leather pouch around his neck.

"Kobar, will you hold this for me so I can get some rocks for myself?" Burt asked as he held out the stick with the trout tied to it.

Kobar took the stick from Burt and continued cooking the fish as Burt got up and started gathering his stones. When done, he returned to the fire and sat next to Kobar, retrieving the almost-done fish from him. Quill returned to Kailon's side. They waited in silence, each deep in his own world of private thought. When the fish was ready, they ate their fill.

****

"Kobar, it is time to go. Please lead us out of this Elves' Treasure," Kailon requested as he stood and, with cane in hand, adjusted his green cape.

Kobar walked to the far right side of the cavern and Burt, Quill and Kailon followed behind. In just a few short steps, behind several of the bigger stalagmites, Kobar disappeared into a small tunnel that was well hidden. Quill thought about it for a second. If he and Burt had found this tunnel when they first entered the cavern, they would have been out of here much sooner. But fate was not to have it that way. They had been led along a certain path for the sole purpose of finding Kailon. That had certainly become very evident.

Upon entering this tunnel, the first thing Quill noticed was its uphill slant. It was just the right size for elves and dwarves but Kobar was having a hard time squeezing his way out. His seven-foot body was not made to walk up and down this tunnel! It took about twenty minutes until each of them stepped out into the bright sunlight. By now they were so accustomed to the darkness that they had to cover their eyes to protect them from the blinding light.

"Quill, take a good look at this place. Remember it well. Your life depends on it," Kailon instructed as he sat down on a boulder just outside.

Quill backed away and stared at this strange place. The entrance was directly under a huge, ancient oak tree where gnarled and twisted roots hid the entrance to all but a sharp eye. It was then that Quill thought he knew where Kailon's cane had come from. It too was as tangled and knotted as the roots of that tree—and was made from the same type of wood!

"Kailon, is this where you got your cane?" Quill asked.

"No, Quill. The King of Zin gave me this cane. He made it from the roots of a tree very much like this one, but it was an oak that grew near the entrance to the power room within the Kingdom of Zin itself. I believe that after all this time the tree is no longer there."

"What happened to the King of Zin? You told us that you put the kingdom in hiding. Were the King and the people with it when you hid it?" Quill asked.

"No. It is believed that the Dark Elf killed the King and hid the body. The people hid before I cast my spell." With that, Kailon fell silent, his explanations over for the time being.

Before long, and without another word, they rose and fell into step behind Kobar, who had already found the trail. They walked for the remainder of the day.

Chapter Nine

The sun had already disappeared behind the trees marking the trail's edge. Night's velvet darkness settled over them as they made their way down the small, narrow trail. Quill was exhausted. He needed to stop and rest. Burt was falling far behind because of the weight of the shield still on his back. Every now and then Quill could hear Burt mumbling something about being a packhorse. As they came to a small clearing, Kobar stopped. He knew it was time to let Quill and Burt rest; they did not have his endurance. Without sleep, they could go on no longer.

"Oh, am I tired," Burt moaned as he fell to the ground.

"Kailon, I'll go hunt for some food. Do you think Kobar will go with me?" Quill asked.

"Quill, haven't you noticed? Kobar never lets me out of his sight. He protects me just as he will protect you after I die. He will not go with you," Kailon stated flatly.

"Well, then I'll go by myself," Quill retorted.

"What about me Quill? I'll go with you." Even as tired as he was, Burt did not want his friend to go into the woods alone.

"No Burt. You need to stay here, collect some firewood and build a fire. That's more important. I'll be fine," Quill said trying to make Burt feel needed.

Quill entered the woods and removed the bow from around his neck. He then drew an arrow and placed it on the bowstring, carefully holding it, ready for whatever he might find. He continued to walk for a while, stopping every now and then to listen and look. It wasn't long before he heard something. He stopped and listened. It seemed to be only a few feet in front of him. It was not a sound he recognized. He moved a few steps closer but was having a hard time seeing anything through the thick underbrush. Large green ferns covered the ground under the trees. Again he edged closer. Something moved. It was black and low to the ground. Quill's heart began to pound. He thought it would jump out of his chest! All he could think of was the Dark Elf. What should he do? Run or fight? Crouching low, he was afraid to even breathe. He mustn't let it see him. Then a familiar sound—a wild boar! It was using its snout to dig in the dirt for food. It grunted and squealed as it rooted around. He had been letting his imagination run wild!

Quill moved in a little closer now and could see the boar clearly enough to take his shot. He raised his bow and drew the arrow back all in the same graceful motion. He would not miss this shot. But, all the same, he was hoping that this was not a two-hundred-pound boar or he would never get it back to camp! The tension of the bowstring made his arm ache. He took careful aim. A quick release—and the arrow found its mark, sending the boar to the ground without another sound. Quill cautiously approached the animal and gave it a nudge with his foot, just to make sure it was dead. Not a bad size, Quill thought, around sixty pounds; plenty of meat for the remainder of the trip home. He field-dressed his kill and lifted it to his shoulder. With his bow in his left hand and the boar over his right shoulder, he was an impressive sight as he made his way back to camp.

Being the first to spot Quill with his load, Kobar ran to help him. He easily took the boar from Quill's shoulder and carried it to the edge of the trees where he started to skin it. Soon it would be ready for the fire. Without saying anything, Burt began building a spit so he and Kobar could roast the welcome meat.

"I can see that you are a great hunter, Quill. Thank you for finding us a good meal," Kailon remarked, smiling broadly.

Quill hunkered down next to Kailon by the warm, flickering fire. He then pulled out his knife and, taking a handful of dirt, rubbed it over the short blade as his father had taught him. It was the woodsman's way of cleaning the knife after gutting the animal. His father always said that if you cut food with a dirty knife you would get sick. When Quill was finished, he put the knife back into the sheath he wore on his belt and stood up to see how Kobar was doing with the skinning. But Kobar was already coming toward the fire, the boar already skinned and tied to a stake, ready for the spit. Quill stared at this impressive man and shook his head. How did he manage to do things like that so fast? If it were he or Burt it would have taken much longer. Maybe he used his sword? Quill wondered.

"What a fine looking boar! Where did you kill it?" Burt roused Quill from his daydream- ing with his question.

"Not far from here. It was digging in the dirt for roots. It didn't even hear me!" Quill said as he sat back down and watched Kobar lay the boar across the two limbs that Burt had stuck in the ground on each side of the fire. Each limb had a V shape at the top so the spit would fit together perfectly without falling out. Each limb was also well-braced to hold the boar's weight. Burt had thought of everything. Kobar offered to turn the spit, with Burt eager to relieve him later, and so the roasting began.

"Burt, let's find some pine boughs so we'll all have something to lay on for the night," Quill prodded. The fire's warmth was beginning to make Burt sleepy but he dragged himself to his feet anyway and followed Quill. They gathered enough boughs to make bedding for each of them and then collected more firewood just as total darkness settled over the region. Kobar and Kailon stayed with the fire turning the spit and making sure all went right with the camp meal. When Quill and Burt returned with their loads, they were more than ready to give in to the mounting fatigue. Quill stretched out on the ground near the warmth of the glowing coals and Burt sat with his legs straight out and his back comfortably leaned up against the pine boughs they had gathered. The aroma of roasting meat tantalized their stomachs and waiting to eat became an almost impossible task!

As they all basked in the serenity of the evening, they remained silent, taking in all the many sounds of the night. However, it wasn't long before Burt became irritated at the sound of a cricket that was very close by. He started moving about looking for this intruder, mumbling something about not being able to fall asleep with all of this noise.

"Where is that dumb cricket? It sounds like it's right on top of us," Burt complained as he searched under some of the small rocks lying near the fire.

"Burt, Burt, slow down! Do not bother looking for the cricket. Kobar has it. Look! He will show you," Kailon said as he pointed to a cloth bag hanging from Kobar's neck.

Kobar removed the bag and opened it, carefully reaching into it. When he removed his hand, there, resting on his huge finger, was a small, light brown cricket. Burt moved over for a better look.

"Sure enough, look at this Quill. Kobar carries a cricket around with him." Burt moved his face almost close enough for the cricket to touch his nose.

Kobar put the little cricket back in the bag, tying the leather pulls so it would not get out.

"Kobar, why do you carry a cricket around with you?" Burt asked. Kobar remained silent as he hung the bag around his neck once more.

"He has carried that cricket ever since I have known him," Kailon said. He has never told me why. But, I think the cricket is his watchdog, so to speak. You see, it always wakes Kobar if there is danger nearby. That must be why he keeps it."

****

Close to an hour had passed when Quill forced himself to get up to check the meat that Kobar was patiently turning over the open flames.

"My friends, the meat is done. Let's eat!" announced Quill.

Burt jumped up, eagerly pulling his knife from its sheath. He sliced off a huge chunk and handed it to Kobar. Burt then cut meat for Kailon and Quill and finally took some for himself. The aroma was tantalizing but the taste was even better—finer than any they had ever eaten. They savored each bite as if it were the very first. As the night slowly grew longer, each one cut at the meat several more times until they could barely move. It wasn't long before Quill and Burt were looking for their bed of pine boughs. In no time they slept like babies, stomachs filled and minds at ease. Kobar and Kailon remained next to the fire for most of the night. They were enjoying their new-found freedom after returning from their four-hundred-year sleep!

****

As the soft rays of dawn shimmered upward on the eastern horizon, Quill stretched, got up and was scouring the campsite for bits of firewood when he heard Kobar's cricket. As soon as it started chirping, Kobar sprang to his feet drawing the huge sword that never left his side.

"Kobar! Kobar! Calm down! It's only me, Quill."

Kobar looked around for a moment and then walked over to the edge of the woods. Quill watched. Kobar was looking for something—and it wasn't him. Quill had a strange feeling. He couldn't understand what it was but he knew things were not right in their little camp. He moved over to the pile of boughs where he had put his bow and quiver for the night. Again he eyed Kobar who stared into the trees.

Without taking his eyes off Kobar, Quill bent and picked up his weapon. Quickly slinging the quiver around his neck, he moved toward Kobar and drew an arrow. In one single motion, arrow and bow were ready. Quill pulled up about ten feet behind Kobar, both remaining motionless for several minutes, just waiting. Then Kobar slowly turned to face Quill and as he did, Quill saw a movement. It darted so fast that Quill couldn't get a good look at it, but out of instinct he took his shot—and heard his arrow hit its target.

Kobar jumped to the left at the same instant Quill released the arrow and rolled to the ground. On his knees and facing the woods, sword in hand, he was ready for whatever it was that hunted him from the trees. But Quill had already taken charge, and drawing a second arrow, inched forward just enough to see what he had hit. Kobar moved in the same direction. Quill felt an eerie chill run down the middle of his back. It was a viper! He couldn't believe the size of this snake. It had to be at least twelve feet long! Kobar raised his sword and with one swift motion, beheaded the quivering reptile. He retrieved Quill's arrow and handed it back to him.

"Quill, you are by far the best marksman I have ever seen. But I must clarify something that Kailon was trying to tell you when we were still back in the caves. Those arrowheads you use are the *only* ones that can kill these vipers. You use the clear hard gems that are called diamonds. They represent purity and will kill all that is not pure. Remember this lesson Quill Okon. Your life will depend on it many times in the future. I do not know where you found those gems but you and I are going to need more of them before this is over. Fighting the Dark Elf will not be easy. I know.

I have been there." Kobar raised the remainder of the snake with his blade.

"Kobar, why haven't you said much of anything until now? I mean, you've hardly said a word in the past two days. Why?" Quill was definitely curious.

Kobar dropped the carcass to the ground and answered Quill as he wiped his sword. "I am not one for a lot of talk but there is also another reason why I keep my silence. Now is not the time for you to know. For now, you must trust me. It is better that I am quiet." And then he cautioned Quill, "If there is one viper, then I can bet you there are more. We must wake Kailon and Burt and leave this area. Whenever you come in contact with one, it means you are close to the Black Temple." He then returned to the smoldering embers, still hot from the night before. He doused them with water, stirring the coals with a stick to make sure they were out.

Quill acted promptly, prodding Burt with his foot as he said, "Burt, Burt wake up. We have to leave now." Startled, Burt yelled at Quill "Why is it every time I'm sleeping soundly you either kick me or shake me?"

"This is no joke, Burt. Kobar and I just killed an enormous viper and he said we must be close to the Black Temple. We have to leave right away."

Kobar woke Kailon and the four travelers hurriedly gathered their gear, packed enough meat to last the rest of their trip, and set out once more along the trail.

Chapter Ten

Kobar set a fast pace—his long legs leading the way all morning. Kailon followed and Quill remained behind him, with Burt bringing up the rear. As midday came a storm blew in over the tall trees lining the narrow path. The blackening sky worried Quill. He couldn't remember when he had seen the sky so dark and foreboding.

"Kailon, do you think we should find cover pretty soon? If we don't, we are going to end up in the middle of this terrible storm."

"No Quill. We have to press on. Your village is in danger and the only way to protect your families is to get there as fast as we possibly can," Kailon insisted as he kept up the pace.

"How do you know my village is in danger? Sometimes I don't know if I should believe you or not! So far all I have seen are vipers and some colored stones. If you have so much power Kailon, why haven't you used it yet?" Quill asked, a bit of a peevish tone to his usually understanding and soft voice.

"First of all, Quill, I don't possess my powers anymore. I lost them when the Dark Elf destroyed my Elf Circle; a Light Elf has no strength without his circle. I can understand why you find it hard to believe an old elf who does nothing more than babble on and talk of wizardry and elf power, but right now that is all I can do. When we get to your village, I will show you the power of a Light Elf. For now, let's just work together to get there." Kailon moved on. It was his way of saying that enough talking had been done.

Kailon was right. Quill couldn't understand any of it. Kailon said that he was a wizard, the Light Elf and all of that stuff, and now he says he has lost his powers. Something wasn't making any sense at all and he was tiring of trying to play this game with a little elf with big stories!

"The storm is closing in," Burt called as he ran up next to Quill.

Lightning flashed in the distance, full of immense energy, each powerful bolt followed by a booming crash of thunder. This was going to be a severe storm and it was rolling in fast. Quill could smell the rain. The air was full of moisture as it touched his face during the eerie calm that always seemed to precede a violent storm. Quill's only thought was to find refuge—immediate protection from the ravages of such a storm. But again Kailon came to mind and he kept moving, keeping up the pace set by Kobar. It was but a few minutes more when the winds began to howl and the incredible force of the storm hit, bending trees nearly double and splitting the sky releasing torrents of rain. It continued to whip and thrash around them—so hard they were forced to grab onto each other for they could no longer see the trail. Quill and Burt stayed close behind Kailon and Kobar so as not to lose sight of each other. Lightning bolts crackled and snapped, sending jagged slivers of light slicing through the jet black sky as they moved cautiously toward the edge of the trail.

Suddenly, as if the sky itself were falling on top of them, the water dumped everywhere, carving deep gashes in the ground. The wind howled, tearing limbs from trees in front, around, and behind them. In one horrifying instant, a gigantic bolt of lightning struck the trunk of the tree next to them. Exploding in fury, it blasted tree limbs to shards of piercing knives! Kobar leapt into action becoming a shield as he landed on top of the other three. But the force of Kobar's weight shoved them off the muddy trail. Arms and legs wildly swinging, they tumbled and slid straight for the river! Kobar was in front and Quill followed. Burt was grabbing for anything that came within reach. Terrified, he remembered what he had been through when he and Quill went over the cliff. His hand hit something and he grabbed at it, coming to a sudden stop; he had caught hold of a small tree. Just as Burt thought he was safe, Kailon slid into him from behind, knocking him loose once again. Burt saw the river below and knew he didn't stand a chance. With Molik's shield tied to his back, he would sink like a stone!

"Quill, help me, I'll drown!" Burt screamed as he hit the water full force.

Quill and Kobar had already been washed downstream by the force of the rushing water leaving only Kailon to help. And he hit the water right behind Burt! Kailon sputtered, wiping mud and water from his face, then poked at the river's bottom with his cane, trying to find Burt. Within seconds, he felt Burt's hand pull on the cane. Burt surfaced spouting water everywhere and in a state of complete panic!

"Kailon, I'm sinking! Molik's shield is tied to my back! Untie it!" Burt pleaded, his voice barely audible above the raging storm.

"I can't. If we lose the shield, we won't get into the Kingdom of Zin. We need that shield!" Kailon shouted, trying to be heard.

"Who cares about your old shield? What about my *life*?" Burt yelled back angrily.

Kailon was dirty, soaked, and running out of patience as he called out, "Listen Burt, just hang on to me until we get to Kobar; he will help you." Kailon fought to keep control of himself as he grabbed at Burt trying to get a better hold on him.

Quill and Kobar knew Burt was in trouble and they were both trying to swim back upstream to get to him. Kobar reached Burt first and told him to hang on to his back. Quill struggled through the fast-flowing water, finally reaching Kailon and with all his remaining strength, shifted him up on his back just as the four of them were washed downstream by a flash flood. The downpour continued for over an hour. The lightning flashed and arced across the darkened sky without any letup and the four unlikely companions knew the safest place for them at that moment was right where they were, being swept in another direction—far away from the storm! They didn't even think of getting out of the water. It was then that they saw a huge log being swept along quite near them and, with a desperate lunge, Kobar was able to grab it. Burt and Kailon could hold onto that thus freeing Kobar and Quill who were tiring quickly. It was only then that they became aware of towering cliffs on both sides of the river and no apparent way for them to get out.

"Hey! Look there!" Burt called out, gesturing wildly at the rock face.

Quill looked up and noticed the opening to a cave in the face of the rock. Kobar started kicking his feet as soon as he saw it. He was trying to steer the huge log toward the opening. Burt and Kailon joined in, using their hands as paddles trying to help Kobar bring the log closer to the cave. Using every ounce of remaining energy, they moved the log inch by inch, fighting the strong current every bit of the way. But nearing the edge of the river was to be only half this new battle! There were still at least four feet of rock to climb before they could reach the safety of the cave! Kobar was first. He raised his long arms and caught the edge of the rock at the entrance to the cave, pulling himself up until he was high enough to swing his leg up and inside. He crawled the rest of the way in then turned and reached down yelling for Burt to take his hand and climb up. After Burt it was Kailon's turn and then Quill's. They crawled into the darkness and quiet of the cave as a bear would retreat into its den, collapsing one by one onto the rock floor gasping for breath. Their strength was gone.

****

"Quill, get this shield off me!" Burt's voice was shaking, partly from being wet and cold, but mostly from fear. "This thing almost killed me today, pulling me under the water. I know one thing for sure, turtles must sink like rocks. At least I did." He kept trying to reach behind himself to remove the shield on his own.

"Sit still Burt. I'll untie it. Just take it easy!" Quill said as he reached for the thongs holding the shield fast.

****

They had no way of knowing how long they had just lain in utter exhaustion on the cave floor before really coming to their senses. It seemed like days. It was probably only an hour or so. The cold is what brought them around.

"Everyone check to see if anything is lost," Kailon said as he dipped into his pockets.

"Kailon, do you know where we are?" Quill asked as he finished removing Burt's awkward load.

"We are getting close to your valley. You must understand that you and Burt were out of the valley when we were in the caverns. Remember that Quill. If you don't, you will never find the Elf treasure again," Kailon said.

"How could we have walked out of the valley without even knowing it?" Quill asked.

"It wasn't hard. All you had to do was get lost! The next thing you knew you were on a different trail in a different land. I hate to say this, but you and Burt did just that. You got lost. But, you got lost with the help of the acorns. Remember, I am the one that brought *you* to *me*, and right now I don't think you need to worry about how I did it, just that it was done," Kailon explained as he leaned his cane up against the wall.

Burt was sitting across from Kailon listening to him and Quill talk about where they were while also trying to take off his boots so he could empty the water from them. Kobar stood and adjusted his sword and then Molik's sword. He then wandered off into the inner recesses of their refuge.

"Kailon, we were only lost for about three hours. I don't see how we could have left the valley," Burt said while pouring water from his boots.

"Let me tell you something. The two of you found the black temple and because Quill is the Chosen One, the one to become the new Light Elf, the power of the Dark Elf helped you to find Kobar and me. You see, in order for me to have guided the Chosen One to the Elf treasure, and awaken Kobar and myself, I had to use the power of the Dark Elf. How? Simple. He had destroyed my power, so all I did as he and I were fighting was transfer what little power I had left into those two little acorns that you now have in your pocket. They would act as your guide. When I did that, I knew Syffus would protect them, and anyone who found them, because that would be the only way he could find me and stop you from becoming the new Light Elf. As long as I am alive Syffus will never get into the Kingdom of Zin, and when I die Quill will become the new protector of that Kingdom. Your job will be to keep it safe and hidden from Syffus until it rises again. But as for your first question about being lost, yes, you were lost, but only in *your* eyes. I knew where you were going all the time. Remember when you asked me why the stones changed into acorns? Well, the acorns are the fruit of the oak tree, and as time passes you will learn new ways to use the power of the oak. But for now, we must rest. There has been too much talk already. Keep in mind, we are out of the caverns of Elf treasure so we must be careful of what we say." Kailon held his small finger to his lips.

"What do you mean when you say that the Kingdom of Zin will rise again?" Quill asked, not ready to quit this conversation.

"Quill, no more talk about this until we get to the power room within the Kingdom," Kailon snapped back with a tone of finality in his voice.

Burt was trying to get the soggy food bag untied from his belt and was having a hard time of it because the leather ties had pulled tighter in the water. He was mumbling something about not having a good meal in days.

"Quill, do you and Kailon want some of the boar meat to eat?" Burt asked.

Quill didn't answer; he just sat thinking about all of these things Kailon kept telling him. It seemed like he was only getting bits and pieces of information and it was frustrating. Burt finally got the bag untied and took out some meat and handed it to Kailon. He then helped himself to a piece and heaving a great sigh, he leaned back against the wall of the cave, slowly chewing, not saying another word.

Each deep in his own world of thought, they sat quite still for several minutes, taking advantage of the opportunity for rest. Quill glanced out of the cave and watched the rain falling into the river below.

Suddenly he noticed the water level rising! There were only about two more feet to go before the water from the river would be inside the cave! Looking around he soon realized this cave had been carved by the force of the river and the rock was smooth from the action of the water wearing away the rough surface of the stone.

"We can't stay here! The water is rising and before long we'll be flooded out of here!"

Quill jumped to his feet grabbing for his bow and quiver at the same time. "Where did Kobar go?"

"Further inside the cave. He's been gone for some time now," Burt answered.

"Let us go now—we must find him!" Kailon responded.

"I thought you said Kobar never leaves your side, Kailon." Quill's comment was more of a question than a statement.

"I'm sure he is not far," muttered Kailon.

They were about to head off in search when Kobar appeared. "This is not a cave. It is a tunnel that leads to your valley Quill," Kobar announced, the beginnings of a real smile on his face!

****

Kobar led the way with Quill following and Kailon right behind. Burt hurried along last. What they had thought to be a cave was in fact a tunnel that went right under the mountains opening onto the valley where Quill and Burt had spent all their lives. It wasn't long before they could see light ahead. Kobar stopped and, turning around, pointed at Quill saying, "This comes out under a water fall. Be careful, it is going to be slippery." Like any of them had to be warned about water being slippery after what they had been through!

Quill emerged from the tunnel first. The instant his eyes could see past the falls he recognized his homeland. They had come out just a half day's walk from the village at the head of a small lake. But, why was this the first time he had seen the tunnel?

"Quill, we're home!" exclaimed Burt happily.

Quill stood gazing into the valley—taking note of the incredible beauty of the place. Green fields covered with wild flowers; streams and small lakes dotted the landscape throughout the valley, highlighted by dense forest—trees standing at rigid attention on every side. The sweet sounds and smells comforted Quill. He was home! His excitement grew rapidly as he climbed down from the rock under the waterfall, making his way to a trail no more than twenty feet from the edge of the nearest small lake. Burt scampered along behind him just as excited to be in such familiar surroundings.

"We're only about a half day's walk from the village. Do you remember this place? It's where you and I used to swim and fish when we were kids. I don't remember any tunnel, do you Quill?" In his excitement Burt slipped and bumped into Quill.

It didn't take long before they reached the trail leading back to the village. Each one in turn took one last look at the waterfall. Quill shook his head still not believing there was a tunnel behind there. But now he knew there was and also, where it would take him.

Quill led the way for the remainder of the trip, taking them to the outer perimeter of the village. It was getting dark as the sun slowly slid behind the mountains they had come to know so well. Smoke rose from small campfires in the village and they could hear children talking and laughing as they stopped for a moment to listen.

Kailon's voice was almost a whisper as he turned to Kobar and said, "Listen, a sound you and I have not heard for such a very long time. How good to be back to a place we can call home." His eyes glistened with tears of joy but were quickly brushed dry before anyone could notice.

"Kailon, tonight you will sit at my mother's table and have the best meal ever." Burt rubbed his hand over his large stomach as he extended this generous invitation.

"Hear me. Neither of you will mention the Kingdom of Zin until I say you can, understand?" Kailon's words were not to be taken lightly. They all nodded in agreement.

Burt could wait no longer. He half ran, half walked toward the village, mumbling happily about food. Kobar followed Burt, laughing along with his new-found friend. Quill and Kailon stayed together as they too made their way along the trail—the small village of Okon a welcome sight stretched out before them.

Chapter Eleven

Kailon put out his hand, resting it on Quill's shoulder, as he spoke. "Quill, Kobar and I are going to wait here. I don't think it's a good idea to enter the village right now. Your people will not accept Kobar right away."

"What are you saying Kailon? This is my home and you and Kobar are welcome. Please come with us," Quill pleaded.

"Listen to me Quill." Kailon's voice was barely above a whisper. "Your village has been isolated from everything for four hundred years. Your people believe they are the only living things in this valley. I don't want to start a panic."

"Quill, aren't you coming?" Burt called out excitedly as he stopped and waited.

"Just go," Kailon urged. "We will be fine. We will come to the village after you have explained to everyone about how you found us."

Quill looked up at Kobar and could see in his eyes, visible behind the leather mask, that he too wanted it this way.

"But what do I tell them?" Quill asked. "You've made Burt and I promise that we wouldn't tell anyone about the Kingdom of Zin."

Kailon thought a moment before deciding on a plausible story. "Tell them that you and Burt found us wandering around in the valley and that in the past few days we have become friends. Explain to them that we come from another land but you don't know where."

"You're asking me to lie, Kailon. That's something I cannot do," Quill said with anguish in his voice.

"No, Quill, I am not asking you to lie. An elf cannot lie. What I'm asking you to do is use good judgment and choose your words carefully. I do not want you to confuse the people.

"How long will you stay out here?" Quill asked.

"When I am ready and I feel *you* are ready, I will come. For now, Kobar and I will make camp somewhere else."

"Where?" Quill was deeply concerned.

"We will be close by, but not too close. If the Dark Elf is in this valley he will be drawn to me before he would be to your village. It is safer for everyone if I remain away from the village for now. We have a lot of things to do and very little time in which to do them. We have to find the opening to the Kingdom and then you must start to build your Elf Circle. While we are doing all of these things, we must proceed with extreme caution and look for signs that the Dark Elf is close by. Once we open the power tomb, Syffus will be very near. He wants to destroy everything pure and good around us, so Syffus will stop at nothing to do just that. Keep your wits about you son. Sleep lightly and trust no one right now." Kailon's hands gently rested on Quill's shoulders, reassuring him as he spoke.

By now Burt had returned to the spot where Quill stood and listened as Kailon said, "Quill, give me your hand."

Quill obediently stretched out his hand and watched as Kailon reached into one of his pockets and pulled out a small object. Kailon paused for a moment and looked up at Kobar who was standing right next to him yet towering over these little people. Kobar nodded. He knew what Kailon was about to do. Kailon then placed his small hand on top of Quill's waiting palm.

"Quill, this is the golden ring of the Light Elf. It must be worn at all times. This is the beginning—your first step to becoming the new Light Elf. This ring belonged to the Golden Elf, the only one to ever reach the highest level of magical power. I pass this on to you as it was written long, long ago. You are now on your way to becoming the new Light Elf." Kailon let go of the ring that now lay in the middle of Quill's palm.

"Hey! Look at that!" Burt exclaimed. "It's glowing like a lightning bug!"

The light now exploded into glorious streams, spewing all the colors of the rainbow in every direction radiantly illuminating each awestruck face as they stood closely together. The effect on Quill and Burt was magical and they allowed the light to penetrate their very souls!

"Quill *is* the Chosen One. The ring has verified it," Kobar announced in a soft, almost reverent, voice as he placed his hand on Burt's shoulder. And with that pronouncement, the spell was broken and the light faded as suddenly as it had appeared.

Then, as if someone had shaken the leather pouch where he lived, Kobar's cricket began chirping loudly. Quill shot a glance at Kobar knowing that the last time they had heard the cricket a viper had been close by.

"Don't worry Quill, Twolek is excited for you. He knows we have a new Light Elf," Kobar said as he held the leather pouch high above his head for everyone to see.

"You mean the cricket has a name?" Burt asked.

"Yes, his name is Twolek," Kailon announced.

Quill then took the ring in his left hand and slipped it onto the center finger of his right hand. As he did, his body was instantly bathed in a shimmering aura of soft light. He was shocked and didn't understand, but, for an instant, he did feel a change come over him.

Shielding his eyes from the unexpected happening, Burt trembled, more from surprise than from fear. To his amazement, he actually felt remarkably calm in the face of everything that had been going on in such a short amount of time.

Like a fog gently lifting, the soft glow was gone.

"Can we go home now?" Burt asked in a very tiny voice.

Smiling warmly, Kailon agreed. "Yes, Burt. It is time for you and Quill to go. Kobar and I will be fine. In the morning, come back here and we will begin our search for the Kingdom. Kailon raised his cane, lightly touching Quill's cheek with the end of that small wooden stick.

Quill looked at Kobar, then at Kailon, nodded his head and turned toward the village. He and Burt walked off, side by side in silence Burt was the first to speak. "Quill, do you believe what Kailon said about the Kingdom of Zin and magic?"

"Well, *something's* going on! I can't explain it but I do know those vipers were real and Kobar and Kailon are real. And the light that surrounded us was real. There must be a very powerful force behind it all. For now though, you and I must honor Kailon's request and not say *anything* to *anyone*!

****

"They're back! They're back!" A chorus of excited yells accompanied the wayward travelers as they came into view of the group gathered around a huge bonfire burning in the center of the village.

"Quill, Burt, where have you been?" a nameless voice shouted out. Running up to them the men tripped over each other in their excitement, reaching out to touch the two, slapping them on the back and blurting out a jumble of questions about their journey away from the village. Quill and Burt certainly realized that everyone had been concerned about them and were elated to have them back. In the midst of all this commotion, Quill heard a voice he recognized.

"Quill, you've had us scared to death! Where have you been son?" Quill knew his father's voice immediately—and there in the middle of the crowd of men stood Lore. Next to him was Tobble, Burt's father. For the time being he would let Lore do the talking. After all, Lore *is* the leader of this village called Okon; it was his place to speak first. The village was named after the family Okon, the proud family name of Lore and his son Quill. Okon is a name respected by one and all and a name they had all trusted for centuries. Quill's father is a proud elf, and as their eyes met, Quill could see the strength that they both shared.

For a moment, Quill stopped and took a good look at this man for whom he would do anything. Lore's slate blue eyes highlighted his ageless face, his cheeks rosy from the fire's warmth. His small elfin body was as solid as ever, considering he was approaching his sixtieth year. Lore's silvery white hair glistened in the firelight—the color of time for an elf. He was traditionally dressed as all Okonians have dressed for generations—leather pants, green shirt covered by a leather vest, and boots half-way up to his knees. Lore's knife hung from the right side of his belt just as it had for as long as Quill could remember.

"It's so good to see that you are safe," Lore exclaimed as he pulled his son close and hugged him tightly.

"Father, it's so good to be home again. There were times when I wondered if I would ever see it again!" Quill said. Then he recalled his promise to Kailon.

Burt and Tobble moved closer to Quill. Burt looked nervously at his friend who knew exactly what Burt was thinking. He gave a look of reassurance to his little buddy and said nothing more that would alert Lore to any of the dangers which they had experienced.

"Come. Let's sit by the fire. Tell us where you two have been," Lore invited as he led the way to a log that would serve as good-enough seating.

"But wait, Father. Where's Mother?" Quill asked.

"As soon as someone saw you coming, she and Burt's mother went off to start cooking. You know how they are! A little food is good for the soul—and for the sons who have been away from their tables for a time!" As he spoke, Lore motioned for Quill to sit. As he did so, Quill's eyes took in all of his surroundings. A warm feeling enveloped him and a smile spread across his face. It was only then that he thought to remove his bow and quiver. He was safe. He was home!

"What's that tied to your back Burt?" Lore asked as Burt gratefully removed his burdens.

"It's a shield Quill and I found on a cliff we fell over," he explained. Burt held up the shield for all to see. At that, Tobble took the shield and handed it to Lore. With the glare from the fire reflecting from it, the detail and craftsmanship of this piece of armor became evident. Lore waited a few moments, not saying anything, looking at and feeling the shield. Then he looked at Quill and said, "Son, this is not from our land. Where did you get this?"

His father was a very wise man and Quill knew he could never lie to him. But he also remembered Kailon's advice: Choose your words carefully.

"There's a lot to tell, and we'll tell you all about it eventually, but for now I have to ask you to bear with me for I'm bound to silence for a little while longer."

"What are you talking about Quill? When I ask you a question, I expect an answer," Lore snapped as he jumped to his feet holding the shield in front of Quill's face.

Quill rose and looked squarely into his father's eyes. He had to answer him. He put his hand on Lore's shoulder and said, "The shield belonged to a great warrior, one who lived in another time. Burt and I found his skeleton and with it was this shield."

Grumbling a bit, Lore sat back down with Quill next to him, the tension between the two quickly melting away. Tobble retrieved the shield from Lore's hands. He was fascinated as he studied it in the glare of the huge fire.

"Son, I'm sorry I got angry. But you and Burt have been gone for so long. We were all so worried and we feared the worst. We've had search parties out for the past three days searching for any sign of you. I'm not asking much, just tell us what happened." Lore's voice began to rise once again. Then he noticed the ring. Quill saw his father glance at it and he quickly tried to hide it with his other hand.

"What is that ring on your right hand? Where did you get it?" Lore's voice was insistent.

"It's a gift from a friend. His name is Kailon and he is an elf just like you and I, Father."

"Where is this so-called 'friend' of yours?" Lore pressed, now noticing the small pouches hanging from both Quill and Burt's necks, the ones Kailon had given them to hold the magic stones.

"He's somewhere in the valley. He didn't think it would be wise to come into the village right now," Quill responded.

At that moment, Tobble interrupted. "And what happened to your clothes, Burt?"

"I was attacked by a wolf." Burt ran his hands over his clothes, realizing that he must look pretty shabby by now. After all, the wolf did a really good job of tearing them up and if it weren't for the two acorns, he would have died.

Quill interrupted. "Listen, all of you. Burt and I are very tired and we haven't had a good meal in days. We'd like to get to our homes and eat and get some sleep. We'll answer all your questions. I promise. But first we need to relax; please. Tomorrow is another day.

"Quill is right. We should all go to our homes now. Our prayers have been answered. Our sons are home and safe. Our curiosity will keep!" Tobble spoke with the authority of someone who was used to being listened to. Lore nodded appreciatively at his best friend then looked again at Quill. He stooped to pick up Quill's bow and quiver, then, standing next to his son, said, "We'll do as you ask. Let's go now. Your mother is waiting. Putting his arm around Quill's shoulders, father and son set out for their sod home located at the center of the village. They had gone no more than twenty feet when they were brought to a sudden halt by a shout from behind. Quill recognized that shrill voice before even turning to look. It was Okar, the village priest.

"I say again. Where are you going, Quill?" That screeching voice was not about to be ignored!

Quill turned to face their pursuer and lowered his head in a sign of respect before answering. "My father and I are going home."

Okar is a powerful priest, a power born of faith, not magic, just the strength of his faith. He is a dwarf, small in stature, but squarely built. His wit and temperament are like the fox who roams in the forest beyond the village, always challenging the faith and patience of the people. His ears and nose, in comparison to the rest of his face, are large. The hair upon his head and the beard on his face, are as red as the fur of the fox. His strongest asset is his commanding voice. When Okar speaks, the whole population listens—and sometimes trembles in fear!

"Have you forgotten to thank the Almighty for bringing you home safely?" Okar roared.

Quill stared at Okar and it seemed as though his voice was raising a cloud of dust—all Quill could see was the glare of the fire with dust floating all around it.

"You're right, Okar. We do need to give thanks," Burt said as he jumped to his feet.

Okar reached over and grabbed Burt by the back of the neck. He led him to Quill. Only the crackling and sputtering of the fire broke the deadly silence. It is sacrilegious to challenge a priest, much less question what he does. Quill's legs began to shake and he could feel Burt's fear as Okar pulled him along.

"The two of you—kneel down and give abundant thanks to the Lord in full view of those who love you!" ordered the righteous prelate. Quill and Burt instantly dropped to their knees, heads bowed.

"O Mighty Father, Giver of life, Protector of the weak and the lost, we thank you for returning to us those who have been gone! You have once again proven that you are All Powerful. Forgive these children for their sins and help them to see the right path in life and to always follow your teachings. Amen."

After Okar had finished praying, Quill raised his eyes, though not his head, and saw Okar still standing over them. His arms were stretched over his head and his cream-colored robe fluttered in the breeze. A wooden medallion hung from his neck. It was made from oak and was carved in the form of one upright timber with a second crossing it a little down from the top. About five inches in length and roughly the same across, it was very prominently displayed on the leather thong which suspended it on the old priest's chest. Could it be the same oak tree that fashioned Kailon's cane? Impossible. And yet, if it were from the same tree, then the Kingdom of Zin was right here in this valley! "Why didn't I think of this before?" Quill wondered. He saw Okar's symbol of office in a new light now and noticed what he had never bothered to see before, that carved across the face of it were two circles. Quill couldn't take his eyes off it. And all the things Kailon had told him were swirling like a whirlpool in his mind, each thought fighting for some kind of order but still just a jumble of unrelated facts.

"What is wrong with you, Quill? Why do you stare at me so?" Okar questioned rather impatiently.

"I'm sorry Okar. I guess I'm just tired." Quill lowered his head once more.

Before turning to walk away, Okar spoke to both young men again. "Tomorrow morning I expect you both to meet me in the church. We need to pray together. It is very important, not just fanciful whim on my part. Do you understand?"

They nodded in agreement, casting quick, guarded looks at each other. Quill then turned, went to his father, and they headed home.

"Son, I don't think I've ever seen Okar so upset. If I were you, I would do as he demands. He'll surely come looking for you if you are not at the church early in the morning." Lore's arm draped comfortably around his son's shoulders. Without further conversation they entered their house.

Kara ran to welcome her son, with tears of joy in her eyes, her words of greeting becoming almost a babble in her excitement at the safe return of her pride and joy! "O Quill! It's so good to have you back. Are you all right? Are you hurt? Were you lost? Where have you been? Why were you gone so long?" The words kept spilling out as she threw her arms around him and hugged him to within an inch of his life!

Quill laughed heartily, embracing his mother in a gigantic bear hug in return. "Easy Mother! You'll run out of breath before I have a chance to answer! I'll tell you everything but all in good time." He silently reflected on this beautiful woman. Elfin women have a reputation for beauty and Kara was certainly no exception, in fact, in his eyes, there were none who could compare. Her hair was the color of the new moon and her eyes as blue as the sky on a spring day. She also had a perfectly shaped figure. (Although Quill was a bit abashed to even notice that!) Yet, there was another very important quality worth noting—very smart and clever, elfin women can spot a lie a mile away! Somehow they always know when deception is afoot.

"Are you all right, Quill?" she asked once more.

"I'm fine, just fine. Hungry for your delicious food though—and very tired!"

"Come then. Sit and eat. A good meal and good night's sleep and you'll be fit as a fiddle by morning." Kara grabbed Quill's hand, leading him to the small table in front of the fireplace and practically pushing him into a chair.

Quill relished the sights and aromas of home. Truly there was nothing like it in the whole world. The house wasn't very large, only three rooms, two of which were used for sleeping. This main room was where they spent most of their time and where all family activity took place. A fireplace was on the right as you entered, with a table and five chairs nearby. Burt's father, an excellent craftsman, had made them. Shelves were on either side of the fireplace and extra small tables beneath them. It was on these tables where Kara prepared all their meals. On the other side of the room, a water barrel, a wood box and two large, comfortable chairs completed the furnishings. Here is where his mother and father relaxed at the end of a hard day's work. The roof of the house came to a peak at the center with two vents on either side of the slopes to allow for ventilation, as there were no windows. The wooden support beams criss-crossed under the roof and served as a place for Lore to store the pieces of wood he used to fashion arrows and bows. His mother stored baskets there and dried plants which she ground for spices and medicines hung from each corner.

"Mother, it's so good to be home. I missed you very much," Quill said quietly, looking up at Kara's doting face.

"Well son, we missed you too. But you still haven't answered my questions. Where did you and Burt go? Your father and Tobble looked for you for three days and nights." She spoke while preparing a plate of food for him. Quill was thankful that she was not looking at him because he knew he had to phrase his answers carefully so as not to reveal too much. He also knew he could not lie to his mother. Even if he could fool her, he knew better than to do so. He had never told a falsehood before and wasn't about to start now.

"Well Mother, I don't really want to say anything right now. I need to eat and sleep. In the morning I'll tell you all. I promise. Please understand."

Quill didn't say much for the remainder of the time it took him to eat his meal. Lore and Kara sat with their son, watching him, but not pressing for any more information or explanations. Quill was glad of that. When he had eaten his fill, he embraced each of them lovingly and went to his room, collapsing on the soft, warm bed. Totally exhausted, he was asleep almost before his head hit the pillow.

Chapter Twelve

"Kara, is Quill awake yet?" Lore asked as he carried in a load of firewood.

"No, he hasn't stirred. Not a peep. I really think we should leave him alone. He looked as though he could sleep for an entire week. I keep wondering where he and Burt were and what they were doing." Kara worked at the table making bread while speaking with her husband. She usually made ten loaves at a time and today was no exception. She enjoyed it and was exceptionally good at it.

"He has to get up soon, Kara. Okar wants to see him and Burt this morning. If he stays in bed much longer, Okar is sure to come looking for him. I don't want that crazy priest running around my home. He'll be yelling and blessing everything in sight!"

"Lore, you shouldn't be speaking about him that way. You know that's a sacrilege!" Kara admonished in a very stern tone but with a bit of a smirk on her face. The look wasn't lost on Lore, who sat down at the table while Kara brought him a cup of broth. As she went back to kneading the bread, she asked, "What do you think really happened to Quill and Burt, Lore?"

"I don't know," he answered while brushing some flour off his sleeve. "But from the looks of Burt's clothes and that shield they brought back with them, I would think that Quill has a lot to explain."

"What shield? I haven't seen any shield," Kara asked.

"Burt must have taken it home with him," Lore answered. "It's beautiful, about two feet round, gold in color with inlaid stones around the outside edge. They must be jewels of some kind. I've never seen anything like it before."

A knock at the door startled them both. Without a word, the door opened and in walked Burt. Burt never waited for an invitation; he always just walked in.

"Is Quill up yet?" he asked, yawning.

"No Burt, not yet." Kara replied as she pulled out a chair and motioned for Burt to sit. "There's no need for you to stand in the doorway."

As Burt entered their home, Lore and Kara noticed he was carrying the shield with him. Kara stopped working with the dough and wiped her hands. She sat down at the table, never taking her eyes off the shield.

"Burt, put that shield up here on the table so we can get a better look at it," Lore directed as he pointed to the table.

Burt laid the shield near the edge of the five-foot length, being careful not to lay it too near the bread dough. Lore stood up and ran his hands over the face of this magnificent piece. Kara just sat there watching the different colored stones as they reflected firelight all over the room. She was in awe of their beauty.

"Father, that shield doesn't belong to us." It was Quill who had spoken as he walked into the room.

"You're awake, son!" Lore said as he jumped up from the table and away from the beautiful shield.

"That belongs to Kobar, Father. It belonged to his brother. Burt has it because he carried it back with us."

"And just who is Kobar?" Lore wanted to know.

"The bodyguard of Kailon, the Elf I told you about last night," Quill answered while moving closer to the table and the shield.

"Kobar is very large. He looks mean but he isn't. He is really a very nice person," offered Burt by way of explanation.

Just as Lore was about to respond, there was a commanding yell from outside.

"Quill! Burt! Where are you?"

With a grimace and a shrug of his shoulders, Lore whispered to no one in particular "See, what did I tell you?"

"They're both in here Okar."

Quill opened the door and walked outside. Burt grabbed the shield and followed. There, standing with Tobble, was Okar. He was dressed in a fashion that neither Quill, nor anyone in the village for that matter, had ever seen. A brown robe completely covered his body with a hood brought up to cover his head. Embroidered on the front of the robe were two circles, one white, the other black. They overlapped each other about half way and were about six inches in size. Around his waist a rope of hemp with ten tied knots, evenly spaced apart, cinched the robe loosely. In his right hand he carried a tall staff. At the top of the staff was carved the head of a falcon. In his left hand, Okar carried a large, leather-bound book emblazoned with a letter Z carefully carved across the front cover. He was definitely the image of a powerful leader.

"Quill Okon!" Okar bellowed, "do you want to say something to us? Have you news that we should hear?"

Quill didn't say a word, but held out his arm to hold Burt back when he made a move toward Okar.

"Stay here, Burt," Quill whispered.

"Okar, what are you doing?" Lore asked as he moved toward Okar.

"I have important questions. For four hundred years the Church has been waiting. I will make sure that we wait no longer." Okar took three steps toward Quill.

"Are you the one, Quill Okon? Are you the Light Elf?" Okar screamed.

"Yes. Yes, he is the one," a voice yelled from behind the woodpile next to Lore's house.

All eyes of the assembled crowd now turned to the voice. It was Kailon. He moved from behind the pile of wood and very slowly took his place next to Quill. The murmurings of the gathering hushed in expectation. Even Okar remained silent while eyeing this stranger suspiciously.

Then Kailon spoke.

"Yes, Okar. Quill is the one that the Church has been waiting for." Kailon leaned over and whispered, "I forgot about the Church, son. Forgive me. It *has* been four hundred years! I think we should pray with Okar. It will soothe his soul and give me a chance to think of someway to get you out of this."

"Who are you and how do you know my name?" Okar yelled, not to be upstaged by this interloper!

Kailon did not answer. Instead, using his cane, he ever so slowly approached Okar stopping directly in front of him. He pulled the sleeves of his robe up to his elbows and placed his hands, still holding the cane, on Okar's shoulders. Leaning forward, he whispered into Okar's ear, "I am Kailon. I'm sure if you read that book in your hand, you would recognize my name. I wrote it over four hundred years ago. Now, let us not frighten these fine followers of yours with details they do not need to know at this time. Let us go to the church where my friend is waiting. We will talk there. Quill and I need your help. Do you understand?"

Okar gazed deeply into Kailon's eyes. If it were truth he was looking for, he found it there.

Nodding in quiet acknowledgment, he turned, walking in the direction of the church at the southern end of the village.

"Quill. You and Burt bring your families and follow us," Kailon instructed.

"What is going on?" Lore demanded.

"Father, just come along and you'll find out soon. For now, just trust me. Everything will be fine," Quill said as he took his mother's arm and followed Kailon. Lore was still upset because he didn't know what this was all about, but he went along anyway.

Upon arriving at the sod-walled, sturdy little church, Okar stepped aside, allowing Kailon to enter first. The villagers, who had accompanied this strange procession, gathered in the doorway. Burt entered next and Quill immediately heard him call out Kobar's name. Quill hurried in and, bowing slightly, showed his respect for the holiness of this place. Raising his eyes, he saw Kobar standing next to Burt. A happy smile spread across his face at the sight of this new-found friend. As he walked toward them, he extended his hand saying, "Welcome, Kobar! Welcome to my village."

Lore and Kara followed Quill but came up short at the sight of Kobar. Towering over everyone, he was an imposing sight fully dressed in leather from head to toe, including a leather mask, with two huge swords hanging from a loop on his belt, and in his hand a shield the likes of which they could never have imagined. They stood frozen in fear and Kobar was quite aware of that fact. But then he walked over to Kara and, kneeling before her, gently kissed her hand. As he got to his feet, he looked into her eyes and said, "Kara Okon, you are more beautiful than a white rose sweetly kissed by the morning dew."

A smile crossed her face and, drawing a deep breath, she relaxed a little bit. Lore just stood transfixed to the spot as if riveted in stone. Kobar held out his hand in greeting. Although still in shock, Lore slowly began to relax.

"Father, this is Kobar," Quill explained as he moved to stand next to his father. "Shake hands with him. He won't hurt you."

Lore raised his hand and felt Kobar grab it. He squeezed his eyes shut expecting Kobar to crush his hand, but instead he felt warmth and trust. He couldn't believe it. This was a giant but not mean, only gentle.

It was after all of this had taken place that Okar entered the church closely tailed by Tobble, Burt's father. They too reacted with fear.

"Okar, please bring the book to me," Kailon requested softly.

Okar walked up to the altar where Kailon waited, but he didn't take his eyes off Kobar.

"Please, everyone, sit down. Quill, will you go and shut the door? We do not need anyone else involved in this right now." Kailon then laid the book on a small table in front of the altar. While he was opening the book, Quill took a seat next to his mother.

"I would like to begin by introducing myself and my friend. I am Kailon, a Light Elf from long ago. This is my friend Kobar, also from a time long gone. We are here because of Quill. He has been chosen to be the next Light Elf so that he may protect the Kingdom of Zin from the Dark Elf."

"How do we know that you really are Kailon? He lived hundreds of years ago. There is no way you could be Kailon!" Okar countered gruffly as he stood up and moved next to Kailon.

"What is this all about?" Lore asked. "This is crazy. Have you all lost your minds?"

"Okar, I ask only that you open your mind to what I am about to say. I did live when this book was written. I am that old. Please, do me a favor. I have not read from the book in a long, long time but I can tell you this; if you look, there are several pages missing. Am I right? The missing pages are the ones that tell of the Chosen One and the Kingdom of Zin. They also tell of the secrets that hold the Elf Circles together, and how and where the elves got their power. I can understand, Okar, why you are having a hard time believing any of this. The Church has always tried to hide the truth about elves and their magical power since it is not the way of our God. I must say this though, our God would never hide the truth, and the truth is that elves, some elves, do have great powers. As a matter of fact, *all* elves possess a certain amount of magic. Now is not the time to fight this power, Okar. You cannot drive it back as if it were demons or something. It is here in this valley." Kailon stopped speaking for a moment to reach into one of the hidden pockets of his robe. He pulled out what at first appeared to be some kind of scroll. It was tied together with leather strings. Kailon untied them and unrolled the age-worn dark orange and brown colored paper. "Here are the missing pages of your book. I ripped them out over four hundred years ago. I knew the time was not right for the Chosen One so I hid them to keep the Kingdom of Zin protected. Without a named Protector, Zin would have been destroyed."

Okar's eyes were glued to the pages. He was uncharacteristically silent as he scanned each page with an intensity that held everyone present in a kind of hushed anticipation. Quill could not help but notice that Okar held the pages so close to his face that his nose was almost touching the parchment, giving away the fact that his eyesight was indeed failing him. As he finished with each page, he let them fall to the floor.

"Okar, what is it? What do they say?" Lore asked as he stared at the pages strewn about their feet.

"It is true. He is who he says he is; Kailon, the Light Elf. He speaks the truth. The Church has known about him from the beginning. We feared his name because of the danger that comes with it, so nothing was ever said. It has been my responsibility, just as it has been with all those who have come before me, to see to it that any word of the Kingdom of Zin was ignored. It was told only as legend by the elders to amuse the young. Today it can be hidden no longer. Kailon is right. All must be revealed because it is also written that when Kailon awakens, the Dark Elf will wrench the heart of our valley from us."

"Yes, Lore, the stories are all close to the truth. But all of those stories, those wondrous tales about elves, will die with time if the Dark Elf finds the Kingdom before I can get Quill to it," Kailon explained.

"Well, one thing is for sure, this so-called Kingdom is not in this valley. I have been from one end to another and there is nothing out of the ordinary, nothing that would even suggest some grand kingdom, unless it's this tiny village," Lore said pointing to the floor.

"Lore, I understand you have no reason to believe such a Kingdom exists," Kailon said.

Then, pausing briefly before speaking again, Kailon raised one eyebrow, and with just a hint of a smile and a sparkle in his eyes, offered an irresistible invitation. "But what if it does? Are you curious enough to explore with us and find out for yourself?"

Chapter Thirteen

The morning sun had now ascended to its highest point in the clear blue sky above the small village of Okon. The search party that had gathered near the edge of the village would soon face the hottest part of the day. Quill shaded his eyes with his hand as he looked up at the beautiful blue sky. He searched for the hawk that had been flying overhead earlier. As he held his head back, gazing into the open space of the solid blue above, he felt a slight breeze caress his forehead. Soft and gentle, it reminded him of his favorite pastime, lying in the lush green grass on the side of one of the mountains surrounding the valley—sharing time with the clouds that gently floated by, making their way to some far-off land.

It wasn't long before Quill spotted the great hawk, its powerful wings outstretched across the sky, capturing as a prisoner the same sweet breeze that touched Quill's forehead. The hawk never moved a wing; it just held its position, allowing this gentle wind to suspend it high above Quill's head. Quill stood motionless, entranced by this beautiful sight. Suddenly he felt the same kind of solitude as he imagined was familiar to the hawk—alone, detached from every other living thing on the ground below. Quill refused to move, the pleasure of that moment just too intense for him to let go. Eyes closed now, for an instant he felt the ground melt away as he too began to float. Startled, his eyes popped open in fear, but the temptation pulled at him to continue this strange adventure. How could he float like the hawk? This was not real; or was it? Again Quill shut his eyes, holding them shut as tightly as possible, refusing to open them. In that briefest of instants, he felt the breeze holding him high above the ground. As it did, he could see every inch of land dropping away far below him as he rose high above the trees of the valley. He couldn't let go of this strange feeling; he didn't want to! He had never experienced anything so wonderful! So real! Soaring like the hawk, adrift on the currents of air, he was able to observe every detail below. Quill sensed he had total control, enough power to do anything he wished. He could go higher or lower. As he felt the breeze change, so did he, heading off in a new direction, one that now afforded a different view.

Then, yet another burst of air raised him fifty or sixty feet higher. A totally indescribable feeling! Quill turned his head and could see his friends below. He started to call out to them but as he opened his mouth he saw something he didn't understand. He saw himself standing with his friends! But how could that be? How could he be in two places at once? It didn't make sense, but it strangely excited him to view himself from outside of his own body. Then Quill began to question *why—why* was this was happening to him?

As these thoughts filled his mind, he felt himself descending to the ground. Quill instantly changed his thoughts to the hawk and floating in the sky and felt himself begin to rise again! Is this the life of the hawk? Quill wondered. If it is, I want more than ever to be like the hawk as well.

Someone was shaking his arm and calling his name. Quill looked down and saw that it was Kailon calling him. Why would Kailon want to take me from this wonderful, crazy, magical adventure? Then without another thought Quill opened his eyes realizing that he had returned to his body. He was once again Quill Okon, an elf. The masterful feelings possessed by the hawk were retained however, that feeling of control and power. He didn't want to say anything to Kailon for fear that Kailon would laugh at him.

"Did you learn anything from flying with the hawk?" Kailon asked.

"What? How did you know?" Quill responded, startled by the bluntness of the question.

"How soon you have forgotten, Quill, that I too am a Light Elf. I have spent many hours flying with the hawk. It has much to offer you, more than you realize right now. But soon, you will be as a brother to the hawk," Kailon replied, pointing his cane into the blue sky.

Tears ran from Quill's eyes as a feeling of pure joy coursed hotly through his body. He really *had* flown like the hawk! Knowing this filled him with new desire, a desire to accept whatever Kailon offered. For the first time he *wanted* to become the new Light Elf. He *felt* his destiny. He would once again soar with the hawk and be in total control of himself.

"Is it wrong to want power and control, Kailon?"

"I do not believe that you have a desire for power. What you just experienced has been inside of you from the day you were born, but until now you just never understood how to use this great power. No Quill, it is not wrong to enjoy something you already have, as long as you use it wisely." Kailon again raised his cane high and said, "You must be like the hawk that flies overhead—strong, smart, wise, and with a keen mind to sort out the feelings that will come to you when you are alone. You are different. You are not the same as the others. You are not the same as you were five days ago. You have grown in wisdom and experience and will draw others to you who will seek the pleasure and entertainment that only you will provide—just because you are different. And yet, you will always be alone. Keep the memory of the hawk in the forefront of your mind and remember, being alone is not so bad. But you already know that do you not?" His arms swept upward as he continued. "Look up. What do you see? How did it feel to fly like that great bird?" Kailon then lowered his arms and cane slowly and turned to look at the others who were waiting for them.

"Let us go now. We have a lot of ground to cover in order to find the dolmen at the entrance to Zin," Kailon said walking toward Kobar.

As Quill looked skyward one more time, the hawk swooped into a headlong dive heading straight for him. Just as it appeared this great bird would crash into him, it once again changed direction, returning to the free space of the empty sky. The hawk rushed past Quill so fast that he could barely see it. He did, however, feel the hawk's widespread wing brush against his cheek as if it were telling him that he too knew how it felt and was welcoming Quill to the solitude of this new life.

****

"Lore, you told me that you know this valley better than anyone. Well then, you must be the only one who knows where the entrance to Zin is," Kailon said as he knelt, took the end of his cane and began drawing in the soft soil. As Kailon continued drawing, Lore knelt down as well so as to get a better look at the markings in the dirt. The other members of the small search party gathered in a circle straining to see what Kailon was scratching into the ground. Burt looked over his father's shoulder, with Quill standing behind Kailon trying ever so hard to sneak a look at whatever Kailon was describing to Lore.

He drew four upright lines next to each other and then moved his cane to a position right above the four lines and made one straight line across the top. This line extended past each of the two end ones. His cane moved once again, this time off to the right side of his drawing. There he etched a tree into the dirt, then stood up, not saying a word for several moments, but rather studying this odd picture before commenting.

"Lore, what I seek are four huge stones standing on end, each being ten feet high and with a fifth lying across the top. This top stone is twenty-four feet long, a sight you would not be likely to miss. This is the dolmen I made before I left for the Elf Treasure to begin my long sleep waiting for Quill. The dolmen is a marker meant to enable me to find the entrance to the Kingdom. Also, next to the entrance was an oak tree that stood over seventy feet high, its roots growing right out of the ground. If you have seen this tree before, you know that the roots look like this," Kailon said as he held up his cane for careful inspection.

Lore remained silent for several minutes. Rising to his feet, he paced around his band of friends who were now just staring at him. Lore continued to walk round and round. He would occasionally stop and rub his head as if it would magically jar some memory. Then he would begin his pacing again. Finally he came to a stop facing Kailon.

"I know a place at the southern end of the valley that might be the place you're looking for. But, I'm not sure. You see, all I remember is three stones standing on end; and no top stone at all. Another thing that bothers me is that the three stones are standing all alone in a small clearing; no tree nearby. I can't be sure if that's the place you're looking for."

"How far away?" Kailon asked hopefully.

"It will take us a day and a half to get to the general area and then all we have to do is find this dolmen you speak of," Lore answered.

"Well, it sounds like it could be the spot. After all, it has been in the neighborhood of four hundred years since I hid the Kingdom. In that amount of time a good many things can change. I suggest we not waste any more time; let us go." Kailon took the lead heading south in the direction Lore indicated.

****

They had traveled for the remainder of the day without stopping even once for a rest. Kailon fell to the rear with Lore taking the lead most of the time. Kobar followed right behind him always alert for any sign of trouble. When darkness began to fall upon the intrepid band of travelers, Lore searched for a clearing suitable for a camp.

"We'll rest here tonight," Lore decided as he stopped at the edge of a clearing. "Quill, you and Burt go find enough firewood to last the night. Kailon, you and Kobar clear the ground for places to sleep, and Tobble, you find the pine boughs for bedding, and then dig a pit for a fire." Lore had definitely assumed command and moved to the center of the clearing for a more advantageous look at the site he had chosen.

"Father, what are *you* going to do?" Quill asked, hands on hips and waiting for a good answer.

"Hunt. I'm an elf and that's what elves do best," Lore said decisively, and then headed off into the woods.

An hour or so passed and all the assigned tasks were completed. The weary travelers lay about, enjoying the campfire and the many sounds of the night. Lore had managed to bag a small, but solid, wild boar that made a satisfying meal. The night sky was full of stars, all shining like the gleam of a young of a young child's eyes, full of life and happiness. The moon was full blanketing the land with its silvery light. Having eaten a good meal, and with the evening so perfect, it didn't take Quill and the others long to fall into a sound and peaceful sleep.

****

Dawn brought with it a true test of endurance. Lore set the pace hard and fast but toward mid-afternoon Kailon finally had to give in to Kobar's wishes to carry him on his back. It was about two hours before nightfall when Lore stopped, explaining that they were close to the stone pillars but he wasn't exactly sure of the location.

"Quill, do you and Burt still have the small gems you took from the Elves' Treasure?" Kailon asked as he removed the leather pouch from around his neck.

Without a word both Quill and Burt stepped forward, removing their own pouches as well and handed them to Kailon.

"Burt, I will need Molik's shield as well."

Kobar helped Burt untie the shield from his back—a sigh of relief escaping Burt's lips to be finally rid of the huge metal weight.

"What are you going to do Kailon?" Quill asked.

"I will try to find the entrance to the Kingdom of Zin."

Kailon carefully surveyed the area around the trail. A sparse growth of trees allowed a clear view of the nearby mountains.

"Lore, how far are we from those mountains? I need to go there," Kailon queried.

"Not far. Why do you need to get to them? As I've already told you, the clearing where the stones were is closer to this spot."

Kailon didn't answer; he just started walking in the direction of those mountains. Dutifully, everyone followed. Within a few minutes the trail took an upward grade, the trek becoming more difficult. Still Kailon pushed on until he found a small clearing that allowed him to see the valley below.

"Quill, come and stand next to me. You will learn something." Kailon pointed with his cane to the ground next to him.

"Kobar, give me Molik's sword," Kailon ordered.

Lore, Burt and Tobble looked on intently at what Kailon was doing. Frozen—enchanted really—not one of them uttered a word.

Kailon grabbed the sword and knelt on the ground. Bowing his head he began mumbling to himself and soon, finished with this chant, he stood, raising the sword high above his head, again mumbling something. Then, with one swift motion, Kailon drove the sword into the solid rock in front of him. The others jumped back not believing what Kailon had just done. Unfazed, Kailon bent down, picked up the shield and placed it on top of the sword. It appeared as though the sword were made to hold the shield, which had a rounded center and balanced perfectly on top.

"What you are about to see, Quill, should never be forgotten. This is the only way you can get to Zin." Then Kailon emptied all of the colored gems into his hands. As he held them high above his head, the setting sun cast brilliant light through the gems and downward to the stones mounted in the face of the shield. The light passed through each of the stones and continued down, converging at one central point on the blade of Molik's sword, where it became so intense as to be totally blinding. Each of the spellbound spectators quickly shielded his eyes. Once again the refracted light shot out from the blade, piercing the forest below. Kailon began to dance excitedly in a circle.

Gleefully, arms now waving and head bobbing up and down, he exclaimed, "There it is! The way in! It's the entrance to the Kingdom of Zin! Take note all of you where the light of the Elf Circle shines." As Kailon danced the others stood dumbfounded, totally speechless, not understanding a thing he had said or done, but each staring in the direction of the light. They knew only one thing: the hidden Kingdom, the object of this fatiguing search, had been found!

As Kailon lowered his hand—the stream of light faded, then disappeared altogether. He shoved the colored stones back into their bags and returned them to Quill and Burt.

"What happened to the light?" Quill asked in a soft, measured tone.

"The stones we have been carrying gave me the power I needed to find Zin. It was because I lost my power that I had to use the Elf Treasure to move in and out of the Kingdom. If you remember, when we were in the Elves' Treasure, I told you that the gems within the cavern had magical powers. Well, this is just one example of that power, power you too will use when you come into your own as a Light Elf," Kailon answered, still grinning from ear to ear.

The old master then removed the shield from the sword, giving it back to Burt. With an ease that stunned those watching, he pulled the sword from the solid rock, handing it to Kobar. With that, Lore was already in motion, moving toward the designated area among the trees. Tobble was quickly on his heels.

"Let us go, Quill. We must get there before we lose the remaining light of day," Kailon urged, falling into step behind Tobble.

In only a few minutes the group found the massive stones in the clearing that Lore had spoken of back at the edge of the village. Kailon approached them, and began to look around for the two that were missing. One of the upright pillars and also the top slab were gone. His eyes danced across the surface of the ground searching for a clue. Suddenly, he spotted the fourth upright marker lying about twenty feet from the others, almost totally hidden in the thick brush. He pointed his oak cane at it. Without being told, Kobar rushed to the spot, and immediately began pulling and tearing at the overgrown cover.

"Kobar, we must find the other stone and then the dolmen must be rebuilt exactly as I left it centuries ago," Kailon instructed as he neared the ten foot-long stone lying flat on the ground, tapping it with his ever-present cane.

"Quill, you and Burt make camp. Lore, you and Tobble help Kobar find the top stone." Kailon knew what had to be done and there was no question but his orders were to be obeyed.

It wasn't long before the sun dipped behind the trees and evening quickly made its way upon the clearing where once had stood the great dolmen, a monument to time, marking the years until Kailon's return. The three remaining uprights displayed an aura of strength and magic about them as their moon-made shadows stretched thirty feet or more toward the east side of the clearing, edging the ancient trees. Kobar, Lore and Tobble had returned unsuccessfully from their search for the top stone, which had once so proudly balanced atop the other four.

"I do not understand. How could something so heavy and twenty-four feet long, five feet wide and two feet thick just disappear? I have overlooked something, but what?" Kailon pondered as he sat on the edge of the smaller stone.

Quill was carrying the last armful of pine boughs into the camp when he heard Kailon's remarks. Dropping the branches, he approached the three standing stones. Concentrating on them, he was startled to hear a familiar sound coming from the sky above. Raising his eyes he saw the hawk from the village. How strange that it would follow him on this journey. He closed his eyes and thought of hawk-flying, bringing his body in line with the hawk's, and his mind in tune with the great bird's. In a flash, they were one, soaring above the camp. Quill saw mountains and trees below; felt the breeze brush his face as he drifted in the sky above the remains of the dolmen. Looking down at the clearing, he could see his body standing next to the remains of the dolmen. He turned his head a little more toward the east where Kailon, as well as Kobar, Lore, Tobble and Burt stood near the fire. Looking west, the trailing edge of the sun made its way below the far-off horizon. Using the eyes of the hawk Quill could see things as never before. He scanned the area several times, looking for the top stone. Then, jumping right out at him was its outline! He could only see five or six small spots where rock was protruding from the ground—about eight feet from the site of the dolmen. But it was unmistakable. It was there. Then, to let Kailon know he had found the stone, Quill stayed with the hawk as they dove over Kailon's head. Kailon jumped to his feet in fear but soon realized what was happening. He raised his cane to the sky in tribute and muttered to himself, "Quill Okon, your power is strong even before you are given your Elf Circle. You *are* going to be a truly great Light Elf."

Kobar came running with sword drawn anticipating an attack by this mad bird on Kailon.

"Stop! It is not what you think." Kailon held out his hand to halt Kobar's advance. Quill opened his eyes, severing the link with the watchful hawk, and focused on his newfound friend who drifted overhead in ever larger circles until he disappeared from sight.

"Kailon, I found the top stone!" Quill yelled excitedly, gesturing for everyone to come.

"Where? Where is it Quill?" Kailon demanded, out of breath from hurrying.

"Lying right there!" Quill pointed to the spot just a few short feet away. Kailon spun around, poking the cane at the ground and occasionally looking up at Quill and the rest with excitement written all over his face.

"You are right! This is it! We have the top stone!" Kailon exclaimed.

Quill and the others half walked, half ran to look. They kicked and scratched at the ground trying to expose more of the rock.

"And just how are we supposed to get this thing out of the ground and on top of the others? It must weigh tons!" Burt asked incredulously.

"We will do it. I think I know a way." It was Tobble who spoke up quietly, still deep in thought.

"Well, for now let us sleep on it and begin in the morning." Kailon, smiling broadly, clearly elated, waved his arms to gather them all together as night's soft silence gently embraced the excited little group. Everyone but Kobar returned to the welcoming fire. He remained behind. He would begin work on the excavation alone.

"Kailon, this is not going to be easy. We don't have any ropes, or even tools to cut with. I just don't see how it can be done, at least not without sending someone back to the village for help," Lore said as he threw another stick on the fire. But then, more or less thinking out loud, he offered, "Using levers and a fulcrum could possibly do it. Perhaps if we find some logs, or fallen trees, and then gradually raise the stone to the top we'll be able to complete the dolmen."

Lore and Tobble discussed the problem with Kailon for over an hour. As they talked, Burt fell asleep. He was so tired from walking all day he didn't even eat. Quill stood about ten feet from the campfire looking at Kobar and wondering what he was up to. He remembered what Kailon had told him about Kobar, that he has secret powers unknown to anyone. Quill watched him until he was so tired he could no longer stay awake. By now, all the others had nodded off. Returning to the fire he absentmindedly placed a couple of sticks on the glowing embers, then, wrapping his cloak around his shoulders, he laid down on the make-shift bed allowing the cool softness of the night to wash any thoughts from his mind as he drifted into a welcome sleep.

****

As new light dawned upon the six bodies lying around the smoldering campfire, Quill was the first to be awakened by the sounds of the hawk screeching and flapping its wings. But another familiar sound triggered an alarm. Tworek, Kobar's cricket, was wildly chirping. Kobar was instantly awake, jumping up with sword in hand. Quill looked at him and a chill ran down his spine as he remembered the last time this happened. A viper was not far from attacking them. Kobar looked up at the hawk, drawing Quill's eyes skyward too. The feathery sentinel was almost at the other side of the clearing screaming and flapping its wings but staying in the same position, high in the air at the edge of the tree line. By now the others were awake and alert. Lore grabbed his bow and quiver and stood ready next to Quill who had already placed an arrow on his bowstring, ready to be fired at a moment's notice. Then, while scanning the trees at the other side of the clearing, Quill and Lore saw it—the dolmen was back in its original condition! The fourth stone was in place, upright beside the other three, and the fifth, by far the largest, lay across the others. At first Quill couldn't believe what he was seeing. But then he remembered Kailon's admonition about Kobar. Quill slowly turned to face him and when their eyes met, Kobar gave Quill a knowing wink, then continued to scan the surroundings to find the reason for Tworek's and the hawk's alarm.

By now Kailon was making his way to the dolmen. He moved faster than Quill could have imagined.

"Kailon, wait, there's something out there," Quill shouted but Kailon wouldn't stop. His legs just kept pumping faster and faster. Lore broke into a dead run after him; Burt followed. Quill realized that Tworek had stopped his awful chirping. He searched the sky for the hawk but saw nothing. Quill and Kobar followed Kailon and Burt to the dolmen. Tobble brought up the rear.

Quill was amazed; the dolmen was enormous. The pillars appeared different from the day before. Now smooth like the surface of a pond on a hot summer's day, their color appeared wavy pink and dark gray. Quill raised a hesitant hand—he had to touch one of the stones. The smooth surface felt soft, cool even, and smoother than his own skin. He circled the array inspecting every inch, then noticed a hole in the center of the enormous top stone. It was a small hole but from its location Quill surmised that it did indeed have a purpose. He walked under the dolmen and could see up through the hole to the bright blue morning sky.

"Kobar, we'll need Molik's shield and sword along with the necklace which Quill found," Kailon said as he pointed his cane at Kobar.

Kobar withdrew the sword from his belt leaning it up against one of the uprights. He then removed the necklace which he wore around his neck and handed it to Kailon. Burt was already on his way back to the campfire where he had left the shield. Kailon took the necklace and hung it around his own neck. Burt returned with the shield while Lore and Tobble scouted the area, sure that something ominous was lurking about.

"What are you doing Kailon?" Quill asked, his curiosity getting the better of him.

"I am about to open the passageway to the Kingdom. We have to get to the Elves' Power Room before whatever is out there tries to stop us,"

Kailon replied. "Kobar, can you lift me to the top of the dolmen?" He handed his cane to Quill as he prepared himself to be raised to the top of the structure.

Kobar stooped and cupped his hands allowing Kailon to place his right foot into them and with that hoisted the Master high enough to enable him to get a good hand hold on the edge of the stone. Pushing on the bottoms of Kailon's boots, he boosted him up and over the top.

"Kobar, hand me the sword and shield. The rest of you stand back!" Kailon directed.

Taking the implements from Kobar, he settled them into a slot cut deep into the huge stone. The shield fit perfectly—indeed, the slot had been made for it; running in a north/south direction it allowed the shield to face the morning sun now rising in the east. He took the sword and, moving just past the hole, placed it in another smaller cut. Again, the fit was perfect, the sword sliding into the stone about six inches. Kailon then moved over to the center mark, a hole slicing completely through the top stone and kneeling down over it, he removed Molik's necklace, placing it into the hole. It slid into place as easily as water fills a hole in the sand! Kailon stood, removed the small pouch from around his neck which held ten small colored gems from the Elf's Treasure, and emptied them into his hand. Going back to the sword where, in the end of its handle was a small indentation, he chose a clear stone, placed it into the vacant spot in the handle and quickly replaced the other nine gems in the bag, hanging it once more from his neck. He dropped to his knees and crawled back over to the side of the stone where Kobar helped him down. Retrieving his cane from Quill he said, "Now we wait. When the morning sun is just right, it will reflect off the shield onto the sword and then to the center mark where Molik's necklace lays. The passageway will open."

"Kobar, I am still concerned about what the hawk saw and Tworek heard this morning. I feel the power of the Dark Elf is very near. You and Lore walk to the edge of the clearing and make sure we are safe." Kailon's authority was to be obeyed without question.

"Burt, you and I will rekindle the fire and fix a little food for everyone", Tobble offered. He was beginning to feel like a fifth wheel and desperately wanted to contribute something to this endeavor!

Kailon again spoke to Quill: "You will stay here with me. It is time for you to start your journey as a Light Elf. The power that is about to be bestowed upon you is for the life of all good elves. It is to be used wisely to protect our heritage." Then, laying his hand on Quill's shoulder, and lowering his voice so only Quill would hear, he added, "You are special. I have felt that from the moment you touched my cheek in the Elf Treasure. Your power is greater than any I have ever seen and I suspect that the Dark Elf knows this too. That is why he has tried to stop us. I must tell you, the Dark Elf is going to do whatever he can to hurt you, and hurt you he will. Whatever else he is, he *is* smart. Take much care! But first, he must kill me; so it is written."

"What do you mean 'it is written' Kailon? You've said this before but I don't understand." Quill looked worried as he questioned Kailon.

"You will find out once you are inside the Power Room. Now let us get ready. It is almost time." Kailon spoke with a wisdom that comes from experience.

Quill felt fear begin to creep over him. His thoughts were confused and his breathing and heartbeat raced. Then he heard a familiar sound—his new-found friend, the hawk, circled as if floating in the morning sky. It was as though this vigilant winged sentinel had been sent to guard him from all evils that he would face. Quill closed his eyes, thinking of nothing else but his hawk. He felt the rush of the wind, nothing under him now, and once again he and the hawk flew together. He soared higher and higher, the dolmen and the entire clearing now within his view as he rode the currents of warm air. Turning, he headed for the tree line, looking for Kobar and his father, searching the trees for movement, any sign that would tell him of their safety. Under the trees, just a few yards from the fire where Burt and Tobble went about their business, Quill saw movement. As he closed in, he saw that it was not Kobar or his father. It was one of the Dark Elf warriors and he was creeping closer to the camp! He was huge and menacing, dressed all in black and carrying a sword and shield very much like Kobar's. Quill had to do something. He swooped down toward Burt, flying low over his head. Kailon reacted first, yelling for Burt and Tobble to run away from the fire. Quill opened his eyes—the hawk once again flew alone.

Quill ran the short distance to the campfire and stopped. Drawing an arrow, he readied it on the taut string and knelt, waiting for the intruder to enter the clearing. Soon the dark figure emerged from the shelter of the trees and stopped. At that instant, the hawk screeched loudly, flapping its wings wildly. It was evident from the immense size of this Dark Warrior that only Kobar would stand a chance against him. But where was he? He was nowhere in sight! Quill bravely raised his bow and took careful aim at the center of the intruder's chest. Just as he was prepared to release the arrow a voice spoke softly from behind. "Quill, this is my job, not yours." Quill lowered his bow and turned. Kobar stood within three feet of him, his sword and shield ready for battle.

It was at that very moment when Kailon screamed, "Quill! It is time! The passageway is opening! Get over here!" Quill spun around and gasped at the sight before him.

The ground under the dolmen had begun to collapse causing the dolmen to slowly sink below the surface. An intense beam of light reflected from the shield to the sword and then down into the gem which had been placed in that small hole in the center of the top stone. Quill once again faced the Dark Warrior, his thoughts now with Kobar and not the dolmen.

"Quill, go! I will take care of this and be here when you return," Kobar assured him as he pushed past Quill in anticipation of the stranger's next move. It was all happening so fast, yet Quill felt as though everything was moving in slow motion. Time held no relevance for the events unfolding before him.

But, responding to the command, Quill reacted, more on instinct than by purpose, and raced toward the dolmen that was by now hardly visible. When he reached Kailon, who stood next to it, the top of the monument was all that remained visible. Kailon grabbed Quill's arm pulling him onto the stone beside him.

Together they descended beneath the surface and disappeared, along with any trace of the dolmen.

Chapter Fourteen

It took a few moments for Quill's eyes to adjust to the darkness after the brilliance of the morning sun but when they did he was startled by what he saw. There before him was a beautiful, smooth passageway, carved from the same rock as the dolmen.

"Quill, do you have your flint with you?" Kailon asked.

Reaching into his pocket Quill pulled out the small rock that gave fire. Kailon walked over to the rock wall. Protruding from a hole in the floor were torch handles. He pulled one out and told Quill to light it. Quill removed his knife and struck the stone against the metal blade. Sparks flew everywhere but the torch quickly caught, a tiny puff of smoke and then the first crackling of flame. Kailon grabbed another torch from the repository, lighting it from the first. He handed it to Quill. At that moment they heard the unmistakable sound of clashing metal—sword upon sword—coming from above the ground, from where the dolmen had stood. Kobar and the Dark Warrior were in a fierce battle. Kailon knew if he did not get Quill moving down the passage soon he would insist on returning to help Kobar. Gently tugging at Quill's arm he guided him along the path.

Quill's stomach was tied in knots. He was deserting his friend who was fighting a savage warrior on his behalf! Just so he could become a Light Elf? Was all of this really worth the price they would all have to pay? And yet, he allowed himself to be dragged along deeper and deeper into the underground chambers. He worried that he was being weak, not asserting himself more in defense of his friend. But then his attention was diverted by the imposing sight of a giant oaken door completely closing off any further progress. Carved on the face of this door were two circles identical to those on the robe worn by the village priest. Quill kept silent. Staying close to Kailon, he nervously watched his every move.

There did not seem to be any handle or knob that would open the door. How will we get in? he thought. Then Kailon reached for and felt the left side of the door where a latch would normally have been. As he raised his small cane, placing the tip into a hole near his hand, Kailon glanced at Quill briefly. He pushed the cane in about two inches and turned it. There was a scraping sound, small pebbles caught under the door, and then scratching over rock—and the door began to move. Kailon removed the cane, and reached up to push the door. It slowly swung open revealing a cavern three times larger than Quill's village! There were shafts of light everywhere, streaming from above, just like the ones in the Elf Treasure. The Kingdom of Zin lay before him! Quill's breath came in short gasps, almost out of control, and he was sure that his pounding heart shattered the silence within the chamber!

"Quill, welcome to Zin," Kailon announced triumphantly, stepping through the doorway and swinging his arm in a show of grandeur.

Quietly, Quill followed Kailon as they moved to the top of a long flight of stairs that curved from top to bottom. Just as Kailon stopped, the huge oak door slammed shut behind them. It scared Quill so that he jumped and spun around expecting to see something terrible standing behind him. There was nothing! He turned back only to see that Kailon was now half way down the stairs. Quill practically tripped over his own feet trying to catch up to him. He was not about to be left alone in these strange surroundings! But he could not take his eyes off the sights laid out before him. It was a complete city below the ground! Buildings were carved from stone—seemingly untouched, as though newly erected, and creamy white in color. There were statues in the center of water pools and huge archways leading from one building to another. Along the walkways were pillars with intricate carvings from bottom to top. How could all of this exist so far under the earth? And how had it come to be? How is it taken care of? There were so many questions flooding Quill's mind that he shook his head in an effort to clear away these misgivings and concentrate on the immediate events.

Quill looked down the stairs at Kailon. He moved to his right and began his descent. He kept stopping to enjoy the magnificent carvings along the rock wall next to the stairs. They told stories about the people of Zin, children and family members playing and cooking meals and working at their various labors. The carvings portrayed a very prosperous and happy kingdom.

"Quill, come on, we do not have time to look around," Kailon yelled from the bottom of the steps.

Quill continued on down, yet couldn't help but admire these carvings as he did so. Kailon neared what appeared to be the center of the city and Quill followed. They stopped underneath an arch which was about twenty feet high and made of two white stone pillars etched beautifully all the way to the top. The arch itself, stretching from one pillar to the other was plain except in the very center. On the face of both sides were two circles, each with ten knots carved carefully into them.

"This is the entrance to the Elves' Power Room," Kailon explained, lifting his cane and pointing to the two circles.

Quill saw that he was standing on huge squares of cut stone laid into the ground to make an outdoor floor. Not far from the arch was a small pool of water and in the center stood a statue of a man with a crown on his head and robes covering his body.

"I see that statue, Kailon, but who is it?"

"The King of Zin. His name is Zupan and he was the greatest leader of all time," Kailon responded proudly.

"What happened to him?"

"No one knows," answered Kailon. "When I was fighting the Dark Elf, he disappeared. That is when I hid the Kingdom here."

"Will the Kingdom ever come out of hiding?"

"I do not know Quill. When I put it here, there was a spell cast that only allowed Zupan to raise Zin once more. Look over there at the King's palace. Do you see that small hole in the middle of the face of the domed roof?"

"Yes, I see it."

"That is where a solid gold statue of a falcon once stood. The same falcon carved on my cane. The spell requires Zupan to replace the golden falcon thereby allowing Zin to live again."

"Kailon, if Zupan disappeared four hundred years ago he wouldn't even be alive to raise it, would he?"

"Quill, Zupan had powers that even I could not explain. I do not believe he survived. But I am sure he placed the golden falcon in hiding somewhere and has left instructions on how to find it. He would not leave the Kingdom without hope. He would want it raised again someday. Zupan was very much involved in the magical powers of elves. He created the Power Room for the elves so we would always be able to keep our power alive. If he was smart enough to do that, then I do not believe he would have allowed the Kingdom to die forever.

"Zupan. I've never heard of such a name. It sounds strong—a name that a leader would have," Quill said thoughtfully, as he looked one more time at Zupan's statue.

Kailon then turned his cane upside down so that the head of the falcon-carved handle was touching the rock floor. Walking over to the pillar closest to the statue of Zupan he studied the carvings as if he were looking for something in particular.

"What are you looking for Kailon?"

"For a hole large enough to accommodate the handle of this cane," replied the patient teacher. In reality, he thought that Quill would *never* run out of questions! But who could blame him, he thought. Certainly with everything so new and strange there were hundreds of questions—and not always enough answers!

After only a few minutes, Kailon found the spot he was searching for—an exact fit for the handle as he slid the head of the falcon into the waiting hole.

"Kailon, when we were at the entrance to the Elve's Treasure and I asked about the cane, why didn't you tell me it opened the power room?"

"Well, first of all, you never asked me *that* question and secondly, it was not time for you to know! There are still many things about this small root from that mighty oak that you do not know. Zupan gave this cane to me and made me swear to never reveal the power it holds until my time was near an end. Now is that time, and when I die, *you* will carry it." And with that said, Kailon's manner changed abruptly—from teacher to leader as he quickly returned to the business at hand. "Enough of this. It is time to enter the Elves' Power Room."

Reaching down he gave the cane one complete turn, a full circle, to the right and then removed it from the hole. He walked away from the pillars and across the center of the Kingdom toward another set of steps. Quill obediently followed.

"Why are we going over here? I thought the entrance to the Power Room was back there!"

"No, not back there. When Zupan built it he did not want any elf to abuse the purpose of the Room. He felt that if you spent time to reflect that you would most likely find the answer you were looking for without ever actually *entering* the Room. It was meant to be opened only from the center of the city, in front of all the inhabitants of Zin. Because the Room holds such power, it was located out of sight and away from the people."

As they reached the steps, Quill could see more carvings, but this time the carvings were of elves and each was a Light Elf. They all wore a rope belt like Kailon, and Quill noticed the knots of power. As he moved up the stairs, he reflected upon the carvings which described spectacular deeds performed by these elves in order to earn their knots. Some taught farmers more efficient ways to grow their crops, others assisted the sick or taught the young. There were even carvings of Kailon and the battles he had waged against the evil of the Dark Elf himself. As he followed Kailon to the top step, a small landing with rock walls on both sides, Quill began to relax and actually felt calm. There in front of them was a solid rock door. It was the only door in the Kingdom, Quill noticed, that was small and suited for his size. Carved deep into the door was a rope shaped in a circle with ten knots tied in it. Kailon reached up and pushed on the solid rock. The door slowly, almost painfully, began to open. Quill could just about feel the door open from where he stood as the grinding rock shuddered and echoed throughout the great cavern. There was no doubt that the Kingdom of Zin was in safe seclusion from the destructive power of the Dark Elf!

Kailon proceeded through the solid rock doorway while Quill watched—and wondered what lay beyond.

"Quill, you may enter. Nothing will happen to you. You are an elf and all elves are welcome in this magical place."

Quill inched ahead, cautiously taking the five or six steps necessary to go beyond the entrance into the Power Room. Once inside he stopped to take it all in. The room was nothing at all like he had imagined. About twenty feet wide and twenty feet long, the floor, the walls and ceiling were made of oak. He felt as if he were standing inside a huge oak tree! In the center of the room stood a tree stump about three feet high. It was hollowed out at the top, and inside was a pile of acorns just like the two in Quill's vest pocket. When he saw them, Quill raised his hand and felt his own pocket thinking back to how all of this had started with those tiny acorns. At one end of the room the wall was completely covered by a carving. It depicted one solitary elf.

"Who is that?" Quill asked.

"That is the greatest elf who ever lived; the Golden Elf. The ring I gave to you belongs to him. No one has ever seen him, but it is written that the Golden Elf will come again when Zupan calls for him. Now with Zupan gone, I do not know if he will ever reappear."

"You always say 'it is written'. What do you mean by that?"

Kailon didn't answer. He took a few steps over to the wall with the impression of this Golden Elf. He pushed the center knot carved on his belt and half the wall swung open. Behind it was a very tiny room and sitting in the center was another oak stump, upon which lay a very large book bound in leather and beautifully trimmed with gold. Kailon first caressed the book in a manner of total respect and then slowly, almost religiously, opened the cover.

"This book contains the knowledge of all Light Elves, and you must read and learn until you know every bit of it. This is where you are to remain, in quiet reflection and intense study until all of your questions are answered. When you have learned these secrets you will then be given your Elf Circle. This is how it must be done. For this were you born. For you I have returned. My mission is almost complete."

"Who gives me my Elf Circle?"

"The spirits of all Light Elves who have died. This is where our spirits live and they will guide you. The Elf spirits selected you and it is their job to make you a Light Elf. After that, it is my job to teach you how to use the powers that you will receive. Now you may begin to understand why there is so much power here. I do not have power any longer because Syffus destroyed my Elf Circle. But when I die, my powers will be reinstated. How strong they will be depends on how much good I accomplish during my years in this life. Power in our spirit life is attained at different levels. You will soon know why some elves from the past are more powerful than others. Remember, these elves performed incredible acts of goodness while they were alive and so are now more powerful than the others. Listen to them, as they will make you pure. To become pure light is to be clean; mind and body. Purity is the end result of being totally good. Live your life purely from this moment on, Quill Okon, and you will become a great Light Elf both while you are living and when you one day enter the spirit realm."

"Kailon, why do I have to stay here alone? Can't you remain with me?"

"No, Quill, I cannot be here. This learning and study must be done alone—in the silence of your own heart. The elf spirits will take care of you just as they have doing since you picked up those stones that were in fact, acorns. The acorns are spirits. The fruit of the great oak tree, they are the fruit, or power, of the Light Elves. The Elf Circle is comprised of many spirits. That is its essence—the origin of all magical power. How do you think you have survived for so long against the power of Syffus?"

Quill pondered that, and kept his silence.

Kailon continued, "It was the two spirits you have been carrying around in your pocket who have protected you. Now it is time to return them for they have done their job. They brought you here safely. Everything you do from now on in your lifetime will be connected to the Elfin spirits. Remember that. The Elf Circle you are about to receive is truly a circle of spirits. We call them Elf Circles because they come out of the acorns, circle you at all times, and thus protect you. Only one thing can break that circle—the power of the Dark Elf. No one else, except Zupan, can even begin to match the power of the Elf Circle. Keep in mind; these are Light Elves with magical powers. Most of them earned the level of ten knots, so your protection is tremendous right from the beginning. But your own magical powers must be earned. This you do through good deeds as I have told you before."

Quill nodded his head in acknowledgment and then walked over to the pile of acorns lying on the dug-out stump. Reaching into his pocket he retrieved the two acorns he had been carrying for so many days. With his palm outstretched, the acorns resting there, he stared at them as if they would suddenly spring to life. Then reaching his arm out he gently placed them with the other acorns. He turned back to speak with Kailon only to find Kailon gone—and the door sealed.

He was alone.

At a loss, he wondered what to do first. And how would he ever get out of this room? Narrow shafts of light streamed in from above, evidence that at least it was still daylight. But then he realized he must find a way to light this room when night descended. He scanned the room but saw nothing that even resembled a torch. Nothing that would even serve as a substitute. Shrugging his shoulders, he gave up that particular search and entered the chamber that contained the book. He opened the ornate cover and staring down at the first page, began to read the lessons of the Light Elves.

****

The obedient student read until he could no longer see as the natural light began to fade with the onset of night. He left the small room and sat down against the rock door of the larger room. It occurred to him that he still carried his bow and quiver. They were so much a part of him that he took no notice of their being still slung over his shoulders. And so he removed them, laying them on the oak floor, though still within easy reach. He wasn't *that* trusting of this place! He poked around in his food pouch but it was so dark now in the room that he couldn't see what he was doing. Strictly by feel he removed small cloth bundles of food and unwrapped something. Smoked meat. Not fancy but certainly adequate given the surroundings and the circumstances! What would happen next? he wondered. His entire life had been turned upside down in such a short time! To even think about these past days made his head spin. How could all this be happening to him? The more he pondered, the sleepier he became. Finally, he lay down and closed his eyes, no longer able to ward off the fatigue which fought its winning battle with his jumbled thoughts. He drifted into a fitful sleep, filled with dreams of spirits and giants, soaring hawks and deep, dark caverns.

****

Strange sounds jolted him awake, though he thought he must still be dreaming, because he hadn't noticed any sound at all the day before.

Opening his eyes he expected daylight but instead realized the light came from the acorns in the center of the room. There was a brilliant white glow all about them and the noise he heard came from them! After several minutes the sounds stopped—yet the light persisted. Slowly rising to his feet, he moved closer. He could sense the presence of life in them! He waved his right hand about six inches over the top of the acorns, yet, fearful of touching them, he just stared. Nothing happened; just a continuous glow. He should do *something*—not just stand there gawking all night! Maybe if he read some of the book of knowledge he would begin to understand.

Quill closed the book two days later.

Walking over to the acorns, he thought about what Kailon had said before he left. Quill examined his right hand and looked at the ring Kailon had entrusted to him. He took it off to get a better look at it. Then it dawned on him; the book says that if a Light Elf turns his ring to the left three full turns that the Elf Circle will talk to him. Quill figured it was worth a shot! What did he have to lose? He replaced the ring on his finger and glanced at those acorns again. Was he really ready for this? Had Kailon told him the truth or was it a story from a time long ago that had no reality now? He was about to find out.

The glare of the light emanating from the acorns reflected off the ring and illuminated Quill's face. He tried to fight the queasy feeling that there were life-like beings all around him but he couldn't shake it. He reached down to the ring on his middle finger and slowly turned it; once, twice, three times. It was as if a thousand white doves had been released in the small room. Bursts of light became bright white spirits flying to every corner and literally flooding the room with blue-white light. He couldn't believe his eyes! Frozen in fear and totally awestruck, he remained rigidly erect, unflinching. Only his eyes moved trying to take in all that was happening around him. And then, without warning, the tree stump which had held the acorns rose up from the floor and hovered at the ceiling. At the same time the spirits disappeared and the room darkened. No sound, no light—as if everything had died.

Suddenly, one by one, six spirits rose from the floor, again lighting the room, and stood before Quill. He was stunned. He could actually see them. They were elves, and all identically dressed. One spirit came forward. He didn't walk; rather he seemed to float on a cushion of air across the room. His arms were outstretched, as if he were holding something. Quill could not move; his legs seemed rooted to the floor. Then he saw the rope draped across the spirit's arms. It dangled almost to the floor. The spirit stopped directly in front of Quill who trembled from head to foot. This couldn't be happening to him, could it? But he remembered what Kailon had told him about the Elf rope. Something touched his arms; it was soft, like a breeze but with more direct pressure. His first instinct was to recoil from the unearthly caress but he forced himself to appear calm and when the Elf called out to him he responded by raising his own arms and accepting the gift. He intuitively knew what they wanted. After taking the rope, he noticed it already had one knot in it. He wrapped it securely about his waist and as he did, he heard voices.

"Welcome, brother Light Elf. I am Tercal the first Light Elf. I have been waiting here for over a thousand years to become part of your Elf Circle. Standing with me are four other past Light Elves and there is yet another who is to come. We will be your Elf Circle. Your protection and your guides. Be aware, Quill Okon, that there has never been an Elf Circle as powerful as the one you are being given. You were chosen to be the next Light Elf. This is an awesome responsibility, one not to be regarded lightly. You will eventually possess magical powers the likes of which you have never dreamed—and you will earn some of the required knots of power. But as long as Kailon lives, you shall never reach the tenth power. When he dies, you will be free to earn the tenth power. At that time, and only then, will you become the most powerful Light Elf to walk upon this earth."

Quill was speechless. He found it difficult, if not impossible, to believe that a spirit was actually talking to him. He knew a response was in order. Somehow, from somewhere, he found his voice. "Tercal, I humbly accept your gift and am honored to have you as a part of my Circle. Can you tell me about the others?" Along with his voice, he had also discovered his fortitude, his daring. It became easier to accept the reality of this situation once he actually began to converse with his spirit guide.

"Quill Okon, it is not the time for me to reveal what you ask. I will say this: your Circle is comprised of the best and most formidable elves ever to have walked this land. When the time is right, you will learn their identities, but for now, you must trust me and my judgment. It is written (The Book! Now Quill knew why Kailon had used that phrase!) that our task is to guard you and enable you to reach your tenth power. Most of us are Light Elves to the tenth power. You must trust us. We will do our part to protect and guide you. For now however, you must sleep. You have been two days and three nights without rest. When you awaken you will read the book one more time and then, you will be ready."

"Why must I read it again? I think I can remember most of it right now."

"As Kailon said, you must remember *all* of the great Book of Knowledge. You are the hope of the living—the one to wrest the power from Syffus, the Dark Elf. You must know *every-thing*."

Quill nodded, then turned toward the spot where his bow and quiver lay. Resigned to Tercal's advice, he settled to the floor, but looked up once more to speak to this new-found ally. But he was gone, as were the rest of the spirits. Although he had not spoken with them, he had indeed felt their presence.

And so he slept.

The sound of Tercal's voice wakened Quill and he quickly sat up. Appearing in front of him was his Elf Circle, five powerful spirits who would keep vigil over Quill Okon, to protect and guide his living body.

"Quill, you must re-read the book. Once done, you will leave this Power Room and join Kailon and the others. They need you. The Dark Elf is nearby and they weary of defending the dolmen."

Quill returned to the book, leafing through the yellowed, decaying pages. But this time every word seemed different. He couldn't understand why. Not only did each word seem different, but what the words represented took on a whole new meaning. This time Quill couldn't take his eyes from the print for even one minute. Each word passed through his brain like water running down a brook into a clear, cold pool. He read about Tercal and the other Light Elves and even took note that Kailon's name was mentioned several times. As the hours ticked by and Quill neared the end of the book, his time of learning was also coming to an end. Tercal entered the room and took up his post next to Quill.

"Quill, you have been reading for three days and nights. We are becoming concerned for Kailon and the others. Why has it taken you longer to read this time?"

Quill reflected for several moments before answering. Then he gently lifted the cover of the great book and closed it. With his hand resting on the cover, he felt the leather for some time. Quietly responding to Tercal, he said, "The magic that comes from a Light Elf comes from his heart and from his Elf Circle. You know that better than anyone else and I thank you for sharing your magic with me. I will make you and all other Light Elves proud of what you have done for me." He had not directly answered Tercal's question, but felt that his understanding of the monumental task ahead of him was enough. Tercal knew. It was going to be all right.

"Quill, we know where your heart is and we are prepared to assist you in any way we can. But, you must know now that what lies in the future will not be easy. You will at times feel pain within your heart and may even want to give up. Yet, I can tell you this, be patient my son, because in the end you will be great!"

Quill turned to the Book of Knowledge and, as it was written to be done, picked it up and turned it upside down. This was a sign to any other Light Elf that would enter—that a Light Elf is alive and he has been here. He then quit this small chamber, returning to the outer room where, exhausted, he sank down next to the rock door and once again, fell into a deep, but curiously refreshing, sleep.

Chapter Fifteen

Quill woke to the sound of his own coughing and choking, and the inside of his chest and throat seared with burning pain. It took only an instant to realize fire was nearby. He jumped to his feet trying to escape. His eyes burned, making it impossible to see as he rubbed them in a vain effort to relieve the smoke-induced pain. He only managed a few short steps before tripping over something and falling hard to the ground. Stunned, he lay with his eyes tightly closed, then quickly realized that he was no longer in the Power Room! Sitting up once again, he held both hands over his eyes in another attempt to erase the awful smoke, yet still trying to figure out where he was.

But then he became aware of familiar surroundings and knew that somehow, God only knew, he was back at the camp where Kailon, his father and the others were. Slowly his eyes opened, the pain of the smoke assault ebbed, and he saw that the smoke which woke him so rudely was coming from the smoldering campfire. In his efforts to get away from the choking smoke he had stumbled away from the embers—far enough to avoid any further encounter.

He sat quietly for a moment. How did he get here? Where were Tercal and the Kingdom of Zin? Had it all been a dream? Looking around he located Burt who was sound asleep, as were the rest of his band. But he saw no evidence of Kobar. Where was he, and was he safe? There were no immediate answers to his puzzlement.

And what was this? The dolmen loomed at the edge of the camp! He walked over to the spot and simply stared. Now his curiosity was getting the best of him. Were these past days merely a figment of his overactive imagination? Could all of what he had gone through have been for naught? He had to know! He was almost at the dolmen when he spotted the huge figure lying on the ground in front of him. He stopped dead in his tracks. Kobar? Please God, no! But it was the Dark Warrior! Quill moved forward slowly, coming to a stop next to the body. Clad all in black leather, from head to toe, even in death he was an ominous figure. The warrior's shield lay on the far side of his body. It too was solid black and resembled the one Kobar carried. Quill searched for the warrior's sword but there was no sign of it. His eyes moved again to the body that lay beneath him. There was one single hole in the leather; it was dead center over the heart. A small trickle of blood appeared to have run from the chest down and around to the left side of the massive body. Quill knew then that he had not been dreaming. He had indeed heard the horrible sounds of that final battle raging over his head as he descended to the caverns below. Yet, he still had to inspect the dolmen.

As he turned to face the strange edifice, he spied Kobar! He stood with his back to Quill next to the dolmen. This was indeed a most welcome sight! Sensing Quill's presence, Kobar spun around and with the most uncharacteristic show of emotion, he grinned broadly, then raised his sword high above his head in a grand gesture of salute. But instead of acknowledging Kobar's hail, Quill's whole attention turned to the dolmen. It was no longer complete! It was as they had originally found it; three stones standing on end and the other two strewn on the ground. "Kobar! What happened to the dolmen?"

"It was taken apart for your safety, Quill," answered the happy warrior.

This didn't even *begin* to make sense to Quill as he stared open-mouthed at the sight before him. He placed his hand on the center stone, the cool rock bringing some reality to the whole situation. His eyes fixed on Kobar again. The question (always more questions and few, if any, answers!) "Why?" never escaped his lips. Another mystery that he would have to accept. For now.

Instead he asked Kobar, "Have you ever seen the Kingdom of Zin?"

"Yes, Quill, I have seen the great city that lies beneath the ground."

Quill expected this response but still he had needed some clarification. Removing his bow and quiver, which had mysteriously taken their customary position around his shoulders, he plopped down upon the still-damp early morning grass, his head in his hands. Silently he watched the sun make its way through the trees as if opening a new age over all the land. The morning dew glistened upon the clearing like a silvery blanket, while the dying campfire still smoldered from the previous night. Birds sang their morning song, greeting yet another day, the sun warm upon their backs. A light breeze brushed Quill's face with the softness of a feather and wild flowers that painted the edge of the clearing with their vibrant colors gave off a sweet aroma that pleased him. He became as one with the beauty of the land in a way that was exciting and new. All of his senses seemed more alert and ready to see and feel nature's awesome gift. He remained rooted to the spot for several more minutes, reveling in all of it. He reflected on the magic that had been presented to him in the Book of Knowledge, on the land and all its beauty—everything filled with a mystical, magical quality.

But then Quill remembered the Elf Circle, and Tercal. What had happened to the spirits? Did I earn my Elf Circle? He couldn't help but wonder as he repeated this question to himself once again. Then he said out loud, "Did I earn my Circle?" When the question became audible, he felt something move inside his shirt. It was the small pouch around his neck. He opened it, turned over Kobar's shield and emptied the contents of the bag onto the center of it. There, still rolling around in small circles, were six acorns. Quill had his answer. Yes, he had indeed earned his Elf Circle.

Kobar said nothing but watched every move Quill made. Quill picked up the acorns and replaced them in the pouch. But, as he did, it suddenly dawned on him that the colored stones from the Elves' Treasure were gone! He knew they had been replaced with a much greater power. Quill held the pouch tightly in his hands for a while before draping it once more around his neck. He drew in two deep breaths of fresh air and stretched his arms above his head. Now he took bow and quiver in hand and rose. From the corner of his eye he thought he saw movement in the trees just beyond where the others still slept.

In a barely audible whisper Quill asked, "Kobar, is something moving in the trees over there?" He gestured with the end of his bow to the spot that had caught his attention.

Kobar scrambled to his feet, fully alert now as he grabbed his swords and shield in one swift movement. He slid one of the swords in behind his leather belt and stood ready to do battle with the other. Both he and Quill remained still straining to see what lay hidden within the dense brush at the tree line. It took but a moment for a second Dark Warrior to step from cover.

Kobar broke into a run, headed straight for the camp. He feared the outcome; he knew he couldn't reach the others before the warrior. Quill raced as fast as his short legs would carry him but at the same time watching every move the evil menace made. So far, the warrior had not seen them and he was almost upon the camp. Quill shifted slightly to the right of Kobar to afford himself a better view of the situation. Now the Dark Warrior was aware of the two charging forces and raised his sword for the attack. Quill couldn't see who lay below the evil one's certain blow of death. He screamed in a futile attempt to draw attention away from the attack—but it was too late.

With one single slash the sword found its mark. Quill stopped immediately. There was only one way to stop the warrior from inflicting another devastating blow. In what appeared like one single motion, Quill pulled an arrow and brought his bow down into position, placed the arrow on the taut, quivering string, pulled—and fired. With deadly accuracy the missile found its target in the attacker's neck. Mortally wounded, he spun around and, for an instant, Quill saw the hatred in the dark, evil eyes. And then the lifeless body fell to the ground.

Quill's heart raced in fear. Who had the warrior attacked? And was the victim dead? A small figure lay motionless on the ground, blood streaming from the fatal wound. Kobar reached the scene first, throwing his sword down and gathering the small body to himself. Quill then realized the victim was his own father. Kobar cradled the unmoving body gently in his arms and yelled for Quill to hurry. Already in motion, Quill quickly closed the distance to his father's side. By now, Burt, Tobble and Kailon were already next to Kobar looking up at Lore's tiny body. Kobar was frantically scanning Lore to find where the Dark Warrior's sword had claimed its mark. Burt motioned for Quill to hurry. Kobar found the wound before Quill reached the spot. Quill was screaming, yanking on Kobar's arm, trying to get him to lay his father down so he could be with him. They were all out of control, panicked by what had happened in just so short a time. Then Kailon very somberly raised his cane into the air, commanding silence and order without uttering a single word. Kobar reverently lowered Lore's body to the ground. Quill knelt next to his father, taking his hand in both of his.

"Is he alive?" Quill whispered, tears choking the words in his throat. Kobar's eyes revealed the awful truth. Lore was dead.

Leaning close to his father's face, Quill put his ear next to Lore's mouth in hopes that he would hear his father take a breath. There was no sound. Again Quill looked up at Kobar, and pleaded more than asked, "Is he alive?" The answer was already settling heavily on his heart before he even asked, but he needed to hear the words or he wouldn't believe it. Kailon felt Quill's anguish and moving over behind him, placed his hand on Quill's shoulder while saying, "Your father is dead my son. He is in the land of the spirits now, with his God."

Quill gathered his father in his arms clutching the lifeless body close to his own, sobbing tears of frustration and loss. There was nothing he could do now to help this man who had given him so much. "If only I had the tenth power, if only I had the tenth power," Quill whispered over and over as he rocked back and forth cradling his precious burden.

Kailon heard Quill's whispers and knew then that Quill's Elf Circle was complete. Quill was now the new Light Elf. Kailon reached down and took Quill's arm and instructed him to release his father's body; Quill did as he was told. Rising, he turned, allowing himself the comfort of Kailon's shoulders, softly crying as he was led a few steps away.

Kailon nodded to Kobar and Burt. "Make a litter for Lore's body so we can take him home. Tobble, would you pick up our gear, and all of you, be vigilant. Keep a careful watch. The Dark Elf knows where we are and will seek an opportunity to strike again."

Having thus instructed everyone, Kailon led Quill away, stopping after about a hundred yards, and told him to sit. Quill sat. His tears still flowed uncontrollably. And then, in a voice a bit more stern, Kailon said, "Quill, you must get control of yourself. In order for the rest of us to survive, we are going to need your power." He turned Quill to face him, holding him firmly by the shoulders.

"What power? I haven't seen any power yet; and if I had power my father would still be alive!" Quill wiped the tears from his face as he spoke angrily.

"Quill, who is your guardian? What spirit controls your Circle?"

"His name is Tercal," answered Quill.

"Tercal! He was the very first Light Elf, Quill. The spirits have given you the best. How many others are there with Tercal?"

"There are five other spirits but Tercal wouldn't name them. He said I would know in time." He swiped at his nose with the back of his sleeve.

"*Six* Light Elf spirits?" Kailon exclaimed as he sprang to his feet. "I have never heard of such a large Circle. You are the first with such power!"

In spite of the tragedy which had just occurred, Kailon was practically walking on air! He kept circling Quill, deep in thought, contemplating why the elf spirits had made such a large Elf Circle. Then he stopped and squatted down next to Quill. He obviously had arrived at a conclusion.

"The only answer I can come up with is that it must be connected to Zin. It must definitely be that the Kingdom will rise again!"

"Kailon, I can't worry about Zin and Light Elves right now." Quill still had an edge to his voice—he was irritated that anyone would even think about all of this right now with his father lying dead right there. How could Kailon be so thoughtless?

"I have to take my father home. My mother will need me and all this magic and power stuff will just have to wait." The anger in his voice was unmistakable. Quill found it hard to believe that Kailon would even think that he would care about anything other than his father right now. He stood, grabbed his bow and hastily slung it over one shoulder and tromped off in a huff.

But then he heard a familiar voice; it was Tercal.

"Quill, you must control your inner strength and your heart. The power you seek is from within. Do not let the Dark Elf break you down. You must be strong. Your father was a great leader and now you must be the same. He sends his love. He is with us now. He is part of your Elf Circle."

"How can that be? My father was not a Light Elf." Quill was clearly puzzled.

"Your father *was* a Light Elf and, like Kailon, the Dark Elf destroyed his Elf Circle as well. This all took place long before you were born. He was chosen to draw the Dark Elf away from finding Kailon and the Elf Treasure. Our plan failed and Lore lost his Elf Circle soon after he received it. Your father never told anyone as he feared for the safety of his village and of his family. But, now it must be told. With Lore's knowledge of the valley and his pride in you, we will defeat the Dark Elf. But before we can, you must earn the power knots on your rope." Tercal spoke with an assuredness that comes from experience.

By now Kailon was aware of what was happening. He could see it in Quill's face. The Elf spirits were talking to him. Kailon stood apart, waiting for them to finish so he could learn what was going on.

And so it was at that time that Quill was shaken to his very soul. The next voice he heard erased any lingering doubts he may have had. "Quill, it is I, your father."

If Quill wondered at all about his sanity, this would have been the ultimate test!

Lore continued, "I am sorry son, sorry that I never told you my secret. But now we will be together always and I will help to guide your journey of mind and spirit as you become the most powerful Light Elf ever."

The voices stopped as quickly as they had begun. Quill glanced right and left, all around, and then approached Kailon. He had regained his composure and spoke to Kailon more as an equal than as the student. "My father is one of the spirits. He is part of my Circle. He was a Light Elf, whose job was to draw the Dark Elf away until you awoke and my time neared."

Kailon did not utter a word as he and Quill made their way back to camp. Quill solemnly walked over to the litter so expertly made by Kobar and Burt. He calmly stood before it gazing at the small body of his father. How would he explain all of this to his mother so that she would understand? Kneeling, he looked deeply into his father's face. With every ounce of strength and resolution in his broken heart he vowed to himself that he would make his father proud as he continued on his journey of discovery. This path may not have been chosen by him, but he now knew that it was a path he must take. If it required a decision to be made, then he had made it. This was his life from henceforward. He would not fail this challenge.

Still trembling and in shock from the morning's events, Burt cautiously reached out to comfort his friend. "Quill, I'm so sorry about your father. He was a great leader, and an admirable man. I will miss him as will all the people of Okon." Burt's face was tear-stained as he knelt next to his dearest friend.

Quill looked at Burt. Burt was surprised, and a little taken back, to see a slight smile on Quill's face.

"Burt, I haven't had a chance to explain. My father's spirit is with me now. I'm sad that I've lost his physical presence, but I've been told that he is part of my Elf Circle. It's now complete and I must continue in my efforts to earn my power knots."

If Burt was confused by this sudden change of events, he did not show it. He was used to accepting whatever Quill said as truth and so had no trouble believing what he had been told.

The tiny band of adventurers gathered for a quick meal and then moved on toward home.

They knew the remainder of the journey would be rigorous and non-stop. There would be no complaints. Tobble assumed the lead with Kobar right behind dragging the litter. Kailon and Quill took their places behind the litter, with Burt bringing up the rear.

Kobar pushed on relentlessly, never stopping. He had forged a bond of loyalty with Quill as strong as it ever was to Kailon and therefore it was his privilege to complete this task for him.

Kailon spent most of the day discussing with Quill the lessons to be learned from the great Book of Knowledge. He explained that he was duty-bound to train Quill in the full use of his power. But, with only one power knot, Quill's magic was very limited indeed.

Every now and then Quill would hear Burt mumble to himself about carrying Molik's shield and now, the additional weight from the sword that killed Lore. Quill smiled to himself, and reminisced about all they had been through together. And in spite of Burt's grumbling, Quill knew he was really proud of his responsibility. Indeed, he would have been hurt if someone had offered to relieve him of his burdens!

As the sun quietly sank behind the mountains, the shadows grew longer, slowly giving way to the softness of evening. The trail darkened yet Kobar wouldn't stop. Sometimes the trail narrowed and Quill became nervous thinking that another attack was imminent. As night settled in, Kobar's pace slowed allowing all to stay closer together; it was safer that way. After a few hours of walking in the dark, Burt let out a howl! They all stopped short thinking he was in trouble. But no. He merely had a pebble in his boot and wanted to stop to remove it!

As they breathed a sigh of relief, Kobar lowered the litter onto the ground and went back to help Burt. Quill had suspected there was a softer side to Kobar, one that expressed gentleness and concern for others, a quality that hardened warriors usually did not possess. It was difficult for Quill to understand the very opposite sides of this giant of a man—so kind at times yet able to brutally defend and even kill when necessary. Quill felt something strangely peculiar about Kobar but was unable to put his finger on it. He was more than just a warrior or a guardian—or loyal friend. He was more than the sum of all his parts—greater than anyone he had ever known. Quill approached Kobar, and with hand outstretched, said, "You have been a friend, and more, to Burt and to me, and I feel the need to tell you how much I appreciate it. I know Burt feels the same. You are a kind and gentle man. A good friend."

Kobar clasped Quill's hand and looked into his eyes. "Quill, I am honored to share this time with you, and grateful too to be a part of this great mission. Life never ends my little friend. We will always be together, no matter what happens. It is written."

Quill thought about all the times he had heard that phrase, "It is written", and smiled inwardly. Kobar was so deep. Where did he come from? What gave him such wisdom? The answer would come someday. For now, he would just accept the friendship and loyalty so generously offered.

Burt had his boot back on and they were once more on their way, making headway to the village. Kobar and Tobble maintained a good steady pace. It seemed like they had walked for days. Quill was becoming tired and Burt was complaining more frequently. Even Kailon was showing signs of fatigue. By now there were only about two hours left before daylight, but they were only about five hours from the village. Quill reached back to adjust his bow, mostly to make sure it was all right.

He spotted something moving in the trees just ahead of him. Whatever it was, it was not part of the forest. Not saying a word to any of the others, he stopped, readied his weapon as he had done so many times before, and with one single swift motion, the arrow was fired. At that point his companions heard the arrow being released and came to an immediate halt. Something was wrong. Kobar was the first to appear, with his sword drawn and shield up, ready for battle. Burt was already standing beside Quill.

"What was it Quill?" Kobar asked.

"I don't know. Whatever it was, I got a good hit."

Quill and Kobar edged into the trees for a better look. Fifty yards in they found the spot where Quill saw movement. It had been a trick. The only thing there was a black leather vest filled with tree limbs to make it look like a person. There in the center of the vest was Quill's arrow. Instinctively he and Kobar knew what was going to happen next. Kobar never hesitated. He turned and ran toward the trail. Quill retrieved his arrow and placed it next to his bow ready for the next shot, then joined Kobar in a flat-out run toward the rest of the group. In a flash both Kobar and Quill reached their goal. Kobar, with sword still drawn, walked up and down the trail searching for a Dark Warrior. He must be close by. Quill stood guard next to his father's body, bow ready, waiting for the intruder to strike. But, nothing happened. Quill motioned for the others to be still. He listened but only heard the sounds of the night forest.

Kobar walked back over to the litter, laid his sword next to the body, hoisted the end and resumed his trek down the trail. Everyone stayed close together, following doggedly behind the litter. Quill's senses were keenly on edge and every now and then he would look behind them making sure the trail was clear. And each time he did, he caught a glimpse of fear in his friends' eyes. They all knew it was only a matter of time before they were attacked again. As they hiked along, the path widened and the forest began to thin out. They felt some relief knowing it would be harder for the intruders to hide, making a surprise attack much more difficult. For now anyway, they felt safe. Almost.

****

Morning's first light pushed its way over the mountain struggling to break through the heavy low-lying mist which bathed the valley in a golden pre-dawn glow. Quill heard the birds calling out, as they too were thankful for another day. And as this proud son of Lore looked in sorrow at the small lifeless body lying on the litter, his thoughts turned to his childhood remembering how they would hike into the forest to spend days at a time hunting and fishing. More than just father and son, they were friends. Even knowing that his father was now part of his Elf Circle could not dull the ache in his heart at losing those simple pleasures forever.

"Quill, we'll be at Trout Lake soon. I think we should stop and rest," suggested Tobble.

He held up an empty water pouch as evidence that indeed a stop was in order!

Quill moved up next to Kobar and offered Tobble's suggestion to which Kobar readily agreed. So, with grateful sighs of relief from all concerned, they made the lake their final resting ground before arriving at the village.

They were sitting silently in a circle, chewing on the few pieces of smoked meat they had remaining, each deep in his own world of thought, when suddenly Tworek started chirping. The sound, breaking such peaceful silence, startled all of them. Kobar leapt to his feet, grabbing for his weapon as he did so. The incessant chirping meant danger! And each of them was well aware of what might happen! They froze, listening, straining to hear whatever Tworek had sensed. Kobar silently crept forward about ten yards, reached down and retrieved his shield.

In that instant that another Dark Warrior appeared! He stood about twenty yards away, having stepped out from the obscurity of the small thicket of trees nearby. Quill's bow was ready for the kill. But Kobar motioned with his sword for Quill to lower his weapon. Quill knew he had a dead aim on this warrior and could not miss at this distance. Why would Kobar say no? Quill looked to Kailon for the answer to this unvoiced question. But Kailon only gave a very terse sideways motion of his head, indicating that Quill should not act.

Quill steadied himself, waiting and ready if Kobar needed him. He would respect this giant friend's position of guard and special protector. It was difficult to hold back, but he reluctantly understood Kobar's dominance. He was learning patience.

The adversary advanced, stopping about five feet from Kobar who was in position for battle. Burt, Tobble and Kailon stood elbow to elbow, eyes glued to the scene unfolding before them. Kobar would do battle with one of the Dark Elf's personal bodyguards.

Without warning the Dark Warrior lunged toward Kobar and their swords locked in conflict. The awful clang of steel on steel resounded throughout the forest. It seemed clear from the start that Kobar was the more powerful. He was at least a foot taller and his strength overpowered the evil messenger. Quill watched their eyes. Kobar's reflected confidence whereas the Dark Warrior's glared with only hate. Quill trembled at the horrible sight. Each blow from the massive weapons, each echoing of clashing steel, carried the tale of battle for miles. Quill marveled at the incredible strength in their hands as they savagely gripped the swords and fought to the death. The fierce struggle continued for several more minutes with neither showing fatigue. The fighting was relentless, maintaining a hard and fast pace.

Suddenly, the Dark Warrior broke free and charged straight at Kailon! Quill was directly in his path. Quill instinctively raised his bow but because of the short distance between himself and the charging enemy it was not possible for him to take a shot before the deadly figure reached him. He could hear Kobar screaming for him to get out of the way but it was too late. The next thing Quill knew, the Dark Warrior was close enough to touch. With that, Quill's Elf Circle exploded with a raging fury never seen before! The cataclysmic force of the spirits coming to Quill's aid slammed against the Dark Warrior, driving him backwards fifty feet or more, totally destroying his sword and shield. Then, in one of the most terrifying events Quill had ever witnessed, the evil one's body, now lying still upon the trampled, rock-strewn ground, crumbled to dust, with nothing but his black leather garments remaining.

In a blinding flash of light, as quickly as they had appeared, the spirits were gone. The only evidence of the violence a grayish dust floating on the rays of the morning sun.

Quill sank to his knees, bow and arrow falling to the ground unnoticed. Kobar ran over to him, helped him to his feet, and picked up the dropped weapons. He slid the arrow into Quill's quiver and hung the bow over Quill's shoulder. Still in a state of shock, and not saying a word, Quill clung to Kobar whose arms still supported him.

"Are you all right?" Kailon asked anxiously, his trembling voice betraying the outward appearance of calm.

Quill couldn't answer. His strength was gone, his senses dulled. Too much had happened too fast for him to absorb it all. He just stared at the pile of leather, tangible proof that the encounter had indeed occurred.

"Answer me, Quill!" Kailon shouted as he shook Quill's shoulder trying to get a response.

Burt and Tobble weren't in much better shape as both of them were unmoving and still speechless. Kobar turned Quill around and guided him toward the litter. Quill mumbled something about his father. When he reached the litter, he sat down and looked up at Kailon. "What happened? I don't understand." A mask of bewilderment his only expression.

"Your Circle protected you," explained Kailon. "The spirits will not allow you to be harmed. You are the Chosen One, the new Light Elf. *I* am the one the Dark Warrior was after. He didn't know that a new Light Elf has been chosen. Just pray that no others of his kind were watching or the Dark Elf will surely know you are the One. We must keep your power a secret until you are prepared. Let them continue to believe I am the only Light Elf left. That way you will remain safe."

Quill stood up, still shaken, and glanced down at the litter with its precious load. Still numb, but with more of a sense of purpose, he beckoned to the rag-tag group, none the worse for wear. "Let's go. We must bury Lore." And so, they continued on.

Chapter Sixteen

As the morning sun pushed its way up and over the tops of the great oak trees scattered along the trail, it weighed heavily on Quill's mind that in a matter of minutes he would stand before his mother, trying to explain how her husband was killed. It was a task he dreaded more than any chore he had ever been forced to do. He also realized this morning that from this day forward, he was the new leader of Okon. With the death of his father, it was his place to assume leadership; a responsibility that had been passed down from father to son for as far back as anyone could remember. The name Okon had been revered in this valley for over four hundred years.

Wait! It dawned on him. Wasn't that about the same time Kailon hid the Kingdom of Zin from the Dark Elf? And now he finds out that his father was a Light Elf and, conveniently, it is now *his* place to be the new leader of Okon *and* the new Light Elf? "A bit *too* coincidental if you ask me," thought Quill, speaking to no one but the patiently-listening trees.

He had been walking along at his own pace, not really paying attention to anyone, or anything, else. A pine branch brushed across his face, momentarily snapping him out of his reverie, but he quickly fell into deep thought once more.

Picking up his pace a bit, he tried to remember his grandfather. What did he really know about him? He never knew him that well as Grandfather died when Quill was very young. There was a memory of his dying and of how terribly hurt his father had been. He recalled the small wooden coffin and how all the villagers had come to their home to pay their respects before his burial. The more Quill thought about it, the more things started coming together in his mind. Could it be that *all* of the leaders of Okon were Light Elves? Again he thought of his grandfather and remembered his father removing something from grandfather's clothing before the three boards that covered the coffin were nailed in place. What was it that Lore removed? Did it have anything to do with the Light Elves?

"Quill, are you all right? You haven't said a word since the Elf Circle destroyed the Dark Warrior." Burt expressed his concern while adjusting the shield once more tied to his back. (It was slipping down and banging the backs of his legs.)

"I'm all right, Burt. I've just been giving a lot of thought to all that's been going on."

Quill sniffed the air and then looked skyward; it was clouding over with huge, dark thunderclouds. They were rolling toward the village. "It even smells like rain, doesn't it Burt?" Quill asked off-handedly.

Kobar stopped in the middle of the trail and Quill came up to him from behind. Side by side, they gazed across the cornfields that divided the forest from the neat rows of houses that comprised the tiny village. It was mid-summer and the corn now stood at least four feet high. Each stalk contained five or six golden yellow ears of corn and the silk was beginning to peek through the end of each ear. It would be a good crop. There had been plenty of rain and the earth had been good to the farmers this year. Quill remembered the first time he helped his father harvest the corn and how pumpkins were planted in between the corn stalks. When they were ripe, he and the other children would roll them back to the village because they were too heavy to carry. Those were good times, being young, happy and carefree.

But it was different now. A time of sadness. Quill turned and briefly looked at his father's body and then proceeded to the center of the village at a slow but steady pace. As they passed the last cornfield, Quill heard a familiar sound that lifted his spirits a little. It was the sound of his newest friend, the hawk. He stopped for a minute to scan the sky, and watched the graceful bird make a complete circle over his head. He then took the last few painful steps that led to his home. As they stopped in front of the sod hut, Quill heard the neighbors already running from house to house announcing Lore's death.

"Quill, do you want me to tell your mother?" Tobble asked.

"No, Tobble. It's my place, but thank you for asking. I appreciate it. You're a valued friend." Quill brushed away the hair that hung in front of his eyes, trying to neaten his appearance a bit, took a deep breath, and opened the door, knowing that from that moment on nothing would ever be the same again.

He stepped in and went to the table where his mother was busy kneading dough; she was making a whole-grain bread that smelled deliciously of oats and barley and wheat. But as soon as she saw Quill's face she knew something was terribly wrong. She came to him with both hands held out. Quill wrapped his arms around this suddenly frail and vulnerable woman.

"It's your father isn't it?" she asked, her usually steady voice beginning to shake.

"Yes, Father is gone." Tears welled in his eyes and his voice faltered so badly that his mother could barely understand him.

Kara's legs seemed to go to jelly and for an instant she wobbled as though she would fall. But she quickly straightened, let go of Quill and went to the door. She hesitated for only a moment to collect herself. She would not cry now. Her tears would be reserved for private times. Emotion would not rule. Not now.

She went outside, past the gathering neighbors, friends who had known the family Okon for many years. She looked neither right nor left. Making her way to where Lore's body lay, she dropped to her knees. But she shed no tears even then. Her eyes sought out the gentle face of the man she had loved for so long. Her hand reached out to caress the wrinkled brow and to trace the smile lines at the corners of his mouth. How many times they had enjoyed happy moments, and uproarious laughter! Her soft hands found the zig-zag scar on his chin—the end result of an undignified fall from the ladder as he repaired the roof. Quill had only been a baby then, she recalled. She gently kissed the lips which would be hers no longer.

Tobble went to her, wrapped his arms around her shoulders and held her tight. Kara looked up and saw tears dripping down her old friend's face. She wiped at them with the edge of her apron, took his hand in hers, and quietly said, "He was a good man, Tobble. He lived a full and beautiful life. He was loved and respected, but now, I think, he is needed somewhere else."

Kara let go of Tobble's hand and turned for one more loving glance at her husband. Okar stepped forward and clasped her hands. He had been watching this amazing woman. Her strength and fortitude were a lesson for them all. In a hushed tone he said, "Let us say a prayer for our brother, Lore."

Those assembled bowed their heads as Okar prayed.

"O mighty Father, we ask for your strength in our time of need. We ask for forgiveness of our sins and for the courage to forgive those who have done wrong to us. Our brother and good friend has been called to everlasting life. It is your timing, Father God, not ours. We ask for understanding in our pain. Take him into your waiting Kingdom so that he may find your promise of peace. Our hearts are filled with sorrow but one day we too will know your eternal plan. We pray that you will fill Lore Okon's spirit with happiness as he travels to a better place, one of joy, peace and fulfillment. Keep him in your care till we are all united in that glorious land. Amen."

Kara looked for Quill—he was standing in the doorway—and beckoned him to her side. She took his hand and said in a hushed voice, "Come with me. We have to talk." She then led the way to a brook that flowed into a pond not far from their home. When they had come to a gnarled old tree by the side of the brook she sat down under it. Quill settled next to her.

"Son, I knew your father would die soon and he knew it too. It was written." ("This too?" Quill thought incredulously.) "Your father also knew that his spirit would live forever within the Kingdom of Zin, for he was a Light Elf."

"You knew Mother? Kailon told me, but how come you knew so much about the Light Elves and never told me?"

"I know more than I probably should! Your father would never talk about it because he was ashamed to have lost his Elf Circle to the Dark Elf long before we married. I learned that he was a Light Elf quite by accident. He used to talk in his sleep!" She smiled warmly at the memory of those mutterings. "One day when I was cleaning the church for Okar, I found the book that Kailon wrote. I have never, to this day, talked of this. I couldn't tell you about this because I was afraid for your life. If the Dark Elf found us, the less we knew, the safer we'd be."

"Mother, Father's spirit isn't in Zin. His spirit was chosen along with five others to become my Elf Circle. I have talked to him and he is fine."

Tears flooded Kara's eyes for the first time. She finally knew that the mystery—the secret—she had carried all these years was in fact true! With the back of her hand she quickly brushed away the tears that threatened to ruin her composure.

"Was Grandfather Okon a Light Elf too?" Quill asked excitedly.

"Yes, and his father before him, and so on. All Okon males are chosen to become Light Elves. Didn't you learn this when you studied the Book of Knowledge?"

"You know about that too? I had no idea that only Okon men were Light Elves."

"I haven't said that only *Okon* men can be Light Elves. What I said was that *all* Okon men were chosen to become Light Elves. There could be others from other clans. I don't know."

"What about Kailon? Is he part of our family?"

"That I don't know either," Kara replied. They continued to talk and talk, losing all track of time, intimately sharing their feelings about Lore, about his life, about his life with his family. No more was offered by Kara about the mysterious Light Elves. Finally, she patted Quill's hand, said it was time to go, got to her feet and headed home. Quill scrambled to his feet to catch up with her but kept to himself as he and Kara walked the path home, his mind a jumble of information, half answers—and always more questions.

****

By the time they got home Okar had everything taken care of in the Okon household. Lore's body lay in a simple wood coffin on a table in the center of the open room. There were flowers everywhere, brought by each member of the community as they came to pay tribute to their fallen leader. Quill entered behind Kara and went straight to his bedroom. He hung his bow and quiver, which had been brought in for him by Burt, on a peg in the corner of the room and then poured water from a bucket that sat next to the door into a large wooden bowl. He remembered his father carving out that bowl for him, and polishing it till it was as smooth as a well-worn rock. Removing his vest and shirt, he washed the grime of the road from his face, hands and arms. It felt wonderful to freshen up. He would bathe in the pond later. This would have to do for now. It would be a very long night. He dried off quickly and donned a clean shirt, searched for but couldn't find a different vest, so he gave the old one a good shake and put it back on. He then rejoined his mother who was next to the coffin talking quietly to one of her closest friends. Okar stood next to her, head bowed, saying prayers. Quill allowed a trace of a grin to show itself at the sight of the very intent priest. Burt was over in the corner and Quill made his way across the room to be with him. Or to avoid the priest. Whatever.

It's going to be a long day and an even longer night. Come over to my house and get something to eat," Burt offered.

Kara overheard the invitation and urged Quill to go along with Burt. "You haven't had a good meal in days, I'm sure. And Burt's mother is a wonderful cook. You know you want to go. I'll be fine—you can see I'm not alone!" Quill agreed, secretly glad to escape the reality of his father's death, if even for a short time. And, he was afraid Okar might want to pray with him and he just wasn't up to that right now.

They slipped outside, past the long line of mourners waiting to pay their final respects. Most carried flowers and some even brought food. Many rushed up to Quill and took his hand, expressing their sadness, but, although polite, he abruptly excused himself. All he wanted was to get to Burt's house—and Solla's food!

Solla was an institution in her own right! A proud woman, cooking was her favorite passion. It was obvious that she was Burt's mother, they looked so much alike—a bit on the heavy side, short and with the same features of large nose and big ears that characterized the dwarves in the village. She always wore the same type of clothes; light brown dress, an apron covering it, and sandals on her pudgy, flat feet. But the broad and inviting smile that was always spread across her rather plain face gave evidence of the warmth of spirit she possessed.

Once inside, they were glad to see Kailon and Kobar sitting at the table eating. Solla was by far the best cook in town! The table was full of food; bread, game birds, pudding, potatoes—even a cake! Solla rushed to Quill as soon as he came in and threw her arms around him in a warm, loving hug. Tobble pulled out a chair next to Kailon and told Quill to sit while he poured a cup of wine and passed him a plate. Quill didn't think he would be so interested in food but the tempting aromas of Solla's kitchen quickly changed his mind! He helped himself to small amounts of everything but when he was done preparing his plate, it seemed hardly enough to feed a bird.

"Quill, give me that plate. If you're going to sit at my table, then you must eat!" Solla grabbed his plate and filled it to her own satisfaction. Happy now, she handed the plate back to him and this time there was enough food on it to last Quill a week in the woods! He sipped at the wine Tobble had poured. It felt strong and warm and burned his insides as it went down. But oh, it was good! He looked at the plate before him and wondered how he would ever eat all that. Then he realized that everyone, Kailon included, had stopped eating and were staring at him. There wasn't a sound in the room! Dutifully, he picked up the spoon and started eating. When he did the tension eased and the delicious food again became the center of attention. And conversation flowed easily among the good companions.

"Quill, Kobar and I must leave your village. It is not safe for any of you with me here. Syffus only knows about me. His Dark Warriors are trying to kill me, not you. If I stay I am placing the entire village in danger. No more deaths should occur because of me," Kailon stated emphatically.

But Quill was quick to argue. "You can't leave. You are the one chosen to help train me!" Quill said as he pushed his chair back away from the table.

Raising his hand to quietly hush the eager young elf, Kailon explained, "It is better this way. With Syffus not knowing you are the new Light Elf, you and your people will be safe. As for your training, that has already been taken care of. Learning about your magical powers will come soon. But to earn your knots of power, that, my son, is something that is between you and your Elf Circle. They award the levels of power based on achievement. The only knot that you must earn on your own is the tenth knot and that level of power could be many years in the future."

"What do you mean, many years off?" Quill asked impatiently.

"To build your levels of power and earn your knots will take time. It doesn't happen overnight. The Circle is wise. They will not give you all of this power without your first understanding how to properly use it and care for it. I have known Light Elves who have gone twenty-five years without earning the tenth power knot. So for now, time is on your side. You'll need all you can get before Syffus finds you. That is why Kobar and I must leave; so you will have that time. If I remain, Syffus will just be drawn here."

"Where will you go, to the Elves' Treasure?" Burt asked, as he listened ever so carefully to Kailon's words.

"No, Burt. If I enter the Elves' Treasure, it will defeat my purpose. I want Syffus to follow me. He will not go near that place. It would be deadly for him to enter. The best thing to do is to lead Syffus out of the valley. Kobar and I will find a way out and then Syffus will follow. You must understand. Syffus has hungered for my death all these hundreds of years. He is relentless. He *will* come after me."

"How can he live so long?" Quill wanted to know.

"The tenth power. You will know when you achieve that level," Kailon said.

"I know of no one who has ever left this valley. You will accomplish nothing except to wander around the valley endlessly." It was Tobble who spoke up now.

"If that is all I accomplish, then so be it. But one thing is certain—I will keep Syffus from here. This is a big valley. I will hold out as long as I can. The day I die is the day you become the reigning Light Elf of the lands," Kailon said as he laid his wooden cane across the table.

"How will I know when that day comes, Kailon?" Quill questioned.

"The day of my death will be marked by the appearance of a great white horse in the sky. It will run across the sky that night. Kobar will then seek you out and will guard you faithfully as he does me. Syffus will become aware that you live as well. Hopefully, by then, you will be able to defend yourself from the Black Circle."

"When you say 'a great white horse', what do you mean?" Tobble asked.

"Keep your campfire burning and watch the early morning skies. When it comes, you will not mistake it. It will light the sky as if it were mid-day." Having made all this clear, Kailon got to his feet.

"When will you leave?" Quill asked, fearful of the answer.

"Right now, my son. I do not need to take my farewell of your father, or see that he is buried properly. I know where he is and so do you, Quill. He was, and always will be, a great man, a proud man. But he is desperately needed where he is now." With that, Kailon and Kobar took their leave. Quill, Burt and Tobble followed them outside. Kailon, in an unexpected display of emotion, reached for Quill and hugged him to himself. If Quill didn't know better he could have sworn there was a tear in the old master's eye. Kailon pulled away a little and said, "Quill, you will never see me again as Kailon the Light Elf. But, we will meet again, another time." Kailon released Quill, turned and headed north, away from the village. Kobar followed without a backward glance, nor gesture of farewell.

Quill and Burt watched until they disappeared from sight. Quill had lost not only his father, but now the one who had started all of this. He felt alone. He had so many unanswered questions, questions that he wanted to ask Kailon, but would never have the opportunity to do.

Burt reached out and touched Quill's shoulder, startling him back to reality. "We should go and be with your mother. She needs your support. Also, it's your duty to stand as an honor guard for your father."

"As usual, you're right my little friend. I have to spend these last hours with him. My own problems will still be there when this is finished."

Upon returning to his house, Quill didn't see his mother or Okar. He walked through into his mother's bedroom and found them both. To be more accurate, he *heard* them both—arguing loudly. But as soon as Quill entered the room they stopped abruptly and Okar shook his head, snorted and stomped out to the great room.

"What's the matter Mother? Why were you shouting at each other?"

"Nothing for you to be concerned about Quill. Okar was going over tomorrow's plans with me. The plans for your father's funeral."

"But you were fighting about something. Don't tell me it was nothing!" Quill persisted from his position in the doorway.

"I'll tell you about it tomorrow. I'll explain it all. But *after* your father's funeral." Kara was adamant and Quill knew better than to pursue this any further at the present time. Mother and son spent the remainder of the day and evening near the coffin, talking and reminiscing with their many friends and neighbors.

****

It was late when Quill approached his mother saying, "You haven't eaten a thing all day. Why don't you go over to Solla's house and eat a little something. You know how concerned she is for you." In fact, it was he who was getting concerned—afraid that behind her strong front she was falling apart inside. She and Lore were more than just husband and wife, but also true lovers, friends and confidants. She would indeed be lost without him.

"You're right. I am tired, and probably should eat although food, even Solla's, doesn't appeal to me right now. But just sitting in a quiet place, away from everyone *is* appealing. So Kara quietly slipped out and made her way across the short distance to Solla's comforting arms.

Quill and Burt remained at the house. Neither said a word for well over an hour. They were near exhaustion with all the events of the past few days. Quill's mind was awash with questions, but no answers. He replayed everything time and again. Why did his father have to die and why did Kailon and Kobar leave before he had a chance to learn how to use his magical powers? Okar moved about the room lighting candles and saying prayers. Why had he and Kara argued so heatedly? Quill watched the little priest and wondered where he fit into all of this. Why did Okar and Lore keep the legend of the Light Elves a secret for all these years? And why was the church keeping the book that Kailon wrote in secret? These thoughts and more replayed over and over in Quill's mind. For the most part, none of it made any sense!

"Quill, are you hungry?" Burt asked, breaking the silence.

"No, but thanks for asking," Quill answered, only half aware of what his friend was saying.

"Well, I'm going home for a while to grab a bite. It may not seem it to you but it's been hours since we had dinner," Burt replied, patting his stomach. It was a well-known fact that not much stood in the way of Burt and a good meal!

Quill stayed with his father a few minutes longer, then pulled a chair out from under the table and sat down. He looked over at Okar who was now kneeling in prayer. "He certainly has made himself a fixture in this house," thought Quill, though he said nothing. Okar rose and moved to the coffin, continuing his prayers there, alternately sprinkling holy water on Lore's body and on the wooden symbol that hung on the wall between the two bedrooms. Both that wall hanging and the pendant around Okar's neck were of the same design. Funny that Quill would take note of that now. This symbol was a part of his upbringing, his culture, but it had never really meant anything to him until now. For the first time he understood the message of their faith which this simple icon carried. And then Quill sensed Okar standing next to him. He would not be ignored. But he came out with something totally unexpected.

"Quill, why don't you go and get some sleep? There is nothing for you to do now and you will need your strength if you are going to be of any help at all to your mother."

Quill had expected a lecture about his church-going habits, or about his responsibilities to his mother. He was shocked. *This* he could handle. He didn't have the strength to disagree, nor would he have wanted to. So he respectfully thanked Okar for his consideration, got up and pushed the chair back under the table, went to his room and collapsed on the down-filled mattress. Changing into night clothes never even occurred to him. His eyes were so heavy that he wondered how he had kept them open for this long. A sleep-filled yawn, a warm blanket and a comfortable bed combined to send him into a deep, dreamless sleep.

****

Kara tiptoed into Quill's room and gently nudged him awake. It took a few minutes for him to remember what had happened and that he was safe in his own bed. He sat up rubbing sleep from his eyes as Kara lovingly watched.

"I hated to wake you, but it's time." Kara's simple statement prodded Quill to action and to the reality he would rather have forgotten. Smiling, she left the room.

Quickly rising, he removed his vest and shirt, washed, found clean clothes and even brushed his hair. He certainly wanted to be presentable, as his father would like. He paused. His thoughts were of his father and of how much he would miss him. He hated leaving the safety and solitude of his room to go out where the coffin held the starkness of his loss. But there was no turning back—his destiny was sealed. He straightened, shoulders back, prepared to meet his future. He left his room, stopped, ran back to collect his bow and quiver. He would need them.

Kara, Tobble, Burt and Okar waited for him. Okar motioned for Quill to join the others as he started the last prayer before Tobble would secure the coffin. When he had finished, Tobble lowered the lid, then drove the nails in place that would seal Lore's body away from all eyes forever.

Tobble and Burt carried the coffin outside and placed it in the waiting wagon. Quill, Kara, Solla and Okar followed. All the inhabitants of the village came to offer their final goodbyes to a long-time friend and leader. The funeral bier was a hay wagon, nothing special. It was customary to carry the dead in a common wagon. There would be no horse to pull it because, according to custom, Lore's best friend must do that deed. The honor fell to Tobble. He had already taken his place and slowly moved his sorrowful load. Quill and his mother followed Okar who walked directly behind the wagon praying aloud. A procession formed behind and followed to the burial site.

There were no special burial plots for leaders, or anyone else for that matter. All were interred in a small field not far from the village proper. They walked in silence. Quill's only thoughts were of his father. But then the welcome fluttering of the hawk pleasantly surprised him. He raised his eyes to see his feathered friend swooping down at the wagon—and gracefully land on top of the coffin. The action of the hawk brought everyone else to a startled halt as they stared in awe at the great bird.

The hawk remained on his perch of honor as Tobble continued to the field which was the final resting place of other past Okonians. Lore would lie in an already-dug grave near an impressive oak tree at the edge of the field. Tobble struggled along, grateful that the terrain was mostly flat, finally arriving at the site. He stopped. Even though it was a relatively cool day, sweat poured from his forehead. This may have been a labor of honor, but it nonetheless required a great deal of exertion and his body was feeling the strain..

Burt and Tobble slid the coffin from the wagon and laid it on the ground. The hawk flew away. The wagon was moved a short distance away. Now other friends of Lore's assisted in getting the ropes under the coffin so it could be lowered to its final resting place.

Okar began the ritual prayers and sprinkled holy water in the grave to bless the ground where this cherished man would lie. But before the burial, one last thing had to be done.

Quill reached for an arrow, then stood at attention at the grave's edge. He raised the arrow high in the air, a salute to the great hunter who would rest here, and in tribute to the man who had nurtured him and loved him for so many years. Slowly he lowered the arrow and reverently laid it on top of the coffin. Tears ran unchecked down his face as he bowed his head in respect. Tobble and Burt quietly approached, gathered the ropes in both hands and began to lower the casket into the ground. One by one the mourners dropped single flowers into the grave and then Kara stepped forward, sweetly kissed a perfect white daisy, and placed it on top, next to the arrow.

Quill wrapped his arms around his mother, gently leading her back to the privacy of their home. Her time to grieve had come.

Chapter Seventeen

It was finally over. A day Quill thought would never end—and one he would never forget. He was alone at last, for the first time since he had brought Lore's body home. Lost in thought, he sat on a tree stump just outside the village, looking to the West and the setting sun, the sky a bright orange as the glowing ball began its slow descent behind the trees. Watching the sunset was one of Quill's greatest loves but even more than that, he relished being near the woods. As a hunter, he usually spent much of his time away from home and knew every inch of these familiar haunts. His father had taught him well, taught him everything *except* how to be a Light Elf. He reflected on this honor so recently passed along to him. But because of the threat of the Dark Elf, Kailon had to leave before he could teach Quill how to use the power he had been given. He felt stranded in the middle of a sea of uncertainty, unable to grab a lifeline to pull himself out of this mess! What would he do next? How was he supposed to proceed in the quest for the Kingdom if he were alone? But, he wasn't really alone, was he? His Elf Circle would let him know how to start. And his father was part of that Circle and surely would be there for his son! Quill's spirits started to rise and he felt better. How could he allow himself to get so low?

He sat there until the sun had completely slipped away and all that was left was the gray dusk signaling the onset of evening. He was calmer now. Sometimes talking things over with oneself offered the best solutions! His questions were not answered and he still didn't know where he would start, but somehow the future looked brighter.

When he returned home, his mother had dinner waiting. Nothing fancy but he didn't need much. Just being home again was treat enough.

"Quill," Kara said, brushing a stray wisp of hair from her eyes, "you need to get some rest. Tomorrow is a big day for you." She pulled a chair away from the table implying that he should sit down. He did, and then watched his mother as she dished up a plate of food. She was right. Tomorrow would be a big day. He would be given the title of village leader, and as a sign of their support, the people would come together and build Quill his own home. He felt uneasy about that. After you are officially proclaimed the new leader, you are expected to take a suitable wife and ensure the line of Okon with a new son! He absent-mindedly played with his fork, thinking about all the available girls in the village. Was there any one he liked well enough to consider marriage? He could think of none. Marriage had been the furthest thing from his mind until just a few short hours ago!

"Mother, did you and Father fall in love before he was made the leader of Okon, or after?" He was embarrassed to even ask that question but he needed to know.

"Your father and I grew up together and were best friends," Kara said as she placed the plate of food in front of her inquisitive son. "Even as young children we talked of being married and our parents had already planned it. Why do you ask?"

"Well, I'm not attracted to any of the girls in Okon. I'm a hunter and have never really been around the village long enough to even become friends with any of them. For me to take a wife right now is wrong. I need time but I know the people won't like it if I wait. What should I do?" His dinner was ignored as he wrestled with this problem.

"Son, your father and I were very much in love, and I will always love him. Let your heart decide for you, not the people. Who you take as a wife will be your choice. It would be a tragedy to choose someone you do not love. It would be a terrible injustice to the young woman too. If you aren't ready, then wait." She pointed patiently to the untouched plate. Quill nodded and smiled at his mother. She had a way of making everything sound so simple.

He didn't speak again until he had finished eating. Then he pushed his chair back, stood and went over to his mother and hugged her. "Thanks for your support. At least I know one person in Okon Valley who won't be disappointed in me tomorrow!"

"You're wrong, Quill. There are two, maybe even three."

"What? Who?" Quill asked as he stepped back.

"Your father, for one. He *is* part of your Elf Circle and is still with us. The other is Burt of course, your best friend. You know he would give his life for you and if you decide that this is not the time for a wedding, he will definitely support your decision. It wouldn't even surprise me if Okar took your side."

"Now that *would* surprise me!" replied Quill, trying to stifle a laugh. "And while we're on the subject of Okar, I'm still curious as to why you and he were yelling at each other. You promised to tell me after the funeral."

"You're right, I did. Sit down and I'll tell you," Kara said placing her hand on the back of the chair.

Quill seated himself at the table again while Kara removed the empty plate. She walked to the other side of the room, put the plate on the narrow counter, then raised one of the floor boards in the corner, moving it out of the way. She reached down and removed a cloth bundle and, bringing it to the table, placed it in front of Quill.

She began, "Quill, there are many things about this land that Kailon didn't tell you. I don't know if he didn't want to or what, but they are things you will need to know if you are going to survive your quest as a Light Elf against Syffus."

Kara reached over to untie the leather strands that quite securely held the bundle together. Quill studied her every move and his eyes appeared to get bigger as each strand of leather was removed. At last it was open and the outer cloth fell away. He couldn't imagine what would be hidden in the old faded, dirty cloth. As she opened the last piece of material, he saw what secret had been stashed away under those floorboards for so long. Lying in front of him were three ropes with knots along their length, and a small leather-bound book.

"These ropes were your grandfather's and his father's and his father's before him. The book contains knowledge you will need if you are to use the magic of the Light Elves." Kara dipped into one of the pockets of her dress and pulled out yet another Light Elf rope and laid it on the table with the others. "This was your father's; he lost his power when he was a young man not much older than you."

Quill first ran his fingers along the rope, then picked it up, looking at the four knots that gave evidence to his father's status as a Light Elf. The other ropes he gathered one at a time, noticing that each one held four or five knots. Quill was puzzled. Tercal had told him that each of the spirits that now protected him had earned ten knots. If that was so, then why did Lore's rope have only four?

"Mother, Kailon told me that there were ten levels of power that a Light Elf must earn. Why do these ropes have only four or five?"

"Well Quill, all I can tell you is what your father told me. Most of the Light Elves lost their power when they were young. They didn't have the patience to wait to earn the ten power levels before seeking Syffus. Each one of them, including your father, tried to win a battle with Syffus and each time Syffus would strip them of their Circle. He was able to do it because he is a Dark Elf *with* the tenth power level. Whatever you do Quill, you must avoid Syffus until you are at the tenth power. But I must warn you, Syffus will hunt you down relentlessly knowing that the only chance you have of destroying him is if you are a tenth power Light Elf. Anything less, and Syffus will take your Elf Circle from you."

"I'm surprised you know so much about all of this, Mother."

"My knowledge is limited. I learned some information when I found the book Okar has in the church. Anything else came from the bits and pieces your father unknowingly told me over the years. I do know this much, Kailon didn't tell you everything, and I don't think he wanted to, lest you become confused. Kailon wouldn't lie. He *is* a Light Elf. But I think he realized that, if he told you everything right from the start, you wouldn't have believed him."

Quill put the last rope on the table with the others and picked up the book. At first he was reluctant to open it. He hesitated a moment, looking at the leather cover and with the fingers of his right hand, slowly caressed the top of the two circles that remained after all this time. Then he noticed that there was one page of the book bigger than the rest. It was folded over as if someone were trying to make the page fit with the rest. He very carefully pulled the page out of the book and realized that it was not a page *from* the book, but rather was a folded piece of paper.

Lying the book back on the table he began to unfold the paper very carefully so as not to rip it. Yellowed and brittle, it was obviously very old.

As he gingerly opened it, he saw the definite outlines of a map! Now opened all the way, he held it still with one hand, moved the ropes and book from in front of him, then positioned it better on the table. He moved the still-burning candle from the center of the table closer to get a better look. Kara's curiosity drew her closer as well! She leaned over her son's shoulder, being careful not to disturb him.

Quill pored over the map in amazement noticing first that it was laid out north to south and east to west, with the words Okon Valley and a drawing with mountains all around it in the north. Nothing surprising about that! But then Quill surveyed the rest of the map and was astonished to see other valleys and places depicted that he never knew existed! The map displayed a total of five valleys and a great body of water that ran the entire length of the map, continuing far to the east. The other valleys were named but none were familiar to him, nor to Kara. Thron, Klimack, Juwa, and Jacon. Also a desert named Ebon. Odd names indeed. Quill's hand explored every inch of the map as his mind wandered to these other lands—what were they like? And did they in fact even exist? He mumbled to himself as he wondered if there were other people in these lands whom he had never seen or even heard of.

"What's the matter Quill?" Kara asked.

"I never knew there were other valleys or even any *thing* beyond this valley. I asked Kailon once but he never gave me a direct answer. But here it is, right in front of me. *If* this map is to be believed. It definitely describes other places."

Kara didn't say another word. Quill picked up the small book again. Kara had never looked in it. For all the years she knew where it was, she never had the courage to open it to see what was written about the Light Elves. She did, however, know that it contained some of the knowledge Quill would need to know about his power levels.

Quill opened the cover and there on the first page appeared the words ***Keepers of the Light***. The second page contained only names. The first on the list was Tercal, the first Light Elf. Quickly turning the next two pages he came to the end of the list. His first thought was that he would find his father's name at the end; but no. The last name was Sibon and just above Sibon's name was his own name, Quill Okon, and Lore Okon.

A chill ran down the middle of his back as he realized that his life had been planned for over four hundred years! Quickly leafing through the remaining pages, he saw that they were all blank. Except for the very last page, where he found another map. Odd. It was as if whoever had recorded events in this book had been cut short before completing it. He removed this last map and laid it next to the ropes, then closed the book Unfolding this second map, which was just as yellowed as the first, he discovered it was a map of Okon Valley. At first Quill was puzzled. Why would someone have made a map of *this* valley? This was where, as far as he knew, all of the Light Elves had come from. Or had they? He took a closer look at the map. The more he studied it the more he began to see things he didn't understand. The map was laid out right. Every hill, lake and pond were noted in its proper place. But then he began to see that there were some extra ponds. Quill looked up at Kara and said, "This map of Okon Valley isn't right—there are too many ponds."

"Are you sure?"

"Yes. I know every lake and pond. There are fifteen ponds and three lakes. This map shows *seventeen* ponds and three lakes."

He moved his finger across the map as he counted them. Yes, it showed seventeen. Then he noticed that one of the ponds was shown exactly where the dolmen was located. He didn't say anything to Kara about it but it did puzzle him. Why would there be a pond over the entrance to the Kingdom of Zin? Of course! Only a chosen few knew where certain things were. If somehow the Dark Elf got his hands on this map, the secret would be safe. But now Quill wasn't sure about what else was in the valley. Kailon left before he could find out. He studied the map some more and noticed that two more mountains had been added which he knew weren't really there.

"Quill, it's late and I'm getting awfully tired. I'm going to bed." Kara untied her apron as she walked toward her room, but then stopped and turned to look at her child, this boy who had become a man practically overnight. "It'll be best if I don't know any more about the Light Elves. I've told you all I know. But, I will say this. Your father seemed to struggle continuously with it. He spent days at a time trying to understand what it was he had to do, and he did it without the help of someone like Kailon.

All of his information was guesswork. Your grandfather didn't teach him anything either. I believe you've been chosen to be a much more powerful Light Elf or else Kailon wouldn't have started you on your way. It's true there is a lot of mystery behind the success of a Light Elf, mystery only you can unravel. That's part of the task in building your own power levels. You must *earn* the right to be a great Light Elf, and I believe each one chosen has a different purpose." That said, Kara left the room.

Quill sat for a moment, his mother's words bouncing around in his mind as he tried to sort it all out. He thought of Kailon and how he had only given him selected information. Maybe my mother is right. To become a great Light Elf one must discover the way for himself and uncover the mystery behind what it is all about. He then reexamined the map of Okon Valley but this time with a different attitude. He now knew the map had something to say. Solve the mystery behind it and the answers would be there. He very carefully studied each pond until he found the two that really weren't ponds; the one where the dolmen was and the second, not far from the village. He proceeded to trace all of the mountains that surrounded this valley with his finger until, as with the ponds, he found the two which did not exist. But wait! He remembered when they returned from the Elves' Treasure they walked through a cave. The cave led them back into the valley. He moved his finger until he found the spot, but there was nothing marked on the map to indicate a cave. He gently pushed the paper down with his finger. On the exact spot where the cave had been, there was a crease from one of the folds in the paper. Still he found no markings of the cave. Quill stood up to stretch his legs, yawned and ran his fingers through his hair. He backed up a couple of steps, his eyes still on the spread out paper. Suddenly he realized that the folds in the map were exactly north, south, east and west. The dolmen was to the south and a fold in the map ran right through it. To the west were the places where the cave and another fold in the map were. Quill reached down and picked up the second map which covered the first. Sure enough, the way out of Okon Valley was to the west and beyond lay the other valleys! He put the second map down and wondered to himself what the other folds could mean. There were a total of eight folds in the map. The other four ran northeast, southeast, southwest and northwest.

At the point where all eight lines met was the village! Another thought occurred to him. If he were to search in the direction of each line, it could take him *years* to discover what had been hidden for so many centuries! His eyes were getting heavier and heavier and sleep would not be denied for much longer. So he folded the map the same way he had found it and replaced it in the book. As he reached for the other map, he saw that it was folded the same way leaving eight lines. Incredible! These were not random folds but very purposefully done. There was something in those valleys Quill was supposed to find. But his first thought was of Syffus. What if he ran into him? What would he do? Shaking his head as if to clear his mind of these disturbing thoughts, he folded the second map and slid it too behind the cover of the book. Now, book in arm, he retreated to the solitude of his room, lay on his bed and almost instantly fell into a deep sleep.

With a thud, the book slid unnoticed to the floor beside him, its secrets safe for another day.

OKON VALLEY

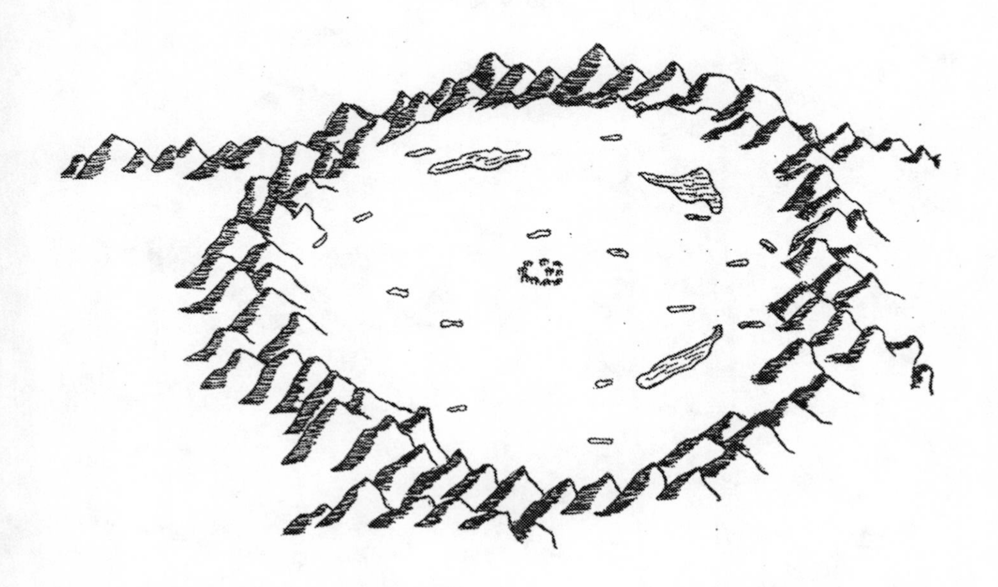

KINGDOM OF ZIN

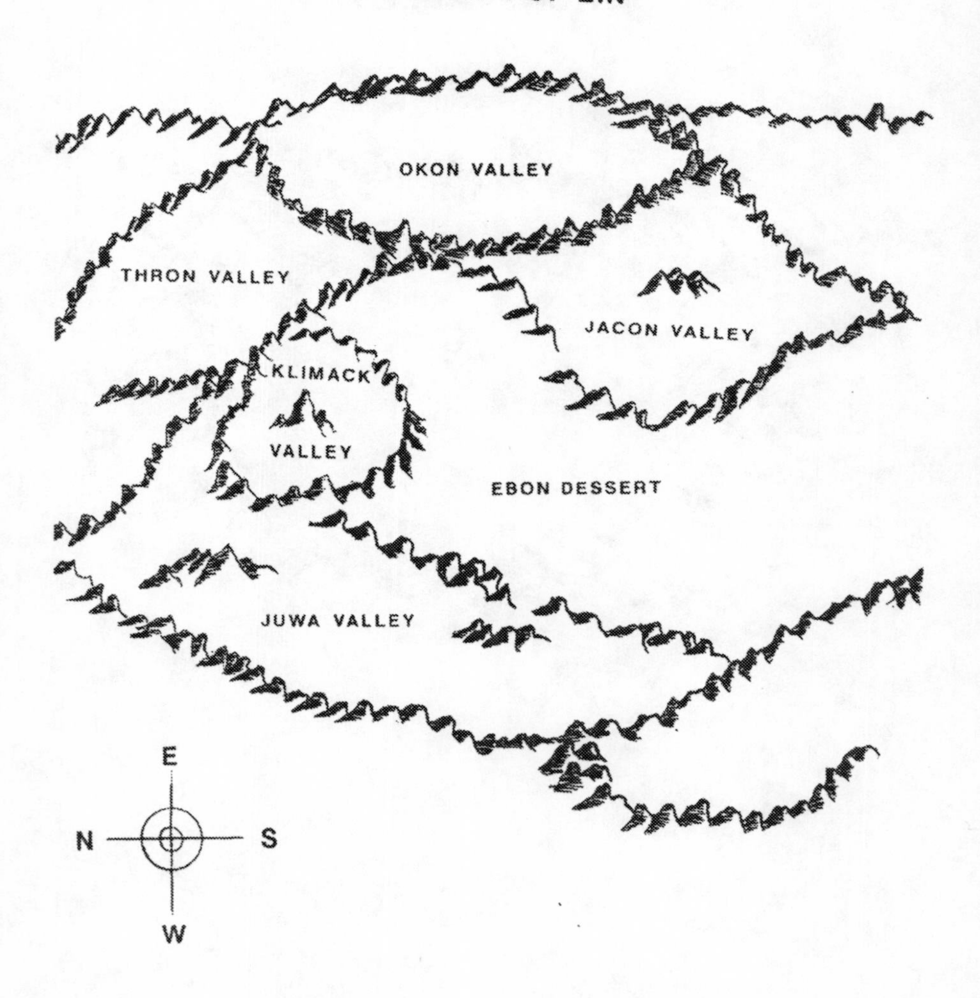

Chapter Eighteen

Quill woke long before his mother knowing what he had to do. He would set out to discover if he was right about the meaning of the folds of the maps. He gathered his belongings and walked very quietly into the main room where he found his food bag hanging next to the door. To his surprise it felt full! Setting it down on the table he opened it and found a note from his mother. She understood what he had to do. She sent him on his quest with her blessing and, best of all, with her love. She told him that the people would celebrate his becoming the new leader of Okon by building him his own home. They too would understand his absence—she would make sure of it! A smile brightened Quill's face as he thought about how his mother always knew what he was up to—and was usually one step ahead of him! He glanced around the room and sure enough, there, hanging on the chair at the end of the table, was his water pouch. Scooping up all of his necessities, and with his bow slung over his shoulder, he grabbed an apple from the barrel next to the door and stuffed it into his pocket. He managed to soundlessly open the door but turned back thinking he had forgotten something. The map! O how stupid! How could he not have taken the map? He tip-toed back into his room where he found the book on the floor where it had fallen. Removing both maps, he stuffed them into his pocket, hid the book up over one of the wooden rafters above his bed, and silently was on his way.

Quill was an early-morning person. He loved the time before sunrise when the clouds hung low and took on an almost soft gray appearance, softly shaded on the edges with a purple-pink brushing. And the dewy grass that tickled his feet seemed to reflect the new-born sun like sparkling gems. He felt at peace with the world as he made his way out of the village heading due South. If he was right about the map, all he had to do was walk southwest and he should find something. As he passed the last house he looked to make sure no one had seen him. The village slept; not a sound to be heard. Only wisps of smoke rose from the chimneys, as the night's fires did no more than smolder a greeting to a new day. A dog scratched at its fleas, then put its head back on it paws, content to drift back to sleep.

Quill was satisfied he had gone undetected and adjusted his course to the southwest, moving at a steady pace to cover as much ground as he could in daylight. He wasn't sure how long it would take, but he had an idea that one day would not be enough. One thing was certain though; he would keep a vigilant eye and keen ear ever ready for any sign of the Dark Warriors!

****

The day wore on without incident, in fact, given the events of the past weeks, it was actually pretty boring—and lonesome! But, as if nature was aware of his inactivity, late in the afternoon the sky took on an ominous look as thunderclouds gathered signaling the onset of a storm. Shelter became the number one priority! Still in the woods, there would be no cave or cliff for refuge—this left only one option; build a shelter, and build it fast. As he began to scurry around collecting pine boughs, he spotted a huge oak tree about one hundred yards to his left. There was a pretty good-sized hole at its base and as Quill approached it, he could see that it was not only old but also hollowed out. Inspecting it more closely he decided that it was a natural shelter—made to order! He would just be able to squeeze through the hole. Removing his gear, he shoved it inside ahead of himself, leaving him ample space to crawl in unhindered. Once inside it had plenty of room and he pushed his belongings against the far side of this wonderful retreat. Then it was back outside to retrieve those pine boughs he had found—they would make an excellent cover for the entrance and would ward off most of the oncoming rain. Now that his shelter was ready, he settled in, ate a little of his mother's delicious food, and prepared to wait out the fast-approaching storm. It wasn't long before the sounds of thunder startled him. He had actually dozed off. But he was wide awake now! It was going to be a vicious storm. Thunder claps deafened his innermost thoughts and lightning flashes zig-zagged through the blackened sky continuously with a tenacity that promised there would be no sleep tonight! The rain poured down in sheets, wind-whipped so that it was impossible to tell from which direction it came. There was no let-up even as night edged into day, the sky barely going one shade brighter to indicate the passage of time. Quill decided quickly to stay right there in his dry cozy little shelter until the storm passed. It was not a difficult decision!

About mid-day the weather started to improve and Quill got ready to leave his safe spot. He pushed the boughs out of his way and squeezed out from under the mighty oak. Taking about five or six steps backward, he took a good look at the tree so as not to forget it. It might come in handy again some time and he wanted to be able to recognize it. He pulled his bow, quiver, food and water out from the tree haven (his knife was secured to his belt where it would always be at hand) and was ready to get on his way again. About two hours later he reached the edge of the forest and just as he thought, the map showed a mountain. But none was there. Mountains were on either side but the only thing in front of him was a strip of lowland where the two peaks met at their bases. It would be a five- or six-hour walk to any other mountain in any direction. What did it mean? Surely there was no way to get out of the valley from here. The cliffs alone rose at least two to three hundred feet straight up. He continued to scan the area to see if he had missed anything, some clue that he just wasn't seeing. But there was nothing.

And then, a sound. At first he thought it was a cat howling, but the longer he listened, the more he thought it sounded like a scream. Moving in the direction of the eerie sound, he found himself at the face of the cliff. And it wasn't just screaming, it was sobbing. Now it sounded like a girl, and she was crying hysterically. But where was the sound coming from? Quill moved forward until he reached some giant boulders that had fallen from the cliff. He climbed up on the biggest one and shaded his eyes to see better. There it was. A huge crack at the base of the cliff and unless you were right on top of it you would miss it. A sharp dip in the ground exposed only a small portion of the crack keeping it mostly hidden from view.

Quill jumped down from the boulder and ran toward the crevice. When he neared the spot, he found a small wagon lying on its side. It had been smashed by a loose boulder that fell from the face of the cliff. It must have happened during the storm. He stopped for a moment trying to figure out who it was that had a wagon way out here. And then the crying began again. He moved slowly now to get a sense of the exact position of the sound. All of a sudden he saw her. Kneeling next to the wagon, almost hidden from sight, was a young girl. She had long blond hair and a beautiful face. She fell back in fear when she saw Quill coming near her and as she looked up, he saw that she was an elf. He also saw a body pinned under the wagon. He walked closer and as he did, the girl jumped up. She didn't say a word. Just stared at Quill—and he at her!

"Who are you?" Quill began.

"Luna," she answered, her voice shaking.

"And who is he?"

"Tran, my father. Please help him. He can't move."

Quill didn't want to upset her any further but he knew that a dwarf could not be her father and that was definitely a dwarf. As he knelt down next to the tiny body he checked to see if he was still alive. Tran opened his eyes and when he saw Quill he said, "This is not the normal position I usually take to greet strangers. Forgive me for not standing up." His words were clipped and shaky, his breath coming in short gasps. He was obviously in great pain. "My name is Tran and I come from the valley of Juwa. And you?"

"I am Quill Okon and you are in Okon Valley."

"Good. That's good. Luna, we made it to Okon Valley."

"We have to get him out from under there. What should we do?" Luna asked Quill, her face mirroring the fear she felt for her father.

Quill stood and circled the wagon. They were loaded down quite well with what looked like everything they owned. The boulder that hit the wagon had rolled away so the only task at hand was to roll the wagon back over.

"I'll be right back. I'll try to find a pole so I can lever the wagon up off him." Quill ran off toward the woods.

"Father, who is this young man?" The question was innocent enough but she hid her suspicions of this stranger who just happened to be at hand when they needed help.

"He said his name is Quill Okon and that this is Okon Valley so I have to guess he comes from a family of leaders." He attempted to raise himself a bit, but the pain was too intense. "Can you get me a drink of water?" His voice was growing weaker.

Luna rifled through the wagon's load and found the water pouch. When she returned Quill had arrived with a long tree limb in his hands. He watched as Luna gave Tran a drink. She was so caring and gentle and again her beauty struck him. Her bright blue eyes reminded him of the sky and her blond hair, falling loosely around her shoulders, gave her a softness which only served to enhance her beauty. But this was not the typical elfin girl. She wore leather pants with boots laced up to her knees. A dark green shirt and brown leather vest completed the outfit. She also carried a knife with a handle fashioned from a deer antler! No, she was absolutely not like any elfin women he knew!

He jolted himself back to the business at hand and said, "Luna, let's try to move one of these smaller rocks." He gestured to one that seemed to be about the right size. Dropping the tree limb, he grabbed hold of the rock and pushed on it, but it refused to budge.

Luna joined Quill and their combined efforts got the rock moving toward the wagon. As they were pushing together their hands touched for the briefest of instants but to Quill it was like a lightening bolt coursing through his body! Something special was happening. Because they were so close, he could smell Luna; a sweet smell, one he had never experienced before. He wished this moment could go on forever but alas, the smallish boulder was in place, exactly where Quill had wanted it. He picked up the limb and wedged one end of it between the wagon and the boulder. As he pulled down on the other end with all of his weight, the wagon began to rise.

He was straining with all his might, sweat beading on his forehead, as he hissed through clenched teeth, "Pull him out *now*!" He didn't know how much longer he could hold the weight off the old man.

Luna grabbed Tran under both arms and with one steady motion, pulled him until he was clear of the wagon. When he moved, he spit out a spine-chilling scream. The pain was excrucia-ting. As soon as he was free, Quill let go of the limb and the wagon crashed down once more. But now the damage to Tran's leg could be clearly seen. It was crushed by the awful weight and torn in several places. Quill inspected it more closely.

Tran's face reflected his pain yet he struggled to speak, trying to sound as if he were not bothered all that much. "Well Quill Okon, what do you think? Am I ever going to dance again?" He tried to raise himself on his elbows to see the leg but quickly fell back down.

Quill looked into Tran's eyes and could see more strength in them than in any man's eyes ever before. He knew he must be perfectly honest and not hold anything back.

"I don't believe your leg can be saved. It's too smashed up. If we don't get it taken care of soon, you could die."

Quill looked up to see tears rolling down Luna's cheeks. He must do something to improve this situation but as he looked at Tran's leg his only thought was that they were easily two and a half days away from the village, given how slowly they would have to travel.

At that moment, quite unexpectedly, Quill heard the cry of the hawk. His friend was circling overhead and calling to him. Quill stood and closed his eyes as Tran and Luna watched in amazement. Soon he found himself looking down at the face of the cliff. He felt the power of the hawk as it climbed higher above the cliff and over the top, descending to the other side of the mountain. It became clear why the hawk had summoned him. Making its way to the opening in the cliff on the other side was a Dark Warrior. He must be following Luna and Tran. The vision flight neared its end as the hawk scaled the peak and cliff again in full view of the two newcomers. Quill opened his eyes.

"We don't have much time Tran. There is a Dark Warrior on his way here. It's impossible to outrun him so we must find a place to hide immediately."

"How do you know this?" Tran questioned, a note of doubt in his voice.

"I can't explain it to you right now, only trust me that I'm telling the truth," Quill answered in much the same tone as Kailon used when he wanted everyone to believe him.

"Why should we hide? Take a stand and fight, Quill. I, Tran, am a great warrior in my own right and where I come from we do not believe in running from danger!" Tran turned on his side to look in the direction of the huge crack in the cliff as if he wanted the Dark Warrior to appear right that very second.

"That's all well and good, Father, but Quill is right. You can't fight with your leg in this condition and Quill can't fight that force alone." Luna had started to gather some of the things thrown from the wagon as she spoke.

"Fetch me my bow and some arrows girl. I'm not about to do anything without them. Whoever heard of someone running from a Dark Warrior when he holds in his hand a weapon that will destroy him before he can be seen? Quill, didn't anyone teach you how to do battle? Luna! Don't forget my sword either!" Tran was insistent and commanded rather than asked for his weapons.

"No one has taught me how to fight but my father did teach me how to hunt," Quill answered, an edge to the tone of his voice. He didn't like being accused of trying to take the easy way out of a fight!

"Well then, make that bow ready. You and I are about to do battle with our enemy." Tran grabbed the bow and arrows Luna had handed him and placed his sword by his side.

Quill couldn't help but wonder who Tran was and how he knew so much about the Dark Warriors. He pulled two arrows from his quiver, sticking the tip of one down along the inside of his boot so that he could grab it quickly after firing the first arrow. This was a trick taught to him by his father which he used when hunting wild boar. Sometimes your first shot misses and you need that second one to be quick. When the boar starts running, you need to be as fast as possible in order to get that second shot off. Putting an arrow in your boot gives you that edge. It would certainly come in handy right now!

Tran kept an eye on Quill as he prepared himself. He knew right away that this was a good hunter.

Quill took his stand next to the wagon waiting for the menacing warrior to appear. As he waited, he could feel his inner strength grow. The Elf Circle was with him, guarding him and bolstering his nerve. He could sense it. Quill looked over at Tran to see how he was doing and was surprised to see Luna on one knee next to her father, bow and arrow in hand and positioned to fire. His eyes went to Tran's leg and he remembered the acorns that he carried in the pouch around his neck. Could they cure him? He laid his bow down next to the wagon and went over to Tran, squatting down next to him.

"Here Tran, listen to me. I want you to hold this in your hand. It will ease some of the pain in your leg." He opened Tran's hand and placed the acorn firmly in the center of his palm. Tran gave Quill a strange look and thought that it was very odd for anyone to hold an acorn to get rid of pain! Quill felt the injured man's uneasiness and tried to reassure him.

"Look," he said, "I've done as you asked by not finding a place to hide from the coming attack; now all I ask is that you do this one thing for me. Please. Just hold the acorn, will you?"

There was no reply. Tran shrugged his shoulders and closed the acorn in his hand. Within moments he had fallen into a deep sleep. The Elf Circle was working as Tran's leg was being healed. Quill moved back to the wagon, once more picking up his bow and arrow and positioning himself for the fight with the ominous Dark Warrior. With Tran asleep Quill felt very much alone. Doing battle with this evil warrior was not his idea of how to have fun! But he also remembered what had happened the last time a Dark Warrior had come close to him. Could, or better yet, *would* the same thing happen? He respected his Circle and knew it would protect him; the more thought he gave it, the more he realized he was safe from such things as these warriors. But Luna and Tran weren't—any more than Quill's father had been!

Not long after that the Dark Warrior appeared. He seemed to come from nowhere and looked huge, dark and extremely cold. The only charge in life for such a warrior is to find the Light Elf. But so far, Syffus believes Kailon is the only one. So they are seeking Kailon, not Quill, the true Light Elf. But the warriors will destroy anything in their paths!

The Dark Warrior stepped out from the shadows and saw the upturned wagon. But nothing else. Quill carefully drew his arrow back, taking deadly aim. He felt his legs weaken as the Warrior closed the distance but took a deep breath, and then another to calm his racing heart enough to steady himself for a good clean shot. The gap narrowed to less than fifty feet. Quill's bowstring slipped along the edge of his fingers giving way to the pressure and his shaking hands. Quill was ready to release the arrow but suddenly, before it left its string, the Dark Warrior howled and fell to the ground, an arrow protruding from the center of his chest. With his mouth open in shock, Quill let the bow go slack, dropping his arrow in the dirt. Where had the shot come from? He found his answer when he spun around and saw Tran standing not ten feet away. He was drawing another arrow just in case the enemy still lived.

"So, you are Quill, the new Light Elf. The one I was sent to find. A friend of yours said to tell you not to worry."

"What are you talking about? What friend? What's going on here?"

"I am speaking of Kailon. You do remember him don't you?" Tran asked with a twinkle in his eye. "He came to me looking for help. He sent me here to help *you*. Understanding the Elf Circle is a difficult task. With my help, Kailon thought it would be easier for you. Here, take your acorn back. Thanks for letting me use it. I'd forgotten the power of the Elf Spirits to cure." Smiling a warm and gracious thanks, Tran handed over the acorn.

"How do I know you're telling me the truth?" Quill asked, while also keeping a watchful eye on the body of the Dark Warrior. "And what do you mean, you *forgot* about the acorn?"

"My father doesn't lie! Kailon did come to our home and ask for help!" Luna shouted in a very angry voice.

"Easy Luna," Tran said, raising a finger to his lips. "Quill is right to question. Kailon said that he hoped you would say that because you must have trust and confidence in your mission. They are what will keep Syffus from finding you." And turning again to Luna, he continued, "Go, get the proof that Quill is looking for." Now he moved closer to the body of the Dark Warrior.

Luna moved around to the other side of the wagon and dug through the tangled mess of belongings strewn all about by the crash. Tran kept his bow ready as he approached the body. Quill followed and stood by Tran's side.

"Look here, Quill. This you must avoid at all costs until you are ready to let Syffus know that you are the Light Elf." Tran was pointing at the huge body before them. He reached down and took the sword from the warrior's hand. Then in a commanding and almost vicious tone of voice, he proclaimed, "Never assume a dark warrior is dead!" To Quill's utter astonishment, he held the tip of the sword to the warrior's back and lunged with all his might—pushing the sword completely through the body!

"There!" he said with a measure of satisfaction. "Now we are certain this one is dead." And he turned away, going back to the still-searching Luna, who as yet had not found what she sought.

Quill was stunned into utter silence. He seemed to be alone in his shock at this act of deliberate brutality. Tran and Luna had fixed their attention to recovering their far-flung belongings.

If Tran had thought their things had been in a jumble from the crash, it was nothing to what lay about now! Luna was tossing things left and right as her frustration grew at her apparent inability to find one simple article! And Quill still stood staring at the body, now impaled on its own weapon. Something didn't make any sense to him. Why did Kailon go to Tran for help? He couldn't know Tran unless Tran himself was over four hundred years old! And what about Luna? She can't be Tran's daughter—anyone could see that. She's an elf; Tran a dwarf. Quill's head hurt from trying to process all of this. Why was it that the deeper into all of this he got, the more questions kept popping up? Not many answers, just more of a mystery!

Quill looked at Tran who now sat near the wagon watching Luna continue her search, a look of amusement on his face. It would do no good to try to help; she was fiercely independent and would find it *her* way.

"Did you say Kailon knew you and came to you for help?" Quill asked as he knelt on one knee next to Tran.

"No. What I said was that Kailon came to me for help. I didn't say I knew him. As you and I both know, Kailon has been in a deep sleep for a very long time. I couldn't have known him.

"Kailon's name in our land is part of our history. He saved our people from Syffus many times. He was the protector of all people until Syffus destroyed his Elf Circle. Since then, we have been fighting the Dark Warriors of Syffus. They have kept up a continuous search for Kailon all this time. Syffus knew Kailon was still alive, merely waiting to turn over his power to the new Light Elf. He would kill Kailon before that could happen! He must prevent the transfer. But now it is too late. Kailon has done his job well—and Syffus doesn't even know it! That is truly the best part! In his belief that Kailon still seeks a new Light Elf, he is in effect being led around by Kailon, led away from *you* until you are ready to assume your position. *My* belief is that Syffus thinks Kailon will lead him and his warriors to the new Light Elf, and at that time he can destroy both of you, the old and the new."

"Aha! Here it is!" exclaimed Luna triumphantly. "Here is the proof that my father is not lying!" She held out a long, narrow bundle to Quill. He stood and took it from her outstretched hand and untied the leather strand that bound the cloth. As he removed the material, he instantly recognized Kailon's twisted oak cane with the head of a falcon carved on the top. Quill knew there was only one way Tran could be in possession of this cane—truly, he was not lying.

Tran put a hand on Quill's shoulder and spoke to him as a father would to a favorite son. "Kailon said to give this to you. He said that it would assure you that he is well and would also remove any doubts you may have about what I say. He also instructed me to tell you that the cane is now yours as the new Light Elf, and to remind you where it came from."

Quill ran his fingers over every inch of the gnarled old cane and lingered on the falcon head remembering the story Kailon had told him about its origin. It all seemed so long ago, and yet such a short time had actually passed since Kailon had come into his life. How he wished the old master were with him now, this very minute, to help him understand what being a Light Elf *really* meant!

"Luna, we'll stay here tonight. We have a lot to do. I'm going to try to find our horse, unless you feel like pulling this wagon for the rest of the journey," he said laughing. "I'll be back as soon as possible. Actually, he probably hasn't gone very far—just far enough to be a nuisance in catching him! Quill, pay attention, son. While I'm gone, see if you have any luck getting that wagon back up on its wheels, would you?" He picked up his sword, checked his quiver for arrows, slung his bow crossways over his shoulders and, following a fairly good set of tracks, went out in search of the wayward animal.

Quill listened and nodded his assent to what was being said. He was still dumbfounded at this whole turn of events. He was alone no longer and he still wasn't sure whether that was such a good thing, but he also knew with absolute certainty that the spirits were keeping a very watchful eye on him.

Yes, it would certainly be an interesting journey!

Chapter Nineteen

Dawn found Luna, Tran and Quill packed into the now upright wagon and ready to leave for Okon village. Quill felt relieved to be heading home for this was a journey which had just not gone the way he had expected it to. The only part which had pleased Quill was the opportunity of finding out that Kailon was all right. But, running into another Dark Warrior at this point in his life was the *last* thing he wanted to happen, although he was aware that from now on these encounters would happen more and more often. It was also becoming very obvious that his suspicions about the maps were correct—and that he had to find the remaining hidden places, and not only in Okon Valley but also outside of the Valley. He knew about two secret passages which would lead him out of his homeland, and yet he felt nervous and edgy about going to places he had never seen, or never even knew existed!

Quill decided to keep the knowledge about these maps to himself, at least for the time being. If they had remained hidden for this long, it wouldn't hurt anything if he just didn't mention them for awhile. Besides, he wasn't all that sure about Tran. Who was this dwarfen warrior who allegedly had been sent by Kailon? Could he really trust him? Quill looked at Tran who was hitching up the horse to his wagon. It hadn't taken too long for Tran to find the animal—he had actually just gone over a hill and had contented himself grazing on some fresh spring grass! The horse looked as old as his master and it was pretty evident that Tran was getting up there in age! His long, grayish-brown hair and full, scraggly beard certainly matched his clothes that were made from animal hides and looked as unkempt as their wearer. Strapped to his left side he carried a sword which very closely resembled the ones found with the Dark

Warriors. There was also a rather large knife nestled in a sheath worn on his right side.

As Tran proceeded to hitch up the horse, Quill couldn't help but notice what big hands the strange man had; hands that went with his ears, nose, and feet—common features of dwarf men. When Tran spoke, Quill was reminded of Okar, the village priest with the loudest and roughest voice of anyone he knew. It could send chills down one's spine when simply offering a greeting! Scars ran along the right side of his face—scars that looked like the marks of a Dark Warrior—that couldn't be hidden behind that horrible long beard.

But, even with all of this, and his general feeling of uneasiness about Tran, Quill still sensed a gentler side to his new, and a bit unpredictable, companion.

"How long will it take us to get to your village?" Tran asked as he moved away from the old horse and approached Quill.

"Well, first we have to find a trail. I came through the forest to get here and your wagon won't make it back that way."

"So, what do we do, boy? We surely can't carry all of this stuff on our backs!" Tran exclaimed in a booming voice that clearly told Quill he had a short temper.

"My guess would be to follow the mountains north until we find a passage. I know of one but it will be rough going part of the way." Quill pointed to the mountains as he spoke.

"What do you mean by rough? Is it worth trying or are you not so sure of yourself?" Tran snapped back.

Quill felt the heat rising in his blood and his face reddening as he fought to control his own temper. This Tran was arrogant and ill-tempered and he didn't like it one bit! Traveling with him would be no easy thing if this was the attitude he was going to have all the way.

In a somewhat snippy but straightforward tone, Quill retorted, "There *is* a huge swamp between us and the passage to Okon called the Harriet. It is reported to be an evil place, one that all members of Okon have been forbidden to enter for as long as I can remember. My father told stories of strange beings with magical powers, powers that are evil. I've grown up with these stories and learned to stay away from it altogether. So there you have it. We have two choices; go north or south. If we choose south, it could take us days to find a passage. If we chance going north, through the Harriet, we could get there in two, two and a half days."

Tran stood still for a couple of minutes. From the look on his face it was clear that the Harriet enticed him; it was another challenge. A slight smile turned up the corners of his mouth as he went back to the wagon, pulled out what looked to be a shell from a turtle and strapped it to his head!

"All right Quill, the Harriet it will be! I haven't had a good fight with the Mohans in a long time."

"What are you talking about Tran? What is a Mohan?"

"You know so little son, I'm surprised you've survived this long. A Mohan is the swamp being your father told you about. We have them in our valley as well. They are powerful creatures that pray to the moon and eat whatever they kill. You see this turtle shell? ("Like how could I miss it?" thought Quill.) The Mohan King in our valley was kind enough to give it to me. *After* I cut off his left ear! He told me to wear it anytime I entered a Mohan swamp. It is to protect my head. You see, he vowed to relieve me of the burden of my head if he ever saw me again! It was that day the King left the valley never to be seen again. You see Quill, I know what we will be facing in the Harriet; a chance to settle an old score, if in fact this is the swamp the old varmint escaped to. Come on, let's be on our way." Tran left no room for discussion about which direction they would follow as he walked around to the front of the horse, and reins in hand, led him away toward the north.

Luna remained silent through all of this and now walked behind the wagon, carrying her bow on her shoulder and keeping a close eye on the trail. Quill followed her for a while but then picked up his pace and walked beside her.

They kept up a steady pace all day, stopping for nothing. Quill talked to Luna the whole way. They exchanged stories about their childhood and Luna explained how Tran had found her as a baby after the Dark Warriors had killed her parents and two brothers and left her in the mountains to die. Quill told Luna about Burt and how she would surely enjoy having him as a friend as well. He told her about the people of his village and about his mother. They shared some of their hopes and dreams for the future. By the end of the day, Quill felt that he and Luna had become friends. He welcomed that. It was a feeling of intimacy he had only felt with Burt. He liked what he felt. This was the first girl Quill had ever allowed into his life. He liked it. He liked *her*.

It was late in the afternoon when Tran stopped the wagon. They were at the edge of the Harriet. They would make camp here for the night.

"Gather wood for the fire Quill, enough to last for the entire night. We are in the Mohans' territory now but they won't bother us if we keep a fire burning. It goes along with their belief that no harm can come to you if you have a fire burning near you—or something like that!" Tran said as he unhitched the horse from the wagon.

"Or *something* like that?" Quill asked incredulously. "This is our safety we're talking about here, you know!"

"No, no, no Father. The Mohans are afraid of the fire because of the light. Remember, they pray to the dark side and the only light they live by is from the moon. They will not come near us as long as we have fire. The light will hurt their eyes," Luna reminded Tran, shaking her head slowly and giving Quill a knowing glance.

"Women! They always think they know the right answer. I hate that," Tran mumbled as he tied a long piece of rope to the horse's bridle and then tethered it to the front of the wagon.

****

Quill collected firewood for over an hour finding more than enough to last the night. Tran had already coaxed a small fire to life when he returned, and Luna was busy preparing a meal.

"Come, sit here, boy. Luna will have something good for us to eat soon." Tran indicated a spot next to himself.

Quill wanted to tell Tran that he really hated being referred to as "boy" but decided not to ruffle the old man's feathers any more today. This indignity he would accept—for now. Leaning his bow and quiver against the tree where Tran was sitting, he sank to the ground. He really wanted to go and ask Luna if she needed any help but he didn't think Tran would like that. But, he glanced up every now and then, waiting for an opportunity to be near her.

"How far are we from Okon Village right now?" Tran asked.

"Well, I figure it will take us most of the day tomorrow to get through the Harriet, assuming no trouble, and once on the other side, it should take us another good half a day. But remember, I've never been in here before and if we run into problems, it'll take us much longer."

"I know the Mohans, as I've said. They won't allow us to go through their land without a fight. I will give them this much though, they're good fighters; the only ones I know of that the Dark Warriors won't fight!" Tran said this as he removed the turtle shell from his head.

"The Dark Warriors are that afraid of the Mohans?" Quill whispered in a voice that was not as sure of itself as before.

"I don't really know what it is. It's either because the Mohans eat what they kill or because the Dark Warriors are only looking for elves and just can't be bothered with the Mohans. I remember one time being chased by a Dark Warrior right to the edge of the swamp, and then he suddenly stopped. He wouldn't come in after me. Remember that. Someday it could save your life. Use everything at hand to your advantage when fighting a Dark Warrior. Kailon told me you will have a rough time trying to survive against the Dark Elf so listen to what I say, Quill Okon. If you are to be the next Light Elf, you will eventually be found by the Dark Elf and he is no one to fool with!"

"Have you ever seen the Dark Elf, Tran?" Quill now leaned closer so he could listen more attentively. Maybe this old one *did* know what he was talking about.

"It was a long time ago. My father and I were working in the woods cutting trees. Night came and we made camp. I was building a fire and my father was making a pine bough bed. He cut my father's head off. Just like that. Then he hit me in the face with his sword." Tran reached up and touched the scar that ran the full length of his face.

"I'm sorry Tran," Quill replied, feeling genuine sympathy for what this warrior had been through. He knew all too well what it was like to lose your father in such a violent way!

"Don't be sorry, boy. You didn't do it; the Dark Elf did. He is a very vicious force. Maybe I shouldn't say this, but he looked a lot like Kailon. When I first saw Kailon and Kobar, I thought he was the Dark Elf returning. All that I remember of him are his eyes; they are white and evil."

Quill held his tongue for some time. All he did was sit and think about his father and how the Dark Warrior had slain him.

"Quill, without a doubt, tomorrow we will do battle with the Mohans. You should know something about them. They are very strange, have strength beyond belief and they equal that power with magic. Be careful! Some say that the Mohans have more power than the Elves and possess more wealth than all the valleys put together. If we are lucky, we won't encounter them. Maybe we can pass through quickly and undetected—but I wouldn't count on it!" Tran reached for the plate of food Luna offered.

"What makes you think they will even care about us, Tran? We won't be looking for trouble!"

"It's simple boy. I am Tran the warrior. I've spent much of my life killing the Mohans. They killed my wife and son because of what I told you before, for cutting their King's ear off."

"Well, what if you hide in the wagon? Then they won't see you and we can pass without any problems," suggested Quill as Luna handed him his plate.

"You don't understand anything, do you boy?" Tran's voice rose with every word! "Have you been listening to *anything* I've been telling you? *I am a warrior!* We live and die by a code. We are proud and we don't hide from our enemy; we stand and fight! Now, enough questions. Eat, then get some sleep. I'll wake you when it's your turn to watch the fire." Tran stuffed a handful of food into his mouth, letting much of it fall into his scruffy beard.

Quill finished eating and returned the empty plate to Luna. Just when he thought he was beginning to get used to this man, he turned gruff and nasty again. There was no pleasing him.

"Thanks for the meal, Luna. It was excellent!"

"You're welcome, Quill. My father insists that I make him a good meal at least once a day. I couldn't help but hear him tell you that we'll fight the Mohans tomorrow. You have to realize that he's getting old and isn't as sharp as he once was. I'm afraid for him. Is there another way we can go? We can't fight the Mohans!"

"I'm afraid not. We're committed to this course. If we turn around, it will take us several days to reach Okon with the wagon."

"You've never seen a Mohan have you? You don't know what an evil force they are! My father has fought them all of his life and look where it's gotten him!" Luna looked at Tran and Quill saw the concern in her eyes—and the tear that rolled down her cheek.

"He's worn out, tired of trying to rid this land of Mohans and fighting the evil of the Dark Elf," she continued turning away and brushing away the salty drop with the back of her hand.

Holding her squarely by the shoulders, Quill looked intently into her soft brown eyes and spoke firmly but gently. "Luna, after tomorrow, you and your father will never have to fight again. You will both be safe. My village is hidden from evil forces such as the Mohans and the Dark Elf."

"If only I could believe you, Quill. I'm tired of fighting too. For my whole life, all I've done, is fight. I need to be Luna, a young elfin woman, not a warrior defending villages and lands against evil!" She looked up into his eyes hoping to see truth reflected there.

"In my eyes, you *are* a beautiful young elfin woman and I'm glad we're becoming friends." Quill returned Luna's gaze, seeking a response to match his own.

"Quill, you're the first elf I've ever really known. I'm also glad we met." She lowered her eyes. The conversation was over for now. But Quill felt that they would have many more deep discussions. This relationship was just beginning.

He returned to Tran, smoothed a spot of ground with a bough, arranged a bed for himself and settled down for his well-earned rest.

He did not look forward to tomorrow.

****

It would be daylight soon and Quill was sitting his watch by the campfire. It was his turn to keep the fire burning so there wouldn't be a threat of the Mohans attacking during the night. He sat quietly, unmoving, staring into the crackling flames trying to put the pieces of the past couple of days together in his mind. He mulled over the mystery behind the magical power of Light Elves. Of all the tasks he now faced, or had encountered before, the greatest would be to unravel the mystery of how to earn the power levels needed to defend himself against the Dark Elf. With Kailon gone, he knew he would have to rely solely on his own wits to accomplish this hardest-of-all tasks, to take Kailon's place and earn the tenth power level.

Fingering the rope tied to his waist, he mulled over the events which led him to this point. Everything that had already happened had a purpose—and now he would enter the Harriet. What would happen in this swamp filled with beings called Mohans? Fear coursed through his body, a queasiness churning in his stomach, a feeling which was becoming all too familiar since these series of events had begun to take over his life. But he trusted in the power of his Elf Circle to protect him now, as they had so skillfully done before!

Quill looked over to where Luna lay sleeping, and a peaceful, warm feeling swept over him. He had never experienced anything quite like this before. He thought to himself that if he must marry, then Luna would be the only woman he would consider. But then there was Tran. Tran would be a tough adversary if he did in fact decide to ask for Luna's hand in marriage. His eyes shut tight, he shook his head to clear these thoughts from his mind. He must maintain his focus for now—the Harriet and the probable fight with the Mohans had to be his point of concentration. There would be time for other things later.

Picking up a long stick, he poked at the fire, stirring the flames to greater heights, then added a few more pieces of wood for good measure. He wasn't about to let the fire dwindle. And then he settled back down, stretching his legs out in front of him to keep them from falling asleep. As he absent mindedly kicked at a nearby stone, he became aware of a strange smell. At first, he didn't think much of it. But it quickly grew stronger. Was the wind blowing from the direction of the swamp? Was this increasingly nasty odor coming from there? A chill ran down his spine and at that very moment Tran jumped up from a sound sleep, yelling.

"I can smell them! Throw more wood on that fire!" Tran commanded as he fumbled with the turtle shell trying to get it strapped to his head.

"What are you talking about?" Quill asked nervously, as he hurried to pile more wood on the already blazing fire.

"Mohans! I can smell them. They're all around us. If we stay close to the fire till daylight we'll be all right. Wake Luna!"

Quill turned to waken her but she was already sitting up, rubbing the sleep from her eyes. She quickly moved closer to the fire. Snatching up his bow and quiver, Quill stood ready for the next move on the part of these Mohans. Catching a glimpse of Tran, Quill hid a growing smirk at the sight of the old man struggling to tie the turtle shell to his head. By his fumbling it was apparent that he too was afraid. But Quill would not embarrass him by letting him see that he had drawn Quill's attention. Instead, Quill directed his gaze toward the swamp—and noticed movement in front of him, at the very edge of the swamp.

"Tran, something's moving over there!" Quill whispered as he pointed the tip of his bow in that direction.

Tran stepped forward to get a better look, away from the glare of the flames.

With that, a booming voice bellowed out from the darkness. "Tran, this is your last day in this world! You have stepped on Mohan soil for the last time."

"Who *is* that?" Quill asked, his voice actually hoarse from fright.

"Hyslop, the King of the Mohans," replied Tran, stepping forward a bit more. And to the disembodied voice that beckoned him, he yelled, "Hyslop, I have wondered for years where you went. What happened? You didn't like your old swamp, or did you leave because I almost killed you?" Tran was taunting the murky creature, baiting him to come forward to be seen.

"You have killed your last Mohan, Tran," was the raspy response. "You have no idea where you are. This is the heartland of the Mohans. The birthplace of our power. As you and I stand here talking, the Mohan power is crawling toward you like a slow fog, hunting you like a dog on the trail of a rabbit!"

Tran raised his bow and released a shot in the direction of Hyslop's voice. Luna edged closer to Quill as he too raised his bow, arrow set to fly, awaiting the opportunity for the perfect shot.

"Tran, your arrows have no power within the limits of the Harriet. As I have told you, this is the seat of all Mohan power. Throw down your useless weapons and face your destruction like a true warrior!" The air literally vibrated from the roar of the unearthly command.

Quill tried to envision Hyslop's appearance, while at the same time struggling to control his rising fear. It was a given that they were outnumbered and in a no-win situation. Quill lowered his bow, reaching into his quiver for another arrow to have at the ready in his boot, as he had done before. As he did, his hand fell upon Kailon's cane. He had put it in his quiver for safekeeping and now, instinctively, he withdrew the old oak stick and held it tightly. It gave him a sense of security, although his arms trembled and sweat beaded upon his forehead as he lowered the cane in front of him. Slowly Luna's hand reached out, coming to rest on Quill's hand, the one that gripped the carved falcon's head spindle of the old cane. Her silent reassurance encouraged Quill, giving him the confidence he needed to face this menacing threat.

"Tran, I have come myself to settle an old score. You should feel honored. The King of the Mohans will be the one to kill you!" It was a smug, self-satisfied sound that grated from the ogre's throat as he lurched forward, away from the cover of the swamp trees that had until now hidden his massive, grotesque body.

Hyslop's appearance took Quill's breath away. He had never seen anything so ugly! He was scale-covered yet seemed to resemble the same general shape as a dwarf. Blotches of coarse, blackish-brown hair protruded from under the scales of his arms and his face was covered with scabbed and broken skin. It seemed as if he had some kind of fungus living on him. He had only one ear. Quill knew why.

The monster lumbered forward, headed for Tran. But as he came within twenty feet or so of Tran, he changed direction and headed for Quill. Quill felt the pounding of his heart, and Luna squeezed his hand harder. Hyslop stopped about ten feet from Quill and, raising his right arm, pointed at Quill's head.

Quill did not respond. He was frozen in place.

"Answer me, boy. Are you a friend of Tran's?"

Quill was unsure of what he should do. Yet he felt an inner strength beginning to build and almost unaware of his actions, Quill took a step forward. Luna moved with him.

"Hyslop, I am the one you want. Leave the boy alone," Tran ordered.

"You have no say in this old man! I will do as I want with this scrawny, worthless thing you call an elf."

Quill felt his strength growing. His eyesight and hearing were now at fever pitch and he could see the Mohans hiding in the swamp. He could even hear Hyslop's scales rubbing together as he took rasping breaths, swaying from side to side.

"Fall back! Both of you," yelled Tran. "This is *my* fight. Hyslop has no reason to harm either of you." He waved his arm at Quill and Luna, trying to get them to move to safer ground.

Without warning, and with a mere flick of his arm, Hyslop released an enormous surge of power in Tran's direction! Tran was thrown to the ground with stunning force! The protective turtle shell so carefully strapped to his head snapped apart, flying across the campfire and rolling into the swamp.

"I told you, Tran. I will do as I wish. I can suck the life from you with the stroke of my arm and there will be nothing you can do to prevent it!" Then, rising to his full height, Hyslop swung his arms to each side proclaiming in a deafening roar, "I am the most powerful being in this land and no one can stop me. I will soon become the ruler over all living things!"

Quill and Luna rushed over to where Tran lay, face down and not moving. Kneeling down next to him, Quill could not see if he was hurt because Luna had flung herself on top of him, crying hysterically. Quill grasped Luna by the shoulders, trying to get her to regain control of herself.

"Tran is dead whenever I say. I will allow you both a moment for final good-byes before I sever his head from his body, as I have vowed to do!" the evil Mohan King threatened viciously. He proceeded toward them in a slow, deliberate manner.

Luna wrenched free of Quill's hold and sprang toward Hyslop before Quill could stop her. "Luna! No! Don't!" he screamed.

But it was too late. Hyslop never let her touch him. Again, with a flick of his arm, he released his power and Luna smashed to the ground. Quill was instantly up and rushing toward Hyslop, stopping just a few feet from him.

"Try your power on me Hyslop! Or are you afraid to do battle with a boy?" Quill challenged, looking squarely into Hyslop's blazing eyes. All fear had disappeared and, without Quill even being aware of it, his Elf Circle was now in control! Tercal and the other Elf spirits had emerged once again to protect the budding Light Elf. With an enormous flash of light, Tercal appeared. He spoke directly to the Mohan.

"I am Tercal, Light Elf from the Kingdom of Zin!"

Hyslop retreated several feet, covering his eyes from the blinding light of the Elf Spirits as they spun around and around, encircling him.

"There are no more Light Elves! He screeched, his arm still shielding his eyes. "Syffus has destroyed them all and soon I will destroy this Pretender!"

"The Light Elves have ignored you for many years, mainly because you have remained in the Harriet. But now it is time for you to surrender your power. You have not lived up to your promises. When the King of Zin gave you your power, he did so out of compassion, listening to your plea that the Mohans needed the power to survive in the swamps. You lied. You have used the power not to help the Mohans but to harm them. And now you have taken that power beyond the realm of the Harriet. You stand here before the new Light Elf, Quill Okon, and your intent was to harm him. You are not a benevolent soul, but rather, your intentions are of those who relish evil, who are possessed by it, such as Syffus, the Dark Elf!"

"Do you expect me to believe you? The King of Zin himself gave me my power and it is only by his will that the power can be taken away!," Hyslop sneered in scorn.

"His power is our power," replied Tercal. "The Light Elves were entrusted with the same power as that of the King of Zin. It is our task to ensure that all beings are protected from evil and to keep the Kingdom safe until the King's return. You have not honored your agreement and will be punished for that with the loss of all powers!"

Quill was rooted to the spot. Totally silent. For the first time he understood the purpose of the Elf Circle. He listened attentively to every word uttered by Tercal.

Hyslop would not give up. "I don't believe anything you have said. I am more powerful than anyone in these lands and not you nor anyone else will stop me. Light Elf? This scrawny little pointy-eared piece of nothing could never possess more power than I and I will prove it." Hyslop waved his arms again and again to no effect.

"You see, Hyslop, your intentions toward this new Light Elf were not honorable so *he* now possesses *all* of your power," Tercal proclaimed.

Quill found this hard to believe himself! But as his hand moved to the rope encircling his waist, he felt an added knot. And as quickly as they had appeared, the spirits vanished in a flash of light! Quill now understood more about his Circle and felt more confident about becoming the new Light Elf. But he still did not fully understand how the power knots are earned. Was it by finding the courage to face his innermost fears? And by acting on that courage?

"Boy, I can still kill you. I don't need the power of Zin! I can do it with my bare hands," Hyslop yelled taking a step toward Quill. Enraged by this personification of evil, Quill snapped to his senses and raised his cane, pointing it directly at Hyslop. Within seconds, the Mohan King dissolved into a pile of black ash!

Shaken by this sudden turn of events, Quill turned to find Luna. He knelt beside her where she had fallen, and gently shook her.

"Luna, Luna are you all right?"

Blinking her eyes repeatedly, she finally sat up, holding her head in her hands.

"What happened? Where is Hyslop?"

"Gone." It was a statement of fact, but Quill felt it was more of a pronouncement of a better future for all the inhabitants of the land.

He moved quickly to Tran and shook him firmly but there was no response. He rolled him over and, lowering his head to Tran's chest, placed his ear over his heart.

"There's no heartbeat, Luna. Tran is dead."

"No! It can't be. He's a strong man. He can't be dead!" Luna's voice broke as she crawled on her knees to Tran's side. Quill dropped to the ground beside her; he better than most understood her grief. He reached for her, wrapping his arms around her shaking body trying somehow to ease her pain.

"Luna, Tran was old. I think it was just his time. Even you told me he was tired. His heart wasn't strong enough to take the punishment that Hyslop put him through. It was just too much. Let me help you to be strong."

"I'm lost without my father. How will I survive?" Luna wailed. Her tears flowed freely now in desperate grief. He was the only parent she had ever known. "Where will I live? I have to go back to our home."

"No, Luna. You'll go with me to my village. I won't leave you. I want you to be my wife. Will you marry me?" Quill surprised even himself with the suddenness of this proposal, but he also knew that he loved this woman and needed her to be by his side.

He helped Luna to her feet wiping her tears with the tail of his shirt. She regarded Quill silently, then held out her hands to his. In a voice still choked with emotion she said, "You are the kindest and sweetest friend. My *only* friend. But, is it right that I should marry you? I don't know. I don't want to marry because I have no one else to turn to. If I do marry you it will be out of love. For that, I think we need more time together."

"If it's time you need, then so be it," answered Quill. "But my mind will not change. Of that I'm sure!" He knew that for himself, time would only cement the bond he felt with this amazing woman.

Once more, holding onto Quill for support, Luna looked on the body of her father. But out of the corner of her eye she spotted movement—several Mohans were moving toward them!

"Quill, behind you! More Mohans!"

Quill spun around, raising his cane in defense. As he did, a voice cried out.

"Don't! Don't! We mean you no harm Light Elf. Give us a chance to explain. Please. We don't want to hurt anyone!"

"Come forward and speak your peace."

"I am Taid. My father was the King of Mohan until Hyslop killed him. Hyslop was evil and forced us to perform evil deeds. He has killed many of our people who refused to live under his rule. You have freed us from his power and we all thank you for that. You are welcome here and at our tables whenever you wish. With Hyslop gone, his evil power no longer makes cowards of us all! The good life will return to the Harriet."

"Taid, can you and your people show us how to get through the swamp so we can get to Okon Village?" Quill asked.

"Not only that but anything else you need. But first, may I share something with you? Hyslop was not the only one with power from Zin. My father also was given power but was unable to overcome the evil of Hyslop. He feared being killed for control of he power, so before that could happen, he transferred it to me. He swore me to an oath never to use it to do harm. I have kept true to that vow. Now that I know you are the guardian of *all* power within Zin, it will make it easier to understand how and why the power works. I will use it for the good of all my people."

"Taid, you may keep your father's power. Use it wisely and, whatever you do, avoid contact with the Dark Elf as he will destroy both you and your power. And I do have one more favor to ask of you and your people. Will you help us to provide a proper burial for Tran?"

Quill turned to Luna, questioning her with his eyes as to whether she agreed to this. She nodded her head in approval as a fresh tear made its way down her cheek and came to rest at the corner of her mouth. Quill brushed it away with the end of his thumb.

"This will be the last time a tear of grief will ever flow from your heart. If you cry again, it will be from joy," Quill promised as he slid his arm around Luna's shoulders and pulled her close to him.

Chapter Twenty

Quill and Luna stood next to the grave where Tran would lie. Tiad had asked Luna for her approval to bury Tran next to his father, a place of honor within the Harriet. It was now mid-day and Luna was exhausted—both mentally and physically. Quill decided it would be best to spend the night in the Harriet among their new-found friends. All that remained right now were the burial rights for Tran.

Though Quill had known him only briefly, he felt oddly close to the man who had risked everything to keep him and Luna safe. He had lost his own father such a short time ago that the hurt and emptiness were still fresh and raw. He relived his days with Lore with each moment of this final goodbye. He could say with all honesty to Luna that he understood her pain, her grief. His empathy for her loss only served to draw him closer to her; to want to protect her from any harm they might encounter from this time forward.

They stood, arms around each other, listening to the words of the funeral rite so familiar to the Mohans who surrounded them in support. Quill's thoughts retraced the events since his first encounter with Tran and Luna, and then the Mohan people. How strange it seemed to find such closeness among an entire race of people they had not even known existed but a few hours earlier! What an amazing world they lived in! The Creator certainly was good to them and provided for all their needs. Quill looked at Luna tenderly, then gently brushed the tears from her cheeks with his fingers. She quietly leaned her head on his strong shoulder and in that moment knew she would never leave the side of this wonderful man.

Quill's thoughts were interrupted by Tiad's voice as he proclaimed that Tran would forever be regarded a hero among the Mohans and that Quill and Luna would be welcome in the Harriet at any time. At the end of Tiad's farewell they made their way to the Mohan village located exactly in the middle of the swamp. Luna gave one last look at her father's resting place, straightened her shoulders and held her head high. She would carry on in a manner befitting the daughter of such a proud and brave warrior. Her mourning would be private; her outer appearance serene.

"Isn't this a beautiful place Quill?" Luna commented peacefully. She actually felt an amazing calm about her father's death that she never would have expected. "Maybe," she thought, "it's because I have someone strong to lean on."

"Beautiful, yes. Who would ever guess that such a place could exist here?" Quill said.

Everywhere you looked there were flowers and fruit trees growing in and around the Mohans' houses. The houses themselves were built from dried clay somehow formed into blocks, a way of building totally unfamiliar to Quill.

"Tiad, how do you build a house like that?" Quill asked.

"We work the clay with straw, then smooth it into wooden boxes and pack it down. The boxes are placed in the sun to dry." Tiad answered. "This way of working the ground has been handed down from father to son for as long as anyone can remember. When the blocks are dry, they are hard and last for a very long time."

It wasn't until that moment that Quill realized it was the middle of the day, in full sun, and the Mohans were out in the light without the least qualm about it! "Tiad," he began, "Tran told us that Mohans don't like the light. That you fear it. Why is it that you are out now in the full sun?"

"That was never true my friend. *Hyslop* could not stand the light. Evil thrives in darkness. We Mohans relish the sunshine. It's what makes the swamp alive. Just look around you, flowers everywhere! The warmth and brightness of the sun encourages the beautiful growth! Hyslop was infected with a mysterious disease. Some say it was a spell cast upon him by the King of Zin because he abused his powers and the King was angered by that. But *I* believe it was cast by Woba. Before you leave I will introduce you to Woba. She is special among our people. But first we must let Luna rest. Follow me. We'll set you up for the night."

Quill and Luna followed Tiad into one of the small clay houses. Luna was surprised to find all of her clothes laid out waiting for her.

"I hope you don't mind, but the people of my village wanted to do something for you. They cleaned your clothes which had spilled out all over the ground, fed the horse, and did some much needed repairs on your wagon." Tiad seemed very proud of these accomplishments, and of his fellow Mohans! "It's their way of thanking you for ridding the swamp of the evil one."

The visitors were duly impressed and grateful for the kindnesses being shown to them by all of these gentle people. "You and your entire clan have been so considerate. Thank you and please be sure to pass on our thanks to everyone," Luna said. "And now, if I may, I would like to rest for awhile." She went over to the bed at the far side of the single-room hut, swept her hand across the bedcovers in silent approval, then lay down, sinking thankfully upon the soft mattress.

Quill and Tiad stepped outside, closing the door behind them.

"Let's go visit Woba," offered Tiad, leading the way through the village and back into the swamp. They walked for about an hour before they came upon the clay house that belonged to Woba. From approximately twenty yards away, Tiad stopped and called out, "Woba! Woba, it's me, Tiad! May I come in?"

"Yes, come," a frail voice returned.

They proceeded the rest of the way and entered the lone hut. Quill took a sweeping inventory of the single-room home cluttered with an assortment of strange-looking things. Tiad stepped forward to stand next to a table in the center of the room. Woba sat in a straight, hard chair at the table.

"I've been waiting for you Tiad. What happened? You always come in the morning." Her tone was a bit accusatory.

Tiad only smiled, then told her, "Woba, Hyslop is dead! Quill Okon, the new Light Elf, took Hyslop's power."

Woba pushed herself away from the table, quickly stood and, clenching her hand into a fist, raised her arm saying with immense satisfaction, "Finally! Hyslop got what he deserved!"

It was such a sudden outburst that it startled Quill, who had hardly expected such a cry from this old woman! He did notice that Woba didn't look like the rest of the Mohans. She resembled a dwarf! She had no scales, and she certainly wasn't ugly like the others.

"You must be this Quill Okon person," Woba exclaimed coming over to him with hand extended in greeting.

"Yes, I am. And I'm very glad to meet you," Quill answered in his most polite manner. He stared into her eyes and could feel the gentleness of her soul and the wisdom that comes with age. Her hair was gray and time had not been kind to her face for it showed the wrinkled tracks of many years.

"Are you surprised that I am a dwarf?" she asked, her eyes twinkling with a life force which belied her age.

"You might say that I am. You don't look anything like a Mohan," responded Quill as he released her hand.

"Well, let me tell you about that. You see, *all* Mohans are dwarves. When Hyslop became infected with disease, and his appearance began to change many, many years ago, he changed all Mohans so they would look like him. He didn't want to be the only ugly one! So he cast a spell on all but me—I was spared because he feared what I might do. Unknown to him, there was nothing I *could* do. I couldn't reverse one of his spells, but I could inflict him with pain. The disease was my doing." She had a self-satisfied smile on her face.

"Now that Hyslop is dead, can the Mohans be restored to their former appearance?" Quill questioned.

"Yes, but first, come over and sit. Relax. I'll tell you everything." She settled herself in her chair and indicated stools for Quill and Tiad. "If you are really the new Light Elf, *you* can restore them. You are the only one with the power, other than Zupan, the King of Zin."

Tiad leaned across the table and listened intently as Woba continued.

"You see Quill, Hyslop thought he was the most powerful and never believed that Light Elves could harm him so he tried to take control of all living things. Hyslop even believed he would win over the Dark Elf, the most evil being of all." Woba's hand went to her head and she scratched quite incessantly at her tousled mop of hair.

"Where did Hyslop come from?" asked Tiad.

"From another valley, a valley called Jacon. But where he got his power from, I do not know. Some say from Zin, but I could never understand how—or why. The Kingdom was lost over four hundred years ago; at the same time Kailon lost his power. Kailon was the last Light Elf."

Quill broke in quickly, "I know. Kailon is a good friend."

"So, you know what I say is true. How could the King of Zin give Hyslop such power when the King is no longer alive? I really believe Hyslop's power came from the Dark Elf."

"Then how did Tiad's father get *his* power?" Quill asked, his brow furrowed as he tried so hard to understand all that was being said.

Woba went on: "That power was passed from generation to generation for hundreds of years, much like the power of the Light Elves. The only difference is that a Light Elf is the master of *all* power. You possess much more than Tiad's father ever could."

"I don't understand one thing. Before Hyslop died, he said that the King of Zin gave him his power. But if you say it couldn't have been, because the King is dead, then something is not right. How could he have gotten his power from Zin?" It was Tiad who had questioned this.

Quill kept silent. He didn't want to reveal his knowledge of Zin or anything else to Woba and Tiad. The less he told of his knowledge the better, lest he put these kind people in danger and also because of the threat of the Dark Elf using that knowledge to get back at him. Besides, at this point Quill didn't really know whom to trust and it was bad enough that all of the Mohans knew he was the new Light Elf.

"Well, I can't figure it out. I don't see how Hyslop managed his position of power because there was no one to give it to him," Woba said.

Quill just listened, remaining seated and trying to unravel this puzzle. Hyslop received some power from Zin. As he pored over what was being said, it suddenly came to him. Hyslop *thought* he received his power from Zin, but, what if it was from another source unknown to us?

"Woba, when Hyslop came to the Harriet, did he bring his power with him or did he get it after he was here?" Quill wanted to know.

"He came with it demanding that all of the Mohans do as they were told or he would kill them," Woba answered.

Quill didn't continue. He was still trying to put the pieces together. The King of Zin must have given each valley a certain amount of magical power—enough to prevent the Dark Elf from destroying them. But what if somehow Hyslop was able to take a valley's power away? Not only would he now have their magic, but he would also have destroyed the valley because the Dark Warriors would now be able to invade and kill all the inhabitants. So, now the question was, which valley is the one without the King of Zin's power? It's definitely not Okon Valley because Tiad has the power and because Okon Village is where the Light Elves have come from. That leaves one of the other valleys which are drawn on the maps he found in his father's book. Quill felt in his pocket to make sure the maps were still there. Up until now, he had forgotten all about them.

"Woba, Tiad tells me you also possess magic powers. Would you tell me where they came from?" Quill inquired.

"Of course, I don't mind telling you. Get comfortable. It's a long story! Many years ago, some time before Hyslop ever came here, we lived a peaceful life in the Harriet. Then, one night Syffus and several of his Dark Warriors attacked our village. His sole purpose was to destroy everyone in the Harriet. He was searching for Kailon, as he has every hour of every day for these four hundred years or so, and supposed he was here. It was the most horrible night we have ever lived. A night of pure terror and destruction. They tore through the Harriet, slashing and crushing anything that moved—women, children, men—all. He even ordered that all of our animals be killed. But several members of the village managed to flee undetected into the swamp. It was then that I took my chance.

I ran too, but alone. It seemed like I ran for hours before I dared to stop. When I did, I was afraid to move for fear of the Warriors. I stayed in that spot for days. It was during this time that I received my power. I had no food, no water to drink. I was cold, wet and very tired from little sleep and realized that I would soon die if I didn't do something. So I decided to move around the swamp just enough to find shelter. What I found was an old hollowed-out tree with a trunk large enough for me to hide in. It was the biggest tree I have ever seen in the swamp. It was perfect and afforded me all the protection I needed. But something about this tree struck me as very odd. It didn't belong here in the swamp. It was just too huge. Do you know what I mean? But I couldn't turn back—I needed it as my new home! But when I stepped inside, the ground gave way from under my feet and I began falling into a seemingly bottomless pit! I grabbed and clutched at anything that I thought would stop my fall. It did no good; I just kept falling. My heart felt as though it would explode from fear and my mind wandered away from what was happening all the way to my long-ago past, when I was very small."

She stopped talking and seemed to be just staring off into space.

"Woba, are you all right?" Tiad spoke sharply trying to jolt her back to the present.

She blinked her dark brown eyes rapidly several times, shrugged her shoulders a bit, then continued on with her story as if nothing had happened.

"I finally managed to stop myself by grabbing something, but couldn't see what it was because of the inky blackness. I hung there, desperately clinging to my handhold, terrified I would start to fall again. It seemed like hours before my strength gave way. But while I hung on for dear life, I did an awful lot of soul-searching. I remember praying over and over again, begging the Creator to let me live, and at the very moment I could hold on no longer, I thought He had not listened and I was going to die."

Woba fell silent and rose from her chair. Leaning across the table, coming face-to-face with Tiad, she looked him squarely in the eyes. "Tiad, what I am about to tell you must remain between the three of us. You must never repeat it to anyone. Do you understand?"

Tiad nodded his head solemnly in agreement. There would be no way he would break this trust!

The old woman then shuffled to the other side of the room where she knelt down and began pulling up floorboards in front of her. She recovered a small box from its hiding place, returned to the table and placed it in front of Quill. That done, she took her seat once more. Quill didn't touch the box; he sat very still staring at it. It was incredible! Made of what appeared to be pure gold, gold so bright Quill could feel the glare bouncing off his face, it had four small knobs holding it up from the table. Each one seemed to be a large gold nugget! At each end of the box was a handle, and on the face, a gold latch so the lid could be locked. The center of the lid was beautifully engraved. Three hands held a ring with ten different colored stones in it. Running from the upper right arc of the ring crosswise down to the lower part was a sword. The sword's handle contained three stones, each a different color, one at the end and two closest to the blade. Surrounding the entire carving was another ring again set with ten more brilliantly colored stones.

Quill studied the box carefully, and as he did, Kobar came to mind. These rings on the lid were amazingly similar to those on the shields Kobar and his brother Molik had carried. The sword seemed identical to the one Kobar used against the Dark Warrior. He wouldn't mention anything about these coincidences to Tiad or Woba just yet. Maybe the box didn't have anything at all to do with Kobar, but until he was sure it would be best to keep his suspicions to himself.

"Woba, you were about to tell us what happened when you fell into the hole," Tiad said.

"Well, as I was saying, I was dangling there ready to fall because I couldn't hold on any longer and I was sure that I was about to die. I was desperate to find something else to grab on to or maybe even get a foothold. It was so terribly dark but suddenly I felt something. It seemed to feel like a ladder! A *natural* ladder—a network of roots from the tree. I couldn't believe it! At first all I wanted to do was get out of there, but I soon realized that I didn't have the strength left to climb up. My only alternative was to keep going down. It seemed like I descended forever before I reached bottom." Woba reached for the box and slid it in front of her.

"What happened when you got to the bottom Woba?" Tiad asked as he leaned forward even more across the table, hanging on her every word.

"It was pitch dark and I couldn't see a thing. Also, I ached all over from the fall. I guess I was just so relieved to still be alive that I slipped into a deep sleep. I must have slept all through the night, I'm not really sure, but when I woke, I jumped up fully alert and determined to find out where I was and, more importantly, how I could get out! There still was no light so I began feeling around with my hands for something, *anything*, that would give me a clue. There seemed to be a good amount of room, yet, when I moved a bit, I stepped on something and fell down on top of it. Fear instantly grabbed at me once more but I kept searching with my hands and then stopped in horror! What I had tripped over was the skeleton of a gigantic being. It could only have been a Dark Warrior. I knew of nothing else that could possibly be that size! I could take no more! The tears streamed down my cheeks and I sobbed uncontrollably for what must have been ten minutes or more. I was sure I was never going to escape this dark dungeon; a prison of no return! I would die here.

"Gradually I pulled myself together into a semblance of calm and tried to think rationally. The darkness, cold, and fear had combined to make me lose all track of my exact location. I had become disoriented, and no longer knew from which direction I had entered this chamber (if indeed that is what it was). Gingerly, I once more felt the long-dead bones around me trying to find a knife, or anything I might hang onto for security. That's when I discovered a pouch and in it was a stone, perhaps one this dead man had used to sharpen his sword. I dumped it out in front of me and as I did so, the stone must have hit the edge of a rock, or maybe even his sword, because several sparks shot across the skeleton actually lighting up the area! I snatched up the stone and began banging it against the edge of the sword I had seen in the first flash of light. Sparks flew enabling me to see, although very briefly. I thought that there must be some dry twigs or roots down there and I groped around till I found enough to support a tiny fire. By striking the stone again and again I finally managed a puff of smoke and then the beginnings of a fire! I had light! You cannot even begin to imagine what a feeling of relief and safety I felt when I could see at last! It was then that I realized what I had actually fallen into!"

"What? What was it, Woba?" Tiad asked impatiently.

"A tomb. It was the tomb of a wizard—someone from another time and civilization! There in front of me was the accumulated knowledge of the mystical power of a wizard—power that had been contained in this vault and not used for hundreds, maybe even thousands, of years! As I walked around looking at the many objects scattered about and at all the books that were left behind, I realized that his power must have been very great indeed. Then I remembered a story told to me once. If a wizard dies, his power will live on until eventually he will return in another time and in another body! I had always dismissed these stories as just that—stories to capture a child's imagination, but certainly containing no element of truth at all! But I was about to have that doubt proved wrong. In fact, there *are* wizards." She now slowly undid the latch on the gold box sitting in front of her.

Quill and Tiad inched even closer to Woba, each straining for a look at what had been hidden inside this beautiful box for so long. Woba's fingers, bent and gnarled with age, were clumsy in opening the latch but finally it fell away, and she lifted the ornate lid.

Quill stood up to get a better vantage point as Tiad leaned over the lid from across the table, each being unable to control his excitement. But then…

"There's nothing in here!" Quill exclaimed.

"That's right. It was empty when I found it." Woba rose and went to the same spot in the floor where she had lifted the boards, and knelt again. This time she returned with a book. Very large and very heavy. She laid it on the table next to Quill. It was bound with leather and had straps of pure gold securing the binding in place. The symbol appearing on the box was echoed here on the book's cover. Engraved in the same manner.

"This book contains a complete history of the knowledge needed to become a powerful wizard. It also describes the contents of the box," Woba whispered as she very carefully opened the cover and turned to the first brittle page.

Quill saw writing on the page, but he wasn't able to read it. It was in a language totally unfamiliar to him.

"I don't understand this writing. I've never seen it before," Quill remarked.

"I know. It has taken me over four hundred years to decipher it so I could begin to understand what it said."

"Woba, you never finished your story. Remember, you were in the tomb looking around," Tiad said.

"You're right, Tiad. I do need to complete the story. As I said, I was walking around, absolutely in awe at the amount of items just lying all over the place. And then something even more strange happened. At the other side of this tomb I noticed a doorway. It seemed to be carved out of rock. And above the door, carved into the solid stone, was the identical symbol you see on the box here, and on the cover of this book. And it was complete with the colored stones very prominently displayed. I was terrified of what might be behind that door. I could hardly move. Was there another Dark Warrior waiting for someone to open it so he could unleash his wrath? Eventually I summoned enough courage to approach the door and reach to open it. There was a torch leaning against the wall so I took it and went back to the fire to light it. It was when I returned to the door in better light that I got a really good look at the symbol above it. I opened the door. With the first few tentative steps inside all I could see were spider webs and dirt; time's legacy!

"A few more steps inside and I noticed what looked like a huge man-sized box made of stone and three steps leading up to it. Behind it, hanging on a rock, was a shield, again with what I now assume to be a wizard's symbol on it. I raised my foot to the first step trying to look inside but wasn't close enough. So I moved to the second step and could then see that the lid of the box was also carved with that same symbol. When I took the final step up, the stone lid began to move! I leaped down and bolted out of the chamber but could still hear the stone lid scraping, stone against stone as it continued to open! There was nowhere for me to go and I found myself backed up against the wall in the outer room shaking with fear. Yet strangely curious. The grinding stopped. I listened. Not another sound. I summoned all my nerve and moved to reenter the chamber. I took my time and managed to again bring myself to climb to the top of the three steps. I peeked in. And recoiled in horror! There, inside the solid rock tomb, was another skeleton—holding these artifacts; this box and book! It was a horrible experience."

"Woba, I can't believe it! This story is incredible! I've never heard of such a tomb being in the swamp. Never!" breathed Tiad, a long, slow sigh escaping his lips as he spoke.

"Let me finish. My story is not over. For it was at that moment I received my magic powers! I knelt at the tomb to remove the box from the bony hands, and as I opened the latch and lifted the lid, a blinding red light flashed into my eyes, robbing me of my sight for several minutes. A light so powerful that I was knocked off balance, falling off the steps and landing flat on my back. As I lay on the cavern floor, I began to understand what it was I had found. Visions appeared to me, visions of a powerful wizard from another land. They were flashes of insight, gone as quickly as they had come. But from that moment on I have had my power, and, as if the light had somehow communicated with me, I instinctively knew how to *use* it."

"What exactly was in the box, Woba? Where did that red light come from?" Tiad wanted to know.

"I wondered that myself, so when I recovered from the shock of what had happened, I got up and, seeing that the lid had closed, I carefully opened it again. Inside was a magnificent red ruby, the biggest I had ever seen. Only now I knew what it *really* was. Remember, the communication from the light had already told me the answers I sought. I knew that this ruby was actually the wizard's heart! That's why a wizard lives forever; his heart is made from a solid ruby, a ruby the size of a beating heart!"

"But what happened to the ruby? Why isn't it here in this box?" Tiad was totally confused.

"The ruby remained in the box only for a short time after I found it. Then one night the wizard returned to claim it; on a night of a full moon." Woba appeared exhausted from the telling of her tale and leaned her head on the table, across her folded arms.

"So you never saw who the wizard was did you, Woba?" Quill asked.

"No. I've never seen the wizard alive. All that remains is this box, the book and all of the things that I found in the tomb. I removed everything and built this house directly over the spot where the tomb lies. But not even *that* exists now. The night the wizard came for the ruby he also destroyed the tomb. He filled it in with solid rock. All I know is that somewhere out there in our land is the most powerful wizard ever. His name is Zatto." Woba pointed to the first line in the book. The name Zatto was written there.

"Woba, what *is* written in that book?" Quill asked.

"Some day you will know what it says. For now, I have told you enough. But I will tell you this. Zatto is a good wizard and if you find him, he will help you defeat the Dark Elf. It is up to you now Quill, to save the land from the evil power of Syffus. Find Zatto and destroy Syffus. This is your mission Quill Okon."

Quill stood and ran his fingers across the symbol carved in the lid of the gold box. "Woba, you said I have the power to change the Mohans back to their original form, back to dwarves. How do I go about that so I can release them from the spell Hyslop cast upon them?"

"I know that a Light Elf must earn ten levels of power. When you have reached the tenth level you will possess enough power to crush any type of spell. But until then, the Mohans must remain as they are. Now, would you and Tiad please leave? I am very tired and must rest. But Quill, one thing I do know. You and I will never see each other again in this world. The survival of our people is entrusted to you. Don't give up even under the worst conditions!" Woba reached out and took Quill's hand in her own, looking deeply into his eyes.

Quill felt as if he were about to lose an old and trusted friend. How could he have developed such feeling for this woman in so short a time? His attention remained riveted on this wise and caring face. He didn't know how she could be sure they would never again meet but he did believe her.

Without further conversation, Quill turned to leave, grateful for this added instruction as he prepared to fulfill his destiny.

Chapter Twenty-One

As Quill and Tiad left Woba's neat little home, they realized with surprise how much time they had spent with this wise old woman. It was late in the afternoon and the sun was already beginning to outline the trees in a reddish-orange glow. During the long walk back to the village, neither Quill nor Tiad had anything to say, each being preoccupied with his own thoughts; each sorting out all that Woba had told them. So absorbed in thought were they that when they did arrive at the edge of the village, they were amazed at how short the walk had been!

"I'd better go check on Luna," Quill said as he turned in the direction of the house where she rested. Tiad decided to accompany Quill.

"Will you and Luna join my wife and me for dinner? She's an excellent cook and we'd be honored to have you," offered Tiad.

Quill felt that he was the one who should be honored and told Tiad so. "By all means Tiad. That would be fine. Just tell me which house is yours and we'll be there!"

Tiad was very pleased with himself for the way the day had gone. He smiled easily at his new friend, patted him affectionately on the shoulder and set off to tell his wife to prepare extra for dinner!

Quill waited a few minutes before going in to see how Luna was doing. There was so much of what Woba had said today that just didn't make any sense to him. Where did Hyslop really get his power from? Did he steal it from another valley? Where does Zatto the Wizard fit in to all of this? And where is he now? Was Woba right when she said he must find Zatto and seek his help in defeating the Dark Elf? Then of course, there were the Mohan people themselves, still under this terrible spell that has turned them into creatures with scales and an appearance that would make most people run away in fear! How was he supposed to help them? He was supposed to be the one to release them from the spell if what Woba said was true. But how long would they have to wait for his power to allow him the ability to do it? He had set out from Okon Village in search of answers, and what happened? More questions! Again! Would he *ever* get to the bottom of this? He felt like pulling his hair out in frustration, but instead, took a deep breath and, letting it out slowly, forced himself to relax and focus on the matters at hand. The rest would somehow take care of itself. At least that's what he kept telling himself!

"Quill, you're back! Where did you go?" Luna asked.

"Tiad took me into the swamp to meet a dwarf woman named Woba. She has magical powers. Tiad thought I should meet her."

"Well, while you were off with him, I asked some of the Mohans to help me pack for our journey back to your village in the morning. The wagon is a little beat up from being knocked around but nothing's broken and it will still serve us well. We reloaded it and made sure everything was ready. You don't mind that I went ahead with it, do you?"

Quill shook his head emphatically and taking both her hands in his, pulled Luna to himself, wrapped his arms around her and kissed her softly on her forehead. Luna's reaction was not one of surprise, but rather of happy acceptance. She raised her head so their eyes met in a long, loving exchange, soul intermingling with soul, and then surrendered herself to a warm and passionate kiss. Not a word had been spoken yet each knew that their paths had been sealed—they would be together forever.

Luna was the first to speak, almost afraid to break the silence which wrapped them in its gentle folds. "I'm so happy you've come into my life," she whispered. "If it weren't for you I would probably be dead by now."

"When we return to Okon, I want you to marry me," Quill responded. "I know we haven't known each other very long, and I'm not giving you the time you felt we needed, but nothing has ever been so clear to me as the truth of this moment. I want to spend the rest of my life with you, only you. I love you, Luna."

Tears streaked her face as a glow of happiness spread throughout her entire body. She had never felt such bliss! She kissed him once again, though briefly.

"Does this mean you *will* marry me?" Quill asked hopefully.

"Yes, yes. I will be your wife," Luna replied smiling from ear-to-ear.

Quill's heart danced with glee. He felt as giddy as a spring lamb racing around the open field and could hardly believe his good fortune! His grin was so broad his face almost ached and his eyes sparkled with joy.

"Well young lady, I hate to be the one to break the mood here, fantastic as it is, but we've been invited to dinner at Tiad's and we should clean up and get going. He wants us to meet his family and says that his wife is a great cook and we have to eat with them before we leave."

They walked to Tiad's house hand-in-hand and it was the most carefree that Quill had felt in a very long time. What an amazing turn of events in his life! If he had not started out on this journey he never would have met Luna. His spirits were doing a good job watching over him!

They enjoyed their meal with Tiad's family which was served up with ample amounts of laughter, good-natured teasing of one another, and a delicious assortment of foods. From meats, to vegetables from the garden out back to pies made from berries growing along the fence at the side of the house! Truly a feast, and made even more merry when the happy couple shared with everyone their plans to marry as soon as they returned to Quill's home.

That night Luna slept in the same little house and Quill made a blanket bed under the protection of the now-loaded wagon. He had no trouble sleeping even though his dreams focused on his upcoming marriage!

****

Luna was up early, nudging him awake with the toe of her shoe to his shoulder. "Come on. Get up sleepy head! It's time to go."

"All right, all right, I'm getting up. But I'll tell you one thing dear Luna. After we're married, you had better find a better way to wake me up," mumbled Quill.

He managed to get up, pack his things, and within minutes was ready to travel. Tiad met them at the wagon to say goodbye.

"Tiad, I want you to come to our wedding. Luna and I will marry when the moon is full again. Will you come?"

"You couldn't keep me away, Quill! I'll be there with my whole family," answered the happy Tiad.

Luna hugged Tiad, thanking him for everything he had done for them, then let Quill give her a hand up onto the wagon seat. He followed, taking the reins and urging the horse to the trail Tiad had pointed out to him that morning. It would take them in the direction of Okon Village.

Quill had decided that he wasn't going to stop until he reached the village. It was a long trip, but with the trail wide and flat, and with a horse pulling the wagon, it wouldn't take nearly as long as on foot.

As they traveled, Quill's thoughts were consumed by images of the Wizard Zotta and all the things Woba had talked about. He wondered how he could defeat the Dark Elf, something everyone had told him he must do. He thought about fighting Syffus, someone he had never met, yet hated so much. It was one of the Dark Elf warriors who had killed his father and he knew that it would gnaw at his insides until he got his revenge. And what about winning over Syffus? How was he supposed to do that? Could Woba be right? Would he have to find Zatto first?

"Quill, what *is* the matter with you? You haven't said a word for hours." Luna had genuine concern in her voice.

"I'm just thinking about my father, and how I'm going to eventually have to fight the one responsible for his death. Luna, there are times, like now, when I wish there were no such things as Light Elves and Black Elves. I was happy the way I was, not that long ago. Now I've been chosen to be a Light Elf and I must earn the ten levels of power. I was taken to a magic place and given my Elf Circle, which is my magic power. Shortly after that, the Dark Warriors viciously killed my father. But then I met you. To tell the truth, if I hadn't met you, I think I'd go somewhere and hide! I'd hide to get away from the Dark Elf and all his warriors so they couldn't harm any more people of Okon Valley."

"You don't have to hide from anyone. You are the Light Elf," Luna said in her most reassuring tone.

"You don't understand. I won't have enough power to defeat Syffus until I get to the tenth power and that could take years. So what do I do until then?"

"You'll think of something. I'm sure of it. You can solve most problems just by thinking them through; you'll see."

"I hope you're right, because if you're not there will be more of us killed by the Dark Warriors." Quill's face reflected the pain he felt at the thought of losing even a single person. He felt like the survival of the world depended on his every action. And then, another terrible thought! What if Luna were to be hurt? He couldn't allow that to happen! But because he was the target of the Dark Warriors, there was a good chance Luna could be harmed just to get to him. How could he justify putting her in that kind of peril?

The sun was high in the sky, pouring its warmth into the valley, and Quill decided to remove his leather vest. When he reached up to grab the vest, he felt the folded maps which were in his shirt pocket. He abruptly stopped the wagon.

"What's the matter, Quill? Why are we stopping?" Luna asked.

Quill reached in and pulled out the maps, very carefully unfolding them. That's when it came to him! His breathing became more rapid and his hands shook. The maps! They were the key to safety—safety for the entire valley! All of the exits out of the valley were marked on the map—now that he had figured them out it was so obvious! The Dark Warriors were also using those entrances and exits to get in and out of the valley!

"Luna, we have to get to Okon Village as fast as we can! I know how to stop the Dark Elf!" He was the most excited he had been all day.

"How?"

"All of the entrances into Okon Valley must be sealed. If we can close off the valley, then it will remain safe." It seemed so simple. Why hadn't he thought of it before?

Quill pushed the horse to its limit the rest of the day in an effort to reach the village before nightfall. He knew they were getting close when he could smell Solla's cooking! That also brought Burt to mind. His best friend. How would Burt handle the fact that he now had Luna in his life?

"Quill, I can see it. Your village—there it is!"

She was right. The men were going about their nightly ritual of gathering wood for the community campfire, a fire that has burned every night for as long as anyone could remember. It was where stories were told and songs were sung; where he acquired most of his knowledge listening and learning from the elders. Quill stopped the horse just short of the village boundaries. He needed to take a moment to thank Lore's spirit for helping him become the man he was today. Jumping down from the wagon, he held out his arms to Luna easily swinging her down. He then spread his arms to the sides, head slightly bowed and all the while mumbling to himself, now beginning to dance in a circle, around and around. It was an old wives' tale that said if an elf danced in circles, he could conjure up the spirits.

And then a voice. "Quill, it is I, your father."

Quill stopped dancing and turned around to see his father standing behind the wagon.

"Father, Father!" he yelped. "Is it really you?" He could hardly contain his joy at this sudden apparition! "Thank you for coming; I need to talk to you."

"Quill, I walk with you always. Have you forgotten? When your spirit voice reaches out to me I will always listen, will always be with you." Lore held out his arms.

"Father, I want you to know how grateful I am for all the teaching and love you gave to me. I needed to say that and wanted to tell you that no matter what happens, I love you."

"Son, you are going to be a powerful Light Elf. It is already written. You will make your mother and your village proud. And myself as well. Now go to them Quill. They need you. You have been away longer than you should have been. Go and tell them that I am with you and will help to keep them safe."

Quill looked toward the village, then back. But the vision was gone.

"Who was that? I couldn't see him but I heard someone talking to you," Luna asked, a bit shaken by the experience.

"My father. He is one of the spirits in my Elf Circle," answered Quill, still looking around to see if maybe his father was somewhere nearby. "Luna, you must never reveal this to anyone. Do you understand?" And even as he gave her this admonishment, he marveled that she too was able to hear Lore's spirit voice. Truly she was his soul-mate, the one destined to serve by his side forever.

Luna nodded her agreement.

He continued, "An Elf Circle consists of the spirits of Light Elves who have died. It is their responsibility to provide me with the power to protect our people, the people of Okon."

"You can talk to all of these spirits?" asked Luna.

"Yes, I can. And someday I'll explain it all to you. *When* I truly understand it all myself! But enough of this. Let's go to the village so I can introduce you to everybody—I want them to meet my future wife!"

Putting aside this latest encounter, Quill took the horse's reins in his hand and they entered the village.

Friends and neighbors hurried over to Quill, pumping his hand in greeting and showering him with hugs and affectionate slaps on the back. Luna was astounded at the great display of emotion shown by these people—so uncharacteristic of her own home village where the people were much more laid back. Almost spontaneously, first a few, then more and more of the greeters began chanting, "Quill! Quill! Quill! Our leader is back!" A tear formed in Quill's eye at the show of affection. Then, from the middle of the assemblage, an all-too-familiar booming voice was heard—Okar himself spoke.

"Quill Okon, is that you boy? Step forward and let me see you. It is I, Okar!"

Quill let go of the horse and moved out from the group just enough to be in clear view of Okar.

"Silence! I want quiet!" commanded Okar.

Every soul within hearing distance of Okar (which included the entire village given the boisterous quality of this little priest's voice) became silent as he presented himself directly in front of Quill.

"Where have you been, son? And who is the beautiful young woman you have with you?"

For the first time in his life, Quill ignored Okar's blustering words! He didn't answer for his attention was elsewhere as he spotted Kara, her hands to her mouth trying to contain the sounds of her own excitement. When their eyes met they each ran to the other.

"Quill! Quill! I'm so glad you're safe," she cried.

Mother and son grabbed each other in a gigantic bear hug, he swinging her around, her feet just brushing the ground. "Come with me, Mother," he gushed excitedly. "I have someone I want you to meet."

Luna still stood where she had first set foot in the village, waiting for Quill to make an introduction. Or at least for someone to acknowledge her presence! He put an arm around her waist and, still holding his mother's hand, announced, "Mother, everyone, this is Luna. She comes from another valley far away."

No one uttered a word. They simply stared at this stranger. The tension in the air was as thick as a heavy fog! But then Quill continued, "Luna has generously consented to become my wife. We will marry on the next full moon."

All of a sudden, the crowd erupted in wild cheering and began dancing crazily in circles. They started joining hands until the entire village was dancing in one gigantic circle—dancing around Luna, Quill, and his mother. Kara was overcome with joy to think that her son had found such a wonderful girl. With a warm embrace, she welcomed Luna into the family.

"Mother, where's Burt?" Quill asked, suddenly realizing he had not seen his best friend.

"He's out looking for you. Did you think he wouldn't do that? Come on, let's get the two of you inside, away from all this excitement, so we can talk," Kara said.

So they walked home with Quill checking over his shoulder to make sure someone was bringing the horse and wagon. Sure enough, Okar was yelling at people, barking commands, and someone was dutifully leading the horse, wagon still hitched, to the rear of the house.

Outside the house, excitement was building throughout the village. The air was filled with the happy sounds of all the men who were building the fire, the women who were cooking their favorite recipes for all to share, and the children who ran from place to place not quite sure of the cause of all this commotion but very eager to be in on every fun-filled minute! Everyone waited impatiently for Quill to reappear and tell them about his most recent adventure. But Quill was nervous and paced back and forth in the great room of his home.

"Quill, what's wrong with you?" Kara asked.

"I'm worried about Burt. He should have come back by now don't you think?"

"Quill, Burt was sick over the fact that you went off without him. What made it worse was when you didn't return right away. He fretted and stewed thinking you were in trouble and needed his help. He just couldn't sit still and wait. But he's not alone. Tobble and four or five of the better hunters are out there with him," Kara explained. "I'm sure he'll be all right. Please put your mind at ease. When he comes back he'll be glad to see that you are safe and sound."

Patting the bench next to her, Luna said, "Come and sit beside me, Quill. Look at the fine meal your mother has prepared for us." Still not totally convinced, Quill nevertheless gave in and slid into his place at the table.

They had no sooner begun their meal when he heard shouting coming from outside and people yelling for Solla to come. Something was wrong and he could feel it in the pit of his stomach. He jumped up and was out the door in one leap where he found a small group of dwarves and elves standing in a circle over something lying on the ground. Quill went forward to see. Someone handed him a torch as he made his way through the group.

"Quill! Quill! You're home." The familiar voice excited Quill as his turned from side to side looking for its owner. At last, there he was! Burt ran to him, arms swinging and then the two lunged for each other, hugging and twirling each other around. But then Quill saw the tears that ran down Burt's cheeks.

"What's going on, Burt? What happened?" Quill wanted to know.

"It's my father, Quill. One of the Dark Warriors wounded him. It doesn't look good," Burt said as the tears continued to flow.

Quill moved quickly to Tobble's side and without saying a word, put his hands on his most serious wound, not letting go for several minutes. Solla, Burt and the rest of those who had gathered around, watched in amazement. Right before their eyes the wound began to heal! Tobble appeared lifeless, not moving, but Quill wasn't concerned. He could feel Tobble's breathing being restored to a strong and steady rhythm and, after just a few more minutes, he was up and about, perfectly normal! Quill felt a draining of his energy but only momentarily. He soon felt quite normal again. There was no doubt now that Quill Okon was the Light Elf of Okon Valley. They sang and danced, cheering Quill's name in praise of this wondrous deed. Finally, a Light Elf walked among them. His name would be sung in stories for generations to come, for he was truly a hero!

Later that night Quill and Burt made their way to the bonfire. Quill was becoming more and more comfortable with his position and in taking his father's place as the new leader of the Valley. He sat easily with the other men and related the incredible stories of their adventures of the past days and weeks. When he was finished, he withdrew the maps from his pocket and laid them on the ground for all to see. He assigned the men to teams, each team being given the task of traveling to one of the entrances marked on the map. Their mission was to seal each entrance so no one could enter or leave the valley. When this was done, Quill asked if there were any questions. There could be no doubts, no hesitancy on anyone's part. They must all understand how important this was to the survival of the entire population.

"Quill, I have a question." The voice came from the other side of the fire. Quill couldn't see who it was, but he listened.

"What if we encounter the Dark Elf? You haven't told us what we must do."

Quill pondered that one for a moment. They were right. How could he place them in such grave danger? He stared at the ground wondering what made him think these helpless people would risk their lives for him. Then another voice came from across the firelight.

"Quill, if I see the Dark Elf, I'll climb as high as I can to the side of the nearest mountain and build the biggest fire I can. By doing that, it will signal you to come to our aid!"

"I'll do the same," another voice chimed in.

Then still another voice shouted out, "Quill Okon, we are with you. We are the people of Okon and no Dark Elf will drive us from our homes!"

Rising to his feet, Quill felt such an intense pride in his people he could hardly contain himself. They were solidly behind him. No doubts. No misgivings. They trusted him. And he would not let them down. Raising his hands to quiet them down, he began to speak.

"Listen all of you. It shouldn't take any longer than four days for all of this to be completed. But I want everyone to be aware of this. The power of the Dark Elf is nothing to fool with. He and his warriors will kill at first sight. I want everybody to get home safely so be alert at all times; your eyes open and your ears ready to pick up any strange noise. Each team will take at least five elfin bowmen with them. They must be superior marksmen to slay the warriors before they reach you. Before we leave, we will ask the blessing of Okar that our efforts will be successful and our journey without incident. Now go to your homes and get a good night's rest so you will be refreshed in the morning and ready for an early start."

Quill turned to leave but stopped and quickly turned around and added, "One more thing. In case I haven't already made you aware of this…you are all very special to me and I'm proud to serve by your side. And, thank you for your support. Together we *will* get this done!"

A unanimous round of applause and hearty cheering sent Quill off to his mother's house where he would gather his gear for morning and the trip he would take with one of the teams. His mother was waiting for him, sitting at the small table with her hands folded in front of her. "Luna told me what you are doing tomorrow, and why. I too think it's for the best. But please be careful. As your mother, I will always worry about you. You know that don't you? I also wanted to tell you that I think Luna is a perfectly charming, lovely person. I'm so happy for you both! I didn't get much of a chance to tell you that before what with the way things keep happening around here. But I'm sure you know how I feel anyway. And," she added thoughtfully, "you haven't forgotten have you that the villagers have built your home? It's finished and located near the pond, the one you and Burt just about grew up in. Remember?"

Quill enthusiastically nodded his head up and down. How well he remembered those wonderful years. Life was so much more simple then. Do chores, learn from the elders, play.

He and Burt. So close when they were kids—even closer today. He could get lost in those memories—if only there were the time!

"Tomorrow Luna and I will begin to settle your little home. We have to get it ready for your wedding day. All the women are going to help. There's wood to bring in and food to store in the larder. Winter will be upon us in three months and you and Luna must be prepared. Now, relax for a while and then get some sleep. Luna will be sleeping with me."

Quill wondered how he could ever show his appreciation to his mother for all her support and loving care. No matter what happened she was always right there to bolster his spirits or to offer sound advice. He was very fortunate indeed.

The last one to turn in for the night, he blew out the lanterns softly lighting the room and entered his small but cozy bedroom. Undressing quickly, he let himself fall back upon the welcoming bed. The prospect of a good night's sleep sounded awfully good and, wrapping himself in his quilt, he soon drifted off.

Chapter Twenty-Two

It had been several days since the separate groups had gone out from the village to close the entrances to their valley. Their mission had proved completely successful and had met with no resistance whatsoever. The valley had been sealed off from the outside world and there had been no sign of Syffus or his Dark Warriors. This in itself was incredible but no one was questioning the safety of their husbands or fathers or sons who had returned to the welcoming arms of their families! The atmosphere in the village had turned from one of apprehension to one of festive celebration. They were preparing for the soon-to-happen wedding of Luna, stranger-turned-friend, to their favorite son and new leader, Quill.

Okar had spent the past few days scrubbing the old church until it fairly sparkled, and gathering an assortment of colorful wildflowers from the hills beyond the farthest houses of this close-knit community. If truth be told, and if you listened carefully, you could actually hear the gruff old priest humming to himself as he joyfully went about his self-appointed tasks!

Skilled marksmen, and those whose abilities were still being honed to perfection, all combined to bring down a wonderful variety of meats for the occasion. Venison, wild boar, rabbit, turkeys, grouse and even partridge were all prepared according to age-old tradition and favorite family recipes. The aromas filled the air like an elixir of paradise, enticing the appetites of everyone!

Fruits and vegetables were gathered from the multitude of fruit trees and gardens which grew outside nearly every home. The youngsters were enlisted for this chore and, for once, they happily ran to get the job done, and not a complaint from any of them! They too were looking forward to the grand celebration, not so much for the wedding part of course, but for all that delicious smelling food!

The ceremony would take place in the morning—the feasting would go on until…well, let's just say "until". Quill didn't think it was possible to get this excited but he was absolutely beside himself with joy! He walked up and down the paths in and around the village, greeting all those he met with a happy smile and a warm handshake. Times were good!

"Quill! Quill! There's a wagon coming," Burt yelled.

Quill's initial reaction was that he had somehow missed an entrance to the valley and an intruder had come in! But then he remembered Tiad. It had to be the Mohan leader and his family coming to attend the wedding. Quill headed out quickly in the direction of Burt's pointing finger, with Burt falling in behind as usual!

"Quill!" Tiad yelled when he caught sight of his friend.

Quill raced out to the wagon to welcome these happy travelers. Tiad reined in the horse bringing the small two-wheeled cart to a stop and jumped down grabbing Quill by the shoulders and shaking him good-naturedly. "So good to see you my friend!" he proclaimed loudly as Quill returned his eager embrace.

In his excitement at seeing Tiad, Quill almost forgot to greet Tiad's wife and children! "I'm sorry, I didn't mean to ignore you. I guess I've forgotten my manners today," he apologized offering his hand to first one and then the other.

"Don't concern yourself about that Quill! We certainly understand how you can be distracted at a time like this," said Tiad's charming wife.

"Did you have a good journey?" Quill asked.

Tiad answered for them all. "Yes, we started out yesterday and took our time. We looked forward to the trip as well as to the destination. We wouldn't have missed this day for anything!"

Quill turned to Burt and took him by the arm pulling him forward to stand next to him. "Tiad, you must meet my best friend, Burt. And Burt, this is Tiad, leader of the Mohans."

Burt extended his hand in greeting and said, "Quill has told me all about you and about your people. Welcome to Okon Village!" (In spite of his honest and warm greeting, Burt couldn't help but think that these were definitely the ugliest people he had ever met!)

Quill had explained to everyone that Tiad and his family were really dwarves but because of the terrible spell cast on them by Hyslop their appearance had been altered and was unpleasant, to say the least! But, Quill cautioned, he trusted his friends to accept them as the good, and decent people they were, and to treat them with total respect and kindness. He needn't have worried. The Okonians were a very tolerant community, who would go out of their way to make these Mohans feel entirely welcome. It was their way.

"Come on Tiad, let's get your family settled," Quill beckoned.

Together Tiad and Quill led the tired horse into the village where they were met by Luna, who ran straight up to Tiad hugging him with all the enthusiasm of a long-lost relation! For Luna truly felt as close to these Mohans as if they were her real family. She then welcomed the rest of his family in the same way.

Later that evening, after the new arrivals had settled into one of the small Okon homes, Tiad came to Quill and asked if they could go somewhere and talk—alone.

Quill wholeheartedly agreed and they took a long walk to the outskirts of the village near the edge of the wheat field. There they reclined under a large, fully-leafed oak tree.

"Quill, I hate doing this, but I have to give you some bad news. Woba is dead. A Dark Warrior killed her. It happened just two days after you left the village. It's pretty apparent that the Warrior must have been tracking you when he came across Woba's home."

The news hit Quill like someone physically striking him down. *He* was responsible. If he weren't a Light Elf, Woba would still be alive! Yet, he remembered her prophesy—that she would never again see him. She *knew* something like this would happen!

Tiad continued with his story, "We buried her next to my father and Tran. Now that Woba is gone, there is an emptiness in our village that no one can fill. We fear another attack from the Dark Warriors. They must be aware that we know of your existence and your whereabouts. They only bide their time in coming for all of us."

"Tiad, the men of our village and I went to all the entrances to the valley and sealed them. I never thought to consult with you before I had it done. But for now, until we discover what this is really all about, *and* I accumulate enough power to defeat Syffus, I felt the safest course of action was to prevent anyone at all from entering the valley. At least we can live without constant fear of the Dark Warriors slipping in under cover of the night and slaying our loved ones."

"You've done the right thing, Quill. This way I can bring some good news back home with me to my people. They are not sleeping at night out of fear not only of the warriors but of Syffus himself. Your action will bring them peace of mind and of heart. But we know that it's not over, for this is certain—sooner or later, Syffus will find you. He hunts the Light Elf."

"I know you're right. He does hunt the Light Elf which is why Kailon left the valley. He had hopes of leading Syffus away so that I could search out my powers. Understand this Tiad, I will not become the new Light Elf until Kailon dies, and I know that, right now, he is still alive. When he left Okon Valley he instructed me to seek out the white horse running across the sky. That white horse will be my sign that he is dead. But, there is also another problem. I cannot become a full-fledged Light Elf until I earn all ten levels of power, and that could take years. For your sake and the sake of your people, I hope it will *not* take that long! I yearn for the time when I can lift Hyslop's curse from all of you, but Woba told me it would be impossible until I attain the tenth power level—when I have become a full-fledged Light Elf."

"Quill, don't worry about us. We have lived under Hyslop's spell for a long time and have grown to accept it. I do, however, feel good that you are concerned for us and for the safety of our valley. Knowing this makes me feel much better already. I wonder, however, about how long your decision to isolate this valley will be a solution. I'm afraid it's temporary at best. You of all people know the power Syffus has. Sealing the valley will not hold him back forever!"

"You're right. But temporary or not, it's all we have right now, and for as long as Kailon lives, Syffus will continue to hunt for him because he doesn't know about me—yet."

"Remember too, Quill, what Woba told us. If you *are* to defeat Syffus, you must seek out Zatto the Wizard. How can you do that with the valley sealed? If *you* can't leave, how will you ever find him?"

"My first concern is not for myself but for all the inhabitants of this valley." Quill sounded frustrated. "Looking for Zatto is like looking under rocks for someone I'm not even sure is worthy of the search!" His voice continued to rise. "Should we risk our lives for such a fool's errand? All I know about Zatto is what Woba told us. And that wasn't much—not enough anyway to believe he will be of any value when it comes to defeating Syffus!"

"Woba spent years trying to understand Zatto's power and that is where her power came from," countered Tiad. "She *believed* in Zatto's power, believed that it would help you to defeat Syffus and I don't think she would have given that instruction unless she truly meant it!" Tiad's eyes were stern and he was determined to make Quill understand. He turned his back to Quill and looked off in the direction of the village where the evening fire shot giant tongues of flame high into the night sky, virtually lighting the area as bright as day.

Quill had not come out here looking for an argument; this was supposed to be a happy occasion, yet he knew he could not escape the reality of the situation. For whatever reason, he was in the middle of something greater than he and the solution must be found. He reflected on what Tiad had said, and realized he had eliminated any chance of being totally safe in the event something devastating *did* happen. By sealing off the valley, he had virtually trapped himself within its boundaries! He no longer had a passage to the Elf Treasure, the only place where Syffus could not enter. An icy chill made his blood run cold. For the first time he knew that he had put the Elf Circle in danger. If he could not get to the Elf Treasure, Syffus could defeat him.

Tiad was telling Quill that one can't hide. You have to take a stand against danger and Quill knew in his heart that closing off the valley wouldn't work. It would just buy a bit more time. Quill's hand dropped to the rope tied about his waist and he felt the lonely knots. That feeling of dread enveloped him again. His mother's voice came to him too as he remembered her warning about avoiding Syffus until he had achieved that tenth power level. Memories flooded over him too about the trust Kailon had placed in him; Kailon who was continuing to draw Syffus away until Quill became powerful enough to defeat that Dark Elf. But there was something even worse! What if, by closing off the valley, he also stopped the Elf Spirits from awarding him the knots of power? How would he ever earn the tenth level? "Well," he thought, "right now it doesn't matter. The valley needs time to rest and that's what it will have for the time being. I'll give this more thought after the wedding."

Tiad broke into Quill's silence by saying, "Let's go back to the village. Enough has been said between us about Okon Valley. Let's not ruin what is left of the evening." He held out his hand, offering to give Quill a lift to his feet.

They returned to the celebration, their friendship none the worse for the exchange of words between them. Each had spoken in honesty and with respect for the other. These issues had to be addressed and they knew it would be resolved soon. They sat next to each other that night and told stories and listened to the elders share tales of bravery from years long gone. Tiad told the history of the Mohans, and their life in the swamp. He even told them how to build houses from clay and they were amazed. But Quill's thoughts kept returning to the events of the past weeks and about his decision to close the valley. Did he do the right thing?

As morning slid over the mountains surrounding Okon Valley, Quill still sat by the fire, now not more than a deep pile of smoking ashes; he couldn't sleep. He mindlessly poked at the few embers glowing here and there and wondered what he should do. Then he heard the familiar and welcome sound of the hawk, a friend of another sort.

Quill closed his eyes and quickly found himself soaring high above the village, caught on a slight breeze in an effortless glide. He rose higher and higher to the peaks of the mountaintops surrounding the valley and saw all the lakes and ponds which so beautifully dotted the landscape. Looking over the fertile bottom lands which so amply provided food for his people, he saw the wheat fields with their amber-colored crop swaying gently in the morning breeze, and turned to observe the forest where the game was abundant. He turned south and viewed the Harriet, the swamp where the Mohans lived, and also that part of the valley that lay on top of the Kingdom of Zin, still hidden from the evil destruction of Syffus. Again with but a barely perceptible movement of a few feathers, his direction changed and he gracefully descended toward his village. Quill opened his eyes to observe the hawk flying off as soundlessly as he had come. He felt that the hawk was prodding him to look at the bounty of the valley and at the same time reminding him that it could all be lost if he didn't protect it. Okon Valley would never be safe until Syffus was beaten back forever.

Quill acknowledged that in truth this was not the end but merely the beginning of his quest as a Light Elf.

"Come on Quill! You have a lot to do before the wedding," an excited voice from behind shouted. He snapped back to the business at hand to turn and look.

There came Burt, in his half-run, half-shuffle gait, holding tight to a half-eaten apple pie, which he generously offered to his best friend. "Are you going to get ready? You have to eat (first things first in Burt's mind!) and then take a hot bath. My father is already heating water for you!"

Quill noticed that Tiad must have left sometime during the night. He had not even seen him leave! How wrapped up in his own thoughts he had been! Grabbing his bow which lay beside him, he ran after Burt who by now had decided Quill didn't want any of this pie and had dutifully eaten the rest and was wiping his hands clean on his shirt.

Burt steered the soon-to-be groom toward his house where Solla had prepared an ample breakfast and Tobble had the bath water ready. By the time he had finished both, it was less than an hour before the ceremony. Decked out in his finest clothes, complete with a new vest fashioned by his mother, Quill felt scrubbed and polished and ready to meet his bride! Before leaving for the church, he carefully cleaned his bow and neatly hung it from his shoulder. Even the weapon had a role to play in the marriage rite! His quiver was filled with brand new arrows, a special gift from Burt, and was proudly displayed from right to left over his shoulder and across his back. He was set. Let the wedding begin!

Quill's mother concentrated on Luna that morning, helping her to get ready for the biggest day of her life. She had offered her own wedding dress to her new daughter-in-law. As it was custom to pass down the dress from mother to daughter, and since Luna did not have a mother and Kara no daughter, Kara decided that this was the appropriate thing to do! Luna was so touched by Kara's generosity that she clung to her and wept in happiness. The dress was white, just long enough to sweep the ground lightly with each step, and with touches of blue around the hemline and on the cuffs of the long, billowy sleeves. It fit Luna perfectly and she felt like a queen bedecked for her coronation! She too was ready, her heart so full of love for Quill that she thought she would burst!

The townspeople scurried about getting everything ready for the feasting that would follow the ceremony, and Quill watched with pride from the doorway of Burt's home. Such care and effort was being put forth on his and Luna's behalf that it humbled him and he felt he could not possibly be worthy of so much!

"Are you ready old friend?" asked Burt. (Even Burt had ducked in and out of a tub of water this morning in honor of the event!)

"I certainly am, good Buddy! And you know what Burt? *You* even smell good today!" They both had a good laugh and set out for the church.

Now, all the weddings that have ever taken place in Okon Valley have followed a prescribed custom. And this would be no exception. As Quill started toward the church, accompanied by Burt, all the men of the village followed. By law (decreed by Okar) the men entered the church first, to be followed later by the women. Once inside, Quill was struck by the beauty and by how much effort Okar had put into making the building a special place for a special occasion. There were flowers everywhere and a heady fragrance filled the air.

Quill stepped forward and the men filed in and took their seats. Tiad was right up front sitting next to Tobble. Okar stood in front of the altar, and summoned Quill up the aisle. He was actually smiling! He held a tall cane in one hand and a gold chalice in the other.

"Quill Okon. Who brought you here today and for what purpose?" Okar boomed out in his commanding voice.

"We did. We the men of Okon have come to witness to the marriage of our leader, Quill Okon," the men answered in unison.

"Step forward, Quill Okon," beckoned Okar, in his most serious tone. Quill walked up until he stood directly in front of Okar.

"Remove your weapons and give them to your Second," Okar instructed, pointing to Burt.

As Quill removed his bow and quiver and handed them to Burt, he began to chuckle and then his smile broadened so that he thought he'd laugh right out loud! It struck him that the purpose of handing his weapons to Burt, who would keep them for the remainder of the day and through the night, was that Burt must stand guard over the newlyweds and provide protection in case of danger. In that event, Burt was to use Quill's weapons to fend off any evildoers. But both Quill and Burt knew that Burt couldn't hit the broad side of a house with an arrow! Quill's eye caught Burt's and they both broke out laughing. As did the rest of the assembled guests! Even Okar had a difficult time suppressing a laugh!

"Quill Okon," continued Okar, once again the serious priest, "I offer you a drink from the cup of Lore, and if you choose to drink, then she who comes next to sip from the cup must seek you out before the day's end and hold your hands high above hers to show that you belong to each other forever."

Accepting the cup with both his hands, Quill waited for Okar to finish talking before taking a drink.

"Is there any among you who wishes to challenge this drink?" questioned the priest.

No one uttered a word. Quill then raised the beautiful golden chalice, which had belonged to his father, and drank of the wine. With that, the wedding ceremony began.

"Quill Okon, go from here to your hiding place among the stalks of wheat and wait to be found by the one who loves you," Okar commanded pointing to the door.

Quill turned to a resounding cheer from everyone as they also jumped to their feet. He slowly left the church, a huge smile lighting up his face for all to see, and headed toward the wheat fields at the end of the road. Burt tailed Quill, trying not to lose sight of him as Quill went faster and faster toward the field. Burt wanted to keep right up with him so he wouldn't be considered a failure at his task and the wedding be declared invalid!

"Wait up will you?" Burt panted, running as best he could, his little legs pumping hard to catch up to Quill.

Quill allowed his Second, the one in whom he placed his well-being for these twenty-four hours, to catch up to him and they walked toward the edge of the village side by side, as they had always done.

Another voice called out, "Quill, wait a minute will you?" It was Tiad running toward them.

"What's wrong?" Quill wanted to know.

"Nothing's wrong, but I came to your wedding not only to share your happiness but also to bring a gift from my village. For many, many years Woba worked to understand Zatto's language. She was successful, but it wasn't easy. She wasn't an elf like you and had a hard time learning his ways. Now, we want *you* to have everything Woba removed from the wizard's tomb. It's all in my wagon, including the great book and the golden box. I know you don't have plans to look for Zatto right now, but until you do, you'll have time to learn about him!"

"Thank your people for me, Tiad, and you're right. It won't hurt to learn all I can about Zatto—to see what kind of a wizard he really is." Quill placed his hand on Tiad's shoulder, giving it a firm squeeze and a hearty pat.

"Now I'll leave you alone. You have a beautiful young lady waiting for you." He pointed at the doorway to Quill's house. Quill caught just a glimpse of Luna's dress as she ducked away from the open door, grabbed Burt's arm and started running toward the wheat field!

Luna processed to the church, followed by all the women who oohed and aahed at how beautiful she looked. Kara had fashioned a wreath of wildflowers for Luna's head which accented her long, golden hair, draped easily over her shoulders. White daisies, yellow brown-eyed susans, blue cornflowers, and even wild baby's breath, entwined with sky-blue ribbons to make an exquisite hairpiece. Luna had never felt so special! When she entered the church Okar beckoned her to come before him, as he had done to Quill, asking her the same questions. Luna accepted the chalice from Okar's hands and sipped the wine, indicating her willingness to marry. She turned and walked without hesitation down the aisle and out to the road. First she walked, then broke into a run headed straight to the wheat field—and her future!

But she must find Quill, without any help, and the law said that the sooner the bride found her husband, the happier the marriage would be.

At first Luna thought finding Quill among the several wheat fields would be difficult but, fortunately for her, Burt was with Quill and because of his short, but very wide, body, Burt always had a problem walking through the wheat. He kept squashing the grasses beneath his pudgy feet leaving a clear trail for Luna to follow! She ran carefully among the beaten-down wheat and before she had gone very far, she spotted Burt squatting down behind Quill. She rushed up and grabbed Quill by the shoulder, playfully throwing him to the ground, and jumping on his back in pure excitement! She had captured him and now they were married!

Jumping to his feet, Quill scooped Luna into his arms, but quickly set her down in front of him while she took his hands in hers, raising them as high as she possibly could. As their hands lifted toward the sky, the people of the village arrived, having followed Luna in her search for Quill. They were there to witness that these two were, at last, married! Quill lowered their hands and wrapped his strong arms around Luna, in a loving embrace, drawing her to him without once taking his eyes from her face. Her smile was radiant and she had eyes only for him. He gently kissed her lips as the ecstatic elves and dwarves held hands, singing and dancing in ever-larger circles, trampling down the ripened wheat all around the newlyweds, happily chanting the names "Quill" and "Luna" over and over again.

A distinctive flutter caught Quill's attention and he raised his eyes to the blue sky knowing full well that the hawk who so closely monitored his every move was viewing this happy scene too. His kinship with this mighty bird called for his immediate response.

Still holding Luna close, Quill closed his eyes and immediately found himself soaring on the powerful updrafts, once more joined with the magnificent hawk. As he lowered his gaze to the wheat fields he felt an overpowering sense of purpose—and the presence of Tercal and the other spirits of his Elf Circle. They directed his attention to the patterns that had been formed in the fields by the exuberant dancing of Quill's friends and neighbors. Beautiful circles and symbols had appeared where the dancers had been and they seemed to hold a message meant only for Quill!

Deep in his heart, Quill understood what was being shown to him—what it meant to be a Light Elf. It was a message he could not possibly explain, nor would he, even if the words came to him. These images would be burned forever in his mind, proof that his Elf Circle did in fact really exist, yet more than that. He knew with absolute certainty that he was eternally tied to those wise men who had preceded him, all the Light Elves who had ever lived, and would follow in their footsteps to the greater benefit of all the people of the valley!

It was his destiny—and his privilege.

Printed in the United States
106897LV00005B/14/A

9 781604 418620